GR

As Tony drove the E-Type expertly through the Saturday traffic on the King's Road, he looked across at the girl he had picked up the night before. Mandy's dress had slid almost up to her crotch and he knew she was wearing no knickers. He knew that because he'd seen them lying on the carpet when they'd left the flat ten minutes previously. At the next set of traffic lights he leant over and put his hand on her thigh, then slipped it under her minidress. She put her hand on his and pushed it so his fingers slid into her thatch of hair.

'I want to do it again,' she said . . .

Groupies

Johnny Angelo

HEADLINE

First published in 1993
by HEADLINE BOOK PUBLISHING PLC

10 9 8 7 6 5 4 3 2 1

ISBN 0 7472 4091 4

Typeset by
Letterpart Limited, Reigate, Surrey

Printed and bound in Great Britain by
HarperCollins Manufacturing, Glasgow

HEADLINE BOOK PUBLISHING PLC
Headline House
79 Great Titchfield Street
London W1P 7FN

For Hazel . . .

Groupies

PART ONE

1

Tony Parker drove the white E-Type down the King's Road towards Sloane Square feeling well pleased with himself. June 1966, and all was well with the world. The Getaways, the band in which he played lead guitar, had their third single – a song he had written called 'Here We Go' – sitting at number three on the charts, after just two weeks on release. Their first single had got into the top twenty, the second into the top ten, and the new one was top five already and looked certain to be a number one. Only one record could keep them from getting there. The new Beatles' single, 'Paperback Writer'. It all depended how well it performed. It had knocked Sinatra off the top spot that week, but rumour said that it wasn't doing as well as their previous records. Wait and see, thought Tony, only time will tell. And there was plenty of time, he thought, as he drove. He was only twenty-two, and things were looking great.

If The Getaways did take over from The Beatles, it wouldn't be the first time. Three years previously, when the Liverpool group had crashed the British charts for the first time, Tony's band had filled the vacancy they had left at the Star Club on the Reeperbahn in Hamburg. God,

3

but they'd been green then. Green and innocent. Twelve hours a day of seemingly non-stop performing, in front of an audience made up of equal quantities of sailors on shore leave, and prostitutes looking to part them from their cash. Twelve hours a day of jumping around on stage, and little money to show for it. Little money and little food and freezing accommodation. So cold were their digs, in fact, that the drummer who had been with the band then had kept his pyjamas on under his stage suit for the entire six-week engagement. But that was then and this was now. Things had certainly changed. The band's first album was ready for release and they had been paid an advance for the second. Hence the brand-new Jaguar convertible. And thanks to the records, concerts and TV appearances, and of course with a little help from all the cash they generated, hence the blonde dolly sitting next to him in the car. Not that he couldn't have got plenty of birds anyway, with his handsome face, long thick dark hair and skinny, yet muscular, body. But the fame helped. Yes, he thought, it certainly helped.

He looked over at the girl. Mandy, her name was. He'd pulled her the night before at the opening of a new club in Kensington. She'd been high on something and came over and asked if he really was Tony Parker and he'd said that he was, and as he was unusually all alone, he asked her if she wanted a drink. She did. He got two complimentary Scotch and Cokes and they found a dark table in the corner and sat down. Pretty soon she was leaning over to talk to him and they kissed for the first time. Her mouth opened and he pushed his tongue as far down her throat as he could and at the same time ran his hand up her thighs to the hem of the minidress she was wearing. Her legs were bare. The hem was only an inch beneath the crotch of her knickers. He felt her wriggle with pleasure as his hand brushed over her pussy, and he put his fingers under the elastic of her panties and found her pubic hair.

She told him between kisses that she worked for a record company. Not the one that The Getaways were signed to. She told him that she thought it was a shame. He agreed. He would have agreed with anything she said at that point. After half an hour of unsatisfactory snogging and touching up under the table, he suggested they go back to his newly acquired flat in the Chelsea Cloisters. She agreed. They went outside to where the Jaguar was parked. She enthused over it. All women did. He drove home quickly, parked the car in the garage, and they took the lift upstairs. On the short journey they kissed passionately.

As soon as they got into the flat they went to the bedroom. He switched on the radio which was tuned to one of the offshore pirate stations. She stood in the centre of the room and waited for him. She didn't have to wait long. He walked straight over to her and pulled her short dress up over her head and threw it onto a chair. Then, in the dim light from the bedside lamp he had switched on, he looked her up and down. She was wearing just a pair of brief hipster knickers with a flowery pattern on them. Her legs were long and brown. Her hips were full, she had a tiny waist and small pink-tipped breasts that were almost hidden by her long straight blonde hair. He pushed her onto the bed and pulled her knickers off in one action. She didn't say a word. She was still half out of her head and that excited him. He knelt on the floor between her legs and licked and sucked her cunt. She groaned as he did it and opened her legs wider. He nibbled at the folds of skin and she groaned louder. He could feel his cock stretching the tight material of his trousers and he stood up, pulled off his boots and socks, and took off his shirt. He unzipped his trousers and took them off too. His cock was naked beneath them and erect. He lay on the bed next to her and they began kissing. She responded to his kisses and he felt her fingers grasp his erection and begin to gently play with his cock, then she slid her hand round to cup his balls. He adored having his balls played with and their kisses got deeper and deeper still. He put his head down to her breasts and began to lick around her nipples. 'Yes,' she said. 'I love that.'

'Suck my cock,' he ordered, and she obeyed immediately. They slithered around on the bed until her head was at his groin. She licked the length of his shaft from top to bottom, then took one testicle gently into her mouth and sucked it. The feeling almost blew the top of his head off and he put his mouth down to her pussy again.

She put the knob of his cock between her lips and tongued the end, then sucked as much as she could down her throat. As she did so, he pushed *his* tongue as far into her cunt as he could to taste her sweet juices. She was fully open to him and he wanted to fill the opening with his prick. He stopped sucking her and moved so that he could see her mouth working on him. She was wanking his cock with her lips, and the sight of her mouth moving up and down his erect prick almost made him come. He put his hand into her hair and pulled her off him. 'Don't you like it?' she asked teasingly.

'I love it,' he replied. 'Now I'm going to fuck you.'

She rolled over onto her back and opened her legs wide. The way she did it drove him crazy. He mounted her instantly and felt the wetness of her pussy on him, and his cock slid into her in one smooth movement. They began to kiss again and started to move together. The inside of her cunt was slick and hot and he could feel her muscles gripping him. They moved faster, then faster still, until neither could bear it for another moment and he came into her in a hot stream of spunk, and as she felt the liquid burst into her womb she came over his cock with a cry of delight.

As he drove the car expertly through the Saturday traffic, he remembered their first fuck and he looked over at her sitting on the leather upholstery of the passenger seat. Her dress had slid up almost to her crotch and he knew she was wearing no knickers. He knew that because they had still been lying on the carpet, where he'd thrown them the previous evening, when they'd left the disarray of the flat ten minutes previously. At the next set of red traffic lights he leant over and put his hand on her thigh, then slid it under her dress and into the thatch of her hair. She put her hand on his and pushed it, so that his fingers found her crack and slid into the wetness of it. 'I want to do it again,' she said.

'I thought you wanted some breakfast,' he replied, although it was almost two in the afternoon.

'I want both.'

'Which first?'

'A fuck.'

'I'm not going back home.'

'I don't want you to. I want it in the car.'

He laughed. 'It's a bit cramped.'

'So's my cunt,' she said, 'but you fitted in all right.'

He laughed again and, as the lights changed, he put the car into gear, indicated, and turned into the first side-street he came to. He stopped at an empty parking meter, hopped out and put up the roof of the car. 'Get out,' he said as he was doing it.

She did as he said, and he leant in and pulled both seats forward. 'In the back,' he said. Once again she did as she was told. He joined her and, without any preliminaries, pulled down his trousers. She pulled her skirt up to her waist and put one foot on the back of each front seat and slid down until her arse was resting on the edge of the narrow back seat. He knelt between her legs, his cock already hard and red and veined with excitement. She guided him swiftly inside her and he began to move. From where he was kneeling, over her shoulder, through the translucent plastic that formed the rear window of the soft top of the car, he could see pedestrians walking on the pavement outside, but he was pretty sure that they couldn't see in. Not that he cared. He was a star. He was fucking a beautiful chick in a beautiful car. As far as he was concerned the whole world could have a ticket for the show. He felt her breath on his ear as she slid up and down his knob. He pushed harder. He didn't care if she came. He just wanted to shoot her again and, as a policeman turned the corner from the King's Road into the street where they were parked, he did.

2

David Powell, bass player with The Getaways, was wakened that Saturday morning as his girlfriend, top teenage model Jade Dollar, clambered over him to get out of their bed.

David shook his black hair, cut into a Scott Walker bob, out of his eyes and said groggily, 'What's up babe? What time is it?'

'Six,' said the girl as she vanished into the bathroom.

'Six. Morning or night?'

'Morning,' came her voice from the next room. 'The car will be here soon.'

'What car?'

She stuck her head, topped with a mass of black curls, back into the room. 'The car to take me to the airport to catch the plane that's taking me to Paris.'

'Paris. Shit,' he said. And it all came flooding back.

Jade was due to catch an early flight to France where she was taking part in a ten-day fashion show of the best British designs of next year's spring collections.

'Do you have to go?' he asked.

'We've been through this a thousand times,' she said. 'I've got my job, you've got yours. You can't get away

9

because of the single. I can't stay here because of the show.'

'We don't need the money,' said David.

'Maybe we don't, but I'm going anyway. It's been arranged for weeks,' she said firmly.

A moment later Jade came back into the bedroom. She was naked. Her body was tall and slim with tiny breasts, tipped with purple, long thin arms and long thin legs. The perfect figure for a top London model, 1966 vintage.

David stared at the lush black bush that hid her vulva. He loved her cunt. White-skinned and black-haired on the outside, the colour of strawberry mousse inside. 'Come back to bed, love,' he said.

'No chance. I need coffee.'

She left the bedroom and David heard her filling the kettle in the kitchen. He got out of bed and followed in her footsteps.

It was a beautiful morning. The view from the kitchen window over Parson's Green showed that the sun was already warming the flower beds. He crept up behind Jade and slid his hands round to cup the tiny warm buds of her chest, and he slid his cock into the crack of her bottom.

'Stop it, Dave,' she protested. 'Not this morning.'

He slid his right hand down over her belly, as his penis grew and pushed at her flesh.

'Stop it,' she said again, but her protest had less force this time.

'What time's the car coming?' he asked.

'Seven.'

'Then we've got plenty of time.'

'No,' she said. But her voice had lost all its firmness,

and when David turned her to face him, she clung to his nakedness and began to return the hot kisses he showered onto her mouth.

She slid down his body and knelt before him and took his long, veined cock into her mouth. She sucked at the end and pushed it deep down her throat, then pulled her mouth away and kissed his testicles, taking one ball at a time, all the way between her teeth.

Dave moaned as his legs went weak at the sensation. He looked out of the window at the windows of the flats opposite and wondered if any other man in the area was getting this sort of treatment before breakfast.

He pulled Jade to her feet and pushed her back towards the kitchen table. She smiled at him as he did it. She knew what her man liked.

He lay her across the cold pine top of the table, her legs apart and dangling to the floor, then expertly entered her open pussy.

He put one arm each side of her for support and began to move inside her in the age-old act of love.

Jade closed her eyes as she felt him smoothly rubbing his prick up and down the inside of her box, his hairy groin bumping her clitoris. She wrapped her long legs round him and he moved faster and faster towards climax. The girl matched him with every stroke and the sound of their panting breath filled the room.

'Do me,' she cried. 'Do me, David.'

'I'm coming,' he cried back and put more effort into his strokes.

'Come on then, come,' she screamed, and with one last lunge he filled her hot pussy with his come. At the first spurt she pulled him in even tighter with her legs and came in rapture over his penis.

They stayed together, frozen, until their post-coital delight was interrupted by a ring at the doorbell.

'Jesus,' she cried, pushing him away and out of her. 'The bloody car's early and I'm not even dressed yet.'

3

Sylvester Marshall, who had taken the stage name Sly
Mars when he'd been one of the founder members of
The Getaways and now refused to answer to any other,
also woke up at six o'clock that Saturday morning. But
he was definitely not in his own bed. And he was
certainly not with his girlfriend.

Sly didn't believe in girlfriends. Not regular ones
anyway. The rhythm guitarist believed in spreading
himself thin. Find 'em, fuck 'em, and forget 'em, was
his motto, and in the years since the band had been
formed he'd remained true to his code.

It made life more interesting, he found, to wake up
every so often and not know where he was.

That morning, he was lying in a double bed in a white
painted room with no curtains at the windows. The
strong sunlight falling across the bedspread was what
had wakened him.

He was alone. And once again had no idea where he
was, and who or what had brought him here.

He looked round the room. Apart from the bed it
was empty. No other furniture, no carpet, and more
importantly no clothes. Sly looked under the single
sheet and blanket that covered him. He was naked.

Then he looked at the pillow next to him. It was indented and he found one short black hair on it.

He picked up the hair, which was so unlike one of his own blond curls and looked at it.

He was still none the wiser.

Suddenly, the door in the wall opposite opened and a woman entered.

Then, just like David, some miles away, at roughly the same time, it all came back to him.

The woman who came through the door was huge. Not tall. maybe five four, five five, but fat. No, he thought, running his hand through his hair. Not fat. Gargantuan.

She had short, black hair that matched the one he had found on the pillow and wore a purple kimono with a dragon design that did nothing to disguise the size of her.

'Hi, Sly,' she said in a New York accent. 'Did I wake you?'

Sly shook his head. 'No,' he replied.

'Well, good morning to you,' she said. 'How are ya feeling?'

'Just fine,' he replied. 'How are you this morning, Nancy?'

Nancy Goldstein, London correspondent for *Tiger Beat* magazine. The top teen tabloid in the United States.

'Never better, darlin', I had to pee. Now budge over and let your Nancy girl get in there with you.'

She undid her wrap and let it fall to the bare floorboards and stood before Sly in all her glory.

He figured she weighed upwards of fifteen stone. Her shoulders were wide, her breasts – huge, with brown nipples the diameters of saucers – hung down over the folds of her belly until they almost hid the tangle of inky-black pubic hair that grew up to her navel. She saw him looking and did a twirl. Her arse was mammoth, the black hair continuing up between her buttocks and her back to her shoulders and across to her armpits, where two huge, dark tufts peeked out. Her thighs were almost as big around as Sly's waist and dappled with cellulite.

Christ, thought Sly. I wonder what the boys back in Walthamstow would make of this action.

'Like what you see?' asked Nancy, turning back to face him.

Sly grinned and nodded. Sure he did. 'Sure I do, Nance, me old love. Now get back in here and give us a kiss.'

She did as she was told, the bed creaking as she climbed aboard and rolled into Sly's embrace.

As they lay there together Sly remembered how they'd met.

The previous evening *Tiger Beat* had laid on a reception for Nancy. She was new in town and needed to meet some hot rock-and-rollers *tout suite*. Sly had heard about the bash and, being alone, had gone to it.

He'd had his eye on a pretty young thing in the latest brightly coloured, flowered pants suit when Nancy had walked into the room. The combination of her size and the clothes she wore intrigued him. She was dressed like a beatnik, all in black. Shoes, stockings, roll-neck jumper. All black. With the ensemble, she'd worn thick black sunglasses, a black beret on her short black hair and she'd been smoking a black cigarette. Her fingernails were painted black and even her lipstick was such a deep purple that it looked black in the light. The only contrast was a single strand of pearls around her neck.

Sly had fallen like the proverbial brick.

Nancy had recognised him straight off and made her way towards him, just pausing to chat to the celebrities that she met on the way.

Sly could wait. He knew willing quiff when he saw it. And Nancy was willing. More than willing, as she'd proved after the party had finished.

When she finally got to him, shook his hand and said, 'Sly Mars. Hi. I'm Nancy Goldstein. Whaddya say?'

'Do you wear black underneath too, Nance?' asked Sly.

Her face split into a big grin. 'That's for me to know and you to find out.'

Sly grinned back. 'Your place or mine?' he said.

'Not so fast. Later maybe. I've got business to do here. And, talking of business, I think the band is great. When are you going over to the States?'

'Who knows, Nancy?' he replied. 'When we're asked.'

'It may be sooner than you think. I want to do a big spread on you guys. Are any of the others here?'

'Just me, Nance. We're having a couple of days break. We're gigging next week, so everyone's taken the weekend off.'

'Cool. Listen. Why don't you circulate? Like I said, I've got people to see. But don't vanish. Maybe we could get dinner together later and a club. What about it?'

'Sounds good to me,' Sly said. 'I'll be here.'

The rhythm guitarist wandered around the room,

chatting to people he knew, and being accosted by people he didn't who wanted to say hello to part of the latest pop sensation.

Finally, around midnight when the general consensus was that the party was over and other delights beckoned, Nancy Goldstein found him again, talking to a journalist from the *NME*.

'Hi, Derek,' said Nancy to Sly's companion. 'Hello again, Sly. You still up for some food?'

'Starving, babe,' he said.

'Let me get my coat and we're off.'

The *NME* journalist made his farewells and Nancy went off, then reappeared in a black fur, grabbed Sly's arm and said, 'So where's it to be, lover?'

'The Speak. Food, booze, drugs and music. Not necessarily in that order.'

Nancy grinned and squeezed his arm through the expensive leather jacket he was wearing.

They went out to the street and Sly hailed a cab and asked for Margaret Street. Once in the back, Nancy snuggled up to him and he felt her hand on his thigh. During the short journey they kissed for the first time. Her mouth opened and he thought that she was going to swallow his face.

When they got to the club they went through to the comparative quiet of the restaurant, a journey of just a few yards that took over twenty minutes to complete, what with all the hello-ing and goodbye-ing they had to do to the many friends and acquaintances who were hanging round the bar.

They got a table and sat down and gave their order. Nancy insisted that Sly sat next to her on the bench seat looking over the restaurant, and as soon as he joined her he felt her hand on his thigh again. This time just an inch away from his cock. He grinned at her across the six inches that separated their faces. 'Where d'you live?' he asked.

'Hyde Park Mansions. It's just a stroll away.'

'Nice.'

'You?' she asked.

'Chelsea. I have to pass yours to get home.'

'So you do.'

Just then, their order arrived and they settled down to Scotch and Cokes, steak, French fries and peas and listened to the sound of the band in the next room.

Around about two when the place was buzzing, Sly said, 'You fancy leaving soon?'

'It's just getting hot in here,' said Nancy.

'I've been hot since I met you.'

'You Brits are so bold,' said Nancy.

'Do you mind,' said Sly, who was getting drunker by the minute and knew he might not last for too many more rounds at the pace Nancy put the whisky away.

'No, honey,' she said.

'Well, let's go then.'

'OK,' she said. 'Do you want to get the bill?'

'It's on my account,' said Sly and stood up unsteadily. 'Come on, let's take a walk. I need to clear my head.'

They emerged from the depths of the club into the relative cool and quiet of the West End. Nancy took Sly's arm and they made for Hyde Park.

The walk took about ten minutes and, by the time they got to Nancy's address, Sly was feeling much better. They took the lift to the top floor and Nancy let them into her flat.

It was all painted white, with white carpets on the floor and minimal furniture. Nancy dropped her coat onto the floor next to the single sofa in the living room and turned towards Sly.

'You were wondering what I wear underneath,' she said.

He nodded, and took off his jacket and threw it on top of her coat.

Nancy took off her sunglasses, beret and pearls and dropped them onto the floor too. Underneath the glasses, her eyes were thick with mascara. Then she tugged her sweater over her head, unzipped her skirt and let it drop to the floor.

Her enormous tits were restrained by a black bra with each cup big enough to hold a melon. Below the bra she wore a high-waisted corset with suspenders that held up her black stockings. She wore no knickers and her pubic hair was black and shiny in the light.

'Satisfied?' she asked, pirouetting in front of Sly. As she turned away from him he saw that her buttocks were dimpled with fat.

'I will be,' he said. 'Come here.'

Nancy did as he ordered. She went into his arms and he felt the cruel elastic of her underclothes binding in the soft flesh beneath. His arms went round her and to the fastening of her bra and corset.

Drunkenly he unfastened her underclothes and pulled them off, until finally she was standing dressed in just a pair of stockings. Sly pulled at his own clothes until he was naked, then he bore her down onto the carpet. Her skin was incredibly soft and he could hold handfuls of her flesh in his hands. They kissed until their lips were sore, and Nancy grabbed hold of his prick as if it were a lifebelt and she was drowning. Sly sucked at the mountains of her breasts, taking great mounds of them into his mouth. Her nipples were as long as pencil erasers and as thick as Sly's fingers, and he sucked at the warmth of them until they were hard in his mouth. When he was tired of that game he moved his head down between her legs. He pushed her meaty thighs apart until he found the entrance to her pussy. Her juices tasted bitter-sweet on his lips and he pushed his tongue inside her until she cried out in pleasure.

'You're a dirty fucker,' she said. 'I've heard all about you.'

'Nothing good, I hope,' he said as he came up for air.

'Nothing.' And she went down on his cock. Sly watched as her body shook as she sucked at him, her flesh moving voluptuously like waves on the ocean over his skinny body.

Just watching her like that, leaning over his genitals and sucking at his long, meaty prick, excited him tremendously. He found the crack between her buttocks and searched out her arse with his middle finger. He pushed it inside her and the sensation caused her to suck even harder, until he could contain himself no more and he felt himself burst into her mouth. She sobbed as his come hit the back of her throat and sucked harder at his member. He lay back and let his spunk explode into her like a fountain of pleasure. She kept sucking and swallowing, making more animal-like noises as she did so. Only when he was totally spent did she let his cock out of her mouth.

She turned and smiled at him, then crawled over his body and kissed him with her mouth full of Sly's come. They shared his seed, spitting it back and forth between

themselves until they lay back to regain their composure, her body half on his.

Sly felt Nancy's heart beating next to his and shifted
her bulk to get more comfortable.

'Am I too heavy for you?' she asked.

'No, babe,' he said. 'You're beautiful.'

'I want to come,' she said.

'So you shall. Just give me a minute.'

'I thought you guys could fuck all night long.'

He slapped her hard on her bottom and the waves of
fat rolled away from his hand. 'I will,' he said, 'just
have some patience.'

He rolled her right off him and fetched his cigarettes
out of his jacket pocket. He lit two and gave one to her.
She lay back on one elbow and regarded him. 'You've
got a nice bod, Sly,' she said.

'You too,' he said.

'Most guys think I'm too fat.'

'Most guys are stupid. Got an ashtray?'

'In the kitchen. Over there.'

She indicated a door and Sly got up again and
padded into the room and found an ashtray on the
draining board by the sink. On the way back he looked
in the fridge. There was a bottle of champagne cooling
on one shelf. He took it back with him.

'Drink?' he said.

'You're a genius. Get it open,' said Nancy.

Sly did as she said and they shared the bottle,
drinking from the neck. By the time it was half empty,
Sly could feel himself getting hard again.

'It does it every time,' he said, put down the bottle,
stubbed out their cigarettes, grabbed Nancy and began
to kiss her again.

She responded as though she hadn't been with a man in a year. She stroked his hard body with her fingertips, which she wet with a mixture of her own saliva and the wine she had drunk, eliciting moans from the young man as she found his balls, his arsehole, the inside of his ears and his nipples. He reciprocated in kind, driving her mad with his lips and tongue as he explored every inch of her sensitive body. Finally, when she could stand it no more, she mounted him and bore down on his prick until he penetrated her cunt. She rode down on his cock with her groin, the muscles inside her vagina tensing and relaxing as she strove to pull his come out of his balls.

She got faster and faster in her movements, her huge breasts wobbling from side to side and up and down, slapping against the folds of fat on her belly, until she quivered like a white blancmange.

When he could stand it no more, Sly roared like a bull and let go his second orgasm of the night into her honeypot. She bore down on him harder and harder until she, too, cried out as if in pain and came with a splash onto his genitals.

When their climax was complete, they lay next to each other on the white carpet until they had the strength to get up and stagger off to bed.

4

Jud Morgan, the drummer with The Getaways had only one problem: he was terribly shy with girls. At nineteen, the youngest of the band and the newest member – having joined just in time to record the band's first single – he was also technically a virgin.

He could not believe it. Here he was, one quarter of what was considered by many to be the hottest act since The Rolling Stones and he'd never had his end away.

He'd joined the group, after answering an ad in *Melody Maker* and doing several auditions, from his old band, The Houston Jumps, who had been based in his home town of Hastings. They'd been an amateurish blues outfit, of whom Jud had been by far the most proficient, and had never graduated from gigging in small clubs along the south coast, when Jud had been catapulted into what looked like it was going to be very big time.

Jud had spent all the spare time he could muster in his formative years practising his drumming skills in the garage of the house where he lived with his mum and dad on the cliffs above the town. When he wasn't at school, or out earning the money to buy bigger and better drums, he was glued to the stool behind his kit. Before joining his first band, he'd had few friends. None of them female.

When the band had done one of their sporadic gigs, a few girls had latched onto them. But the older and more confident members of the group had grabbed them for themselves. Apart from a few clumsy kisses on the beach, or in the van, Jud's sex life had been non-existent.

After joining The Getaways, things weren't much better. The other members and the road crew were old friends and, although they made Jud more than welcome, once again it always seemed to be them that the girls latched onto. Jud couldn't understand it. But it was true. Neither Tony, Sly nor David knew of his predicament, and he daren't tell, because he knew that they'd make his life miserable with their teasing.

That very same Saturday evening Jud had been invited to dinner at the country home of the parents of one of the friends of the band, Alistair Willoughby. Alistair's parents were minor aristocrats with a fairly stately home on the other side of Guildford. The occasion was the seventeenth birthday of Alistair's sister, Fiona.

Alistair had taken a particular shine to Jud, being roughly the same age and a fanatical fan of rock drummers.

Alistair lived in a flat off the King's Road which his father rented for him until he found his true vocation. This seemed to be taking an exorbitant amount of time, mainly because Alistair spent most nights sitting up, smoking dope and listening to one of the several thousand records he owned, and most of the days sleeping.

One afternoon the previous week, Jud and Alistair had been sitting in the flat listening to the new Manfred Mann album, when Alistair extended the invitation.

'Look, Judley,' said Alistair. 'I know it's probably a terrible bore, but you'll be doing me a big favour if you'll come. I'll get a gold star from the old man. And frankly I could use a few. He's none too happy about me being up here, spending his money and having nothing to show for it. He keeps going on about me getting a job. I mean . . . He's even threatened to fix me up with some frightful position as a clerk with a firm in Guildford. It's run by one of his old pals. He wants me to work my way up to the top. Can you imagine? I'll have to move back home. And what with this chum of his during the day and the parents at night, I won't have a life to call my own.

'Fiona's a bit of a misfit. Seems to run in this generation of the family. Must be in the genes. She goes to a terribly correct boarding school but they've just about given up on her. She loves your band and when she heard we were such good friends she begged Mummy and Daddy to ask me to ask you if you'll pop down for her birthday din-din. Listen, they'll pull out all the stops. Lay on a terrific spread. There's tons of room for you to stay. I'll drive you down in the old Aston and pop you back the next morn. What do you say?'

'What's she like? Your sister.'

'Between you, me and the apple tree, she's a dreadful little frump. All spots and braces on her teeth. No wonder she's got no friends. Frankly I'm not surprised one bit. She resembles a horse if you must know. Mind you, I haven't seen her for ages. She's been at school the last half-dozen times I've been down. And at

Christmas she went skiing. So it's been well over a year. Look, I know it doesn't sound much of an evening, but will you come?'

Jud agreed. He hadn't anything to do that night, it being a day off for the band, and he agreed to call round to Alistair's about four so that they could make an early start.

Alistair made good time in the Aston Martin his father had bought him for his seventeenth birthday and they turned into the drive of the Willoughby residence at just after five.

They were met at the door by a maid, who showed the pair of them to the room where Jud was due to spend the night. It was large and airy, with an en-suite bathroom and french windows that opened onto a balcony that overlooked the grounds at the rear of the house.

'I'll leave you to bathe and change,' said Alistair. 'Drinks in the drawing room, sixish. It's off the hall by the main door. You can't miss it. If you *do* get lost, just holler, someone will hear. I'll see you down there. I've got to have a serious talk with pater about certain problems I'm having with my bank. I want to catch him in a good mood. Having you come down to the ghastly Fiona's dinner might be the ideal moment.'

Jud unpacked his things from the bag he'd brought, including a birthday card and a copy of the band's album autographed by all four members and wrapped in bright paper. He hung his clothes in the wardrobe and went and ran a bath. He sat in the tub for half an hour, washed his hair, then dressed in a white shirt, black velvet trousers and high-heeled boots. He put on a matching jacket, flopped his hair into a fringe, looked in the mirror, winked at his image and, as a distant clock struck six, took Fiona's card and present and made his way downstairs.

He found the drawing room with no trouble. Alistair was standing by the empty fireplace with one elbow on the mantelpiece and holding a glass in the other. He was wearing a plain, dark blue suit, with a matching flower-patterned shirt and tie, and black Chelsea boots. Facing each other from twin sofas across the fireplace were a middle-aged couple. They both rose when Jud entered the room.

'Jud. My dear chap,' said Alistair. 'Come in and meet Mummy and Daddy.'

Jud transferred the card and present he was holding to his left hand and walked into the room.

Alistair's mother was about forty, attractive and sophisticated-looking. She wore her blonde hair in a neat bob, minimal make-up, and a strapless, knee-length cocktail dress in royal blue, with high-heeled shoes in matching leather.

'Jud,' she said, advancing towards him, hands outstretched. 'It was so good of you to come all this way. Alistair's told us so much about you. Welcome.'

Jud shook hands with her. 'Hello, Lady Willoughby,' he said, slightly over-awed, and feeling awkward as usual when faced with an attractive woman.

'Caroline, please,' said Lady Willoughby. 'And this is my husband, Victor.'

Jud walked towards Alistair's father and shook his hand also.

'Delighted,' said the older man, who Jud took to be about fifteen years older than his wife. He was dressed in a dinner jacket and bow tie. 'Fiona will be down directly. Are those for her?' He indicated the items that Jud was holding.

'Yes,' the drummer replied. 'It's our LP. We've all autographed it.'

'That's a lovely thought,' said Caroline. 'I'm sure Fiona will treasure it always. Can I get you a drink? We've got some martinis mixed.'

'Fine,' said Jud and watched in admiration at the way her body moved under her dress as she walked over to a sideboard and poured a clear, oily-looking mixture from a jug into a cocktail glass.

As he accepted the drink, they heard footsteps on the wooden floor outside and a young woman entered the room.

Jud looked at Alistair in surprise. This was hardly what he'd expected. Instead of resembling a horse, the girl who walked through the door looked like a young Brigitte Bardot. Alistair looked equally surprised.

'Fiona,' he said.

'Surprised, big brother?' said the girl.

'I'll say I am. Whatever's happened to you?'

'I've grown up.'

Fiona was wearing a cocktail dress of similar style to her mother's, although slightly shorter, but not as abbreviated as the girls in Chelsea were wearing their skirts. The low-cut bodice and the dark green material showed off her shoulders, which were smooth and slightly tan, beautifully. Her hair, the same shade of blonde as her mother's, was piled up on her head in a loose bouffant.

'This is Jud Morgan,' said Alistair, 'drummer with The Getaways. Jud, this is, as if you haven't already guessed, my sister, Fiona.'

'I recognise you from *Top of the Pops*,' said Fiona. 'I love your record.'

'Thank you,' said Jud and handed her the parcel and the card. 'Happy birthday. I've brought you a copy of our album.'

'That's lovely,' said Fiona and bobbed up and kissed Jud's cheek, which made him burn red with embarrassment. 'It's not out yet, is it?'

Jud shook his head. The young woman was beautiful and all his old shyness flooded back.

'The girls at school will be green that I've got it first.'

She put the record and the card on the coffee table that stood between the two sofas. 'Now, Mummy promised I could have my first martini tonight as it's my birthday and I'm going to take her up on her offer.'

5

As the policeman approached the car, Tony pulled out of Mandy's soaking quim, tugged up his trousers and hurriedly fastened the zip. She pulled down her skirt and they both sat in the back seat of the car as if butter wouldn't melt in their mouths.

The policeman leant down and peered inside the car, then opened the passenger door. 'Is everything all right in here, sir?' he said to Tony.

'Yes, officer,' he replied. 'I heard a terrible squeak coming from the back suspension. We were just trying to locate the source.'

'I'm sure you were, sir. But a lady complained that you were – how can I put it? Engaged in obscene behaviour.'

'Not at all,' said Tony. 'Just looking for the squeak.'

'Did you find it?' asked the policeman.

'I'm not sure. It might take a bit of time.'

'Then can I suggest you look for the – ahem, squeak – somewhere other than off the King's Road on a Saturday lunchtime. Perhaps the privacy of your own bedroom might be better.'

Tony was about to make a crack about getting the car into the lift when he thought better of it. 'Of course, officer,' he said. 'You're quite right. There is a time and place.'

'Precisely, sir,' said the policeman. 'Now it might be a good idea if you resumed your journey.'

'I agree,' said Tony and he pushed the driver's seat forward, opened the driver's door, clambered out of the car and smiled at the policeman. The policeman pulled the passenger seat forward, extended his hand to Mandy and helped her out of her side of the car. The officer smiled surreptitiously as he caught a glimpse of her naked, dripping cunt as he did so. Tony smiled, too, as he got back into the driver's seat, started the E-Type, waited for Mandy to sit back next to him, put the car into gear and slowly pulled away, giving the policeman a friendly wave as he went.

'I think the copper liked you,' he said to Mandy as the car joined the traffic.

'He should have done,' she replied. 'I gave him a good flash of my pussy for his troubles.'

'You're a dirty girl,' said Tony as he reached the Fulham Road and turned left.

'But good fun,' she said.

Tony nodded and headed towards the street where she told him she lived.

The house she lived in was part of a terrace of white and terracotta-coloured houses in a road off Kensington High Street, which had seen better days. 'Coming in?' she said.

'If you like,' he replied.

He locked the car and followed Mandy up the broad stone steps to the front door of the house. It was obviously split into half a dozen flats, hence the bank of bells by the side of the door. She let them in and he walked up the stairs behind her. The way her arse twitched under her tiny skirt and the knowledge that she had nothing on underneath began to excite him again.

Her flat was on the top floor and she opened the door and ushered him in. Somewhere inside music was playing. Tony recognised a track from *Rubber Soul*.

'My flat-mate,' explained Mandy, then called out, 'Trish, I'm home.'

The music stopped and Tony heard footsteps and a tall, dark-haired girl, dressed in jeans and a T-shirt, appeared at one of the doors off the short hall. 'Where have you been?' she demanded, ignoring Tony. 'I've been worried.'

'I stayed at Tony's,' said Mandy. 'Trish, this is Tony Parker. He's with The Getaways.'

Trish looked at Tony for a moment. Then turned on her heel without acknowledging him and went back into the room. The music started up again. Louder this time.

Mandy looked at Tony and pulled a face. 'Sorry,' she whispered. 'Trish gets a bit over-protective at times.'

Mandy went into the room after her friend and Tony followed. The girl was sitting in an armchair in front of the fireplace. 'I'm sorry, Trish,' said Mandy and knelt next to the chair. 'I know I should have phoned. I was a bit stoned.'

Trish looked at her, then over at Tony. 'I bet you were,' she said. 'Got anything with you?'

'Just a bit of dope,' said Mandy.

'Roll it up then,' said Trish, 'and I might forgive you.'

Mandy's face brightened, and she opened her handbag

and got out the makings of a joint and went to work on it.

Trish looked at Tony again. 'Are you really in The Getaways?'

'Sure,' said Tony.

'They're not bad,' said Trish grudgingly. 'Your record was on the radio this morning. Three times.'

'That's good,' said Tony. 'What do you do?'

'I work for a book publisher?'

'Interesting?'

'It can be.'

As they spoke, Mandy finished expertly rolling the joint and lit it, then passed it to Trish and said, 'Are you sure you're not cross with me?'

Trish took a long hit, breathed deeply, exhaled and said, 'I might have to punish you a little.'

Tony's ears pricked up at the words and he wondered what was going on.

'Oh Trish,' said Mandy, 'I wasn't that bad.'

Trish put her hand up Mandy's skirt, felt around the girl's bottom, pulled her hand back out, rubbed her fingers together, sniffed them, pulled a quizzical face and said, 'Is that right?'

'Maybe a bit bad.'

'Very bad, I'd say.'

'What are you going to do?'

'You know very well, Mandy. You leave me to sleep alone, go off with some guy, get fucked, stay out all night, come home with your cunt soaked with spunk and expect to get clean away with it. No chance. You must have known that I'd have to be severe with you when you got home. It was no good bringing him with you. He won't be able to protect you.'

'I thought . . .' mumbled Mandy.

'You thought wrong. Don't you think she deserves punishment Tony?' asked Trish.

Tony reached over and plucked the joint from between her fingers. 'Yes, I do,' he said as he took a long drag at it.

Trish smiled dreamily as the dope hit. 'A man after my own heart,' she said, got up and left the room.

'What's all that about?' asked Tony.

'Trish looks after me,' said Mandy.

'You sleep with her?'

Mandy nodded.

Tony smiled. It might turn out to be a very interesting afternoon, he thought.

A minute or two later Trish returned. Tony's eyes nearly popped out of his head. She had changed out of her jeans and was now wearing thigh-length black leather boots with spiked heels at least six inches high, a tiny leather miniskirt and a pointed leather bra. In her right hand she carried a long, plaited leather bull-whip. In the other a riding crop with a handle made of horn, tipped with filigreed silver.

She stood in the doorway and crossed her arms. 'Get in here, Mandy,' ordered the dark-haired girl. 'You can come if you want,' she said to Tony, 'but don't try and interfere. This is between her and me.'

Mandy did as she was told, looking apprehensively at Tony as she went. Tony followed. He had no intention of interfering. Just the opposite, in fact.

The two girls went through another door off the hall. It led into their bedroom. It contained a neatly made double bed, a chest of drawers and a wardrobe. Clothes hung from every available space. The curtains were half drawn and the room was warm and dim.

'Take off your dress,' Trish said to Mandy.

Mandy pulled it over her head and stood naked in front of Trish and Tony. Tony felt his manhood growing at the sight of her and the knowledge of what was to come.

'On the bed, bitch,' ordered Trish.

Once again Mandy obeyed.

'Face down,' said Trish.

Mandy rolled onto her stomach.

Trish went to the chest, opened the top drawer and took out a handful of scarves. She went over to the bed, dropped the whip and crop next to Mandy, knelt on the mattress, grabbed Mandy's left hand and tied it to the bed head, using one of the scarves. As she did so, her skirt rose up and exposed the naked orbs of her bottom. Tony smiled and kept watching. Trish lashed both Mandy's ankles and other wrist to the bed, then gagged her with the last of the scarves, picked up the whip and cracked it over the blonde's supine body.

'You little bitch,' she hissed, and brought the whip down on Mandy's smooth bottom. The girl grunted and bucked at the blow, and Tony saw a perfect pink reflection of the plaits of the leather spring up across her buttocks. 'You've been unfaithful again, you whore,' said Trish through gritted teeth and laid the whip across Mandy's shoulders. Once again the girl grunted through the gag and her body jumped as if she'd been subjected to an electric shock.

'You horny cow. You're mine,' said Trish, and the whip went down for the third time. This time across the delicate skin at the top of Mandy's thighs, just under the swell of her arse. She rose off the bed again in agony and her head moved from side to side in denial of the pain.

Trish dropped the whip and picked up the crop by its handle. A short loop of leather was attached to the other end.

'Cunt! Slag! Bitch! Whore! Cow! Tart! Slut!' she cried as she dealt out more blows, concentrating on Mandy's arse and the sensitive area where her legs joined in the curls of her pubic hair, until it was a mass of red weals.

With one last blow, Trish dropped the riding crop and knelt by the side of the bed and covered Mandy's bottom with kisses, sinking her nose into her slit, which Tony noticed was glistening with slimy juice. The dark-haired girl kissed and licked at what previously she had punished, and instead of shouting insults she began to say words of love between the kisses.

The whole episode excited Tony tremendously, as did the fact the Trish's skirt had ridden up again and he could clearly see the mass of black curls between her legs which were equally wet, if not more so, as her girlfriend's. The smell of their sweat and femininity was tangy in the warm air of the room.

Without thinking, Tony loosened his trousers, knelt behind Trish, pushed her skirt all the way up around her waist and slid his member into her soaking slit.

The girl screamed at the intrusion, then relaxed and concentrated once more on Mandy's crack as Tony filled hers to bursting point.

As Tony fucked Trish, he saw that Mandy had moved her head round to watch. Her eyes were full of tears from the pain of the beating she had taken but they were filled with pleasure, too, as one of her lovers fucked the other and the first licked out her treasure chest.

He felt the leather of Trish's boots on the naked skin of his thighs and smelt the odour of it mixing with the girl smell, which made him work harder and harder at Trish's slippery pussy. She pushed back hard at him as he slammed into her until he felt the tickle of orgasm and shot his load into her waiting cunt. As he did so, she bit down on Mandy's arse until all three of them were shivering with pleasure as if they were a single organism.

Tony stood up and pulled free from the glue of sex between Trish's thighs, grabbed her hair and tugged her to her feet. 'Untie Mandy,' he ordered and twisted the handful of curls he grasped in his right hand until she screamed in pain. He threw her onto the bed next to Mandy. 'Do it,' he said. 'And quick.'

Terrified, the girl complied.

When Mandy was free of her bonds, Tony threw Trish onto the top of the bed, picked up the whip from where she had dropped it and began to lash at the girl's body. She lay, accepting the blows with a satisfied smile on her face.

Mandy watched in amazement, then grabbed the riding crop and joined in the beating.

Tony stood back exhausted as Mandy continued raining blows on her girlfriend's body. Then the blonde girl fell upon Trish's form and they began to kiss each other as if Tony wasn't there. He smiled, got dressed and crept out of the flat. The last thing he heard was a scream of joy as one of the girls came.

6

When Jade had dressed and left in the car to take her to the airport, David returned to bed and fell asleep once more.

He awoke again just after eleven and lay on his back watching the reflection of the sun coming through the gaps between the curtains as it moved slowly across the room.

Finally at noon he got up, shaved, showered, cleaned his teeth, put on a wildly patterned silk shirt, ancient blue jeans and a pair of black desert boots.

Then he went into the kitchen and made a cup of coffee before deciding what he would do with the rest of the day. He got out his address book and sat in the kitchen at the table where he'd fucked Jade a few hours earlier and turned the pages slowly.

When he got to the 'J's, he saw the name Jane Price, a phone number and address in the King's Road in a hand that wasn't his own. He thought for a moment, puzzled, then remembered. Jane Price. Of course.

Jane was a junior press officer at The Getaways' record company, Zenith. He'd met her a few weeks earlier at a dinner held for owners and managers of important record shops in the south east.

She was new at the company and the dinner had been the first major project for which she'd been respons-ible. David had been the guest of honour, as the single was the priority release for that week.

Jane had been very nervous but David had charmed everyone, including her, and the meal had been a great success. Afterwards they had shared a limo home, dropping her off first in Chelsea before taking David to Parson's Green.

He remembered that she was a tall, big-boned blonde with thick hair, cornflower-blue bedroom eyes, a sexy mouth, nice tits, a great arse and long legs that he would love to have wrapped round his waist.

On the drive back she'd told him about the other musicians she had been out with and he knew he was on to a certainty, especially when she'd written her own address and phone number in his little black book and invited him to drop in at any time. David decided to make it that very afternoon and not to call her first, in order to make the visit a pleasant surprise, and an even more pleasant one for both of them when he fucked the arse off her.

He hung around the flat for another hour, then went out to the green and caught a cab to Chelsea.

David knocked on Jane's flat door at two in the afternoon. She opened it and said, 'David! What a nice surprise.' She was wearing a short black skirt and a thin white shirt with the tails knotted under her full breasts. In the heat, the shirt was damp with perspiration and the shape of her tits and her nipples were clearly outlined against the almost transparent material.

'I said I'd come round soon. I hope you're not busy.'

'Busy? In this heat, on a Saturday afternoon. Not likely.'

'Are you on your own?'

'Totally.'

He held up a bottle of wine. 'I got this at the offy. Straight out of the fridge.'

'You're an angel. Come in.' She opened the door fully and allowed him to enter. She looked admiringly at his body in the silk shirt and jeans, so old and tight that where his cock coiled against the inside of the material the pressure had worn them white. She wondered if he was wearing anything underneath and the thought made her hot between her legs, hotter even than the day was, and she wanted to hold his prick in her hand and feel it grow between her fingers.

'There are glasses in the kitchen,' she said. 'It's through here.'

She led the way, and she let her hips sway more than usual as she walked and hoped that he was looking at her arse under the brief miniskirt. She got glasses from the top shelf of the cupboard. As she went up on tiptoe to get them she knew that he could see her long bare legs almost up to the tight black silk knickers she was wearing. She didn't look but knew that he was admiring them. When she turned towards him, a wine glass in each hand, he was smiling. She smiled back.

'Bottle opener?' he said.

'In the drawer beside you.' He opened it and found the implement.

'Come into the living room,' she said. 'It's cooler in there. I've got the curtains drawn. I'll put on some music.'

Once again he followed her and once again she felt his eyes on her backside.

The living room was cooler, but not much. The curtains that covered the long windows shifted slightly in the sultry breeze off the river and as they moved back and forth the sunshine dappled the carpet. Four storeys up, the afternoon traffic on the King's Road was muted to a distant buzz. David went and sat on the sofa. Jane switched on the stereo. The new Dylan album was already on the turntable and she started it and placed the needle at the start of side one. 'Great album,' he said. 'I wish Tony could write songs like that.'

'No one can,' said Jane. 'Anyway, you've got a different kind of sound.'

'You can say that again,' he agreed.

She went and sat on the armchair opposite him. She didn't want to rush things and frighten him off. She was going to add this musician's scalp to the growing list of pop stars she'd fucked but she wanted to take her time. Or at least not jump on him the first minute she had him alone and maybe frighten him off altogether. Not that there was much chance of that. She crossed her legs and let her skirt ride up another inch or two.

He opened the wine bottle and poured two glasses and came over and gave her one of them, before resuming his seat. 'Want a joint?' He asked.

'Sure. What is it?'

'Red Leb. The best.' He took a lighter and a ready-rolled joint out of the pocket of his shirt and lit it. He inhaled deeply, then let out the smoke in a thin grey stream, smiled and passed it to her. She felt a tingle as their hands touched.

She took a blast of dope. 'That *is* good,' she said and leant back in her seat.

'God, it's hot,' he said.

'Take off your shirt,' she said. She could already feel the drug in her bloodstream, relaxing her and slurring her speech slightly. He'd been right, it was the best.

'If you'll take yours off too.'

'*David*!'

'If you do I'll show you a way to cool down.'

'How?'

He unbuttoned his shirt and took it off, then rolled the freezing wine bottle over his boney chest. 'It really works,' he said. 'Try it.'

She took the bottle from him and touched it to her naked belly, under her knotted shirt. 'It feels good.'

'Do it properly,' he said.

She felt herself blush and hesitated, but the dope and the wine had relaxed any inhibitions she might have had and she untied her shirt and slipped it off her shoulders. She saw him looking at her naked breasts and felt the nipples swell up under his gaze, and she breathed in deeply so that they stood up proudly and she placed the cold bottle between them and rolled it across the hot flesh. It felt delicious and she involuntarily opened her legs. He stood up and came over to join her on the sofa. He took the bottle from out of her hand and leant down and kissed her breasts. She felt the heat between her legs again and the tight material of her panties cut into the delicate membranes of the wet flesh of her cunt. David lifted his head and kissed her lips. She opened her mouth and his tongue explored the inside of it and, getting bolder, she stuck her tongue into his mouth and licked his teeth and sucked on his full lower lip. He put his hand between her legs and she opened them even more. His fingers found the tight curls of her pubic hair, then slid into the hot, wet slit of her pussy. As she felt him probe her, she gasped with excitement and pleasure.

She placed her hand on his thigh and felt the muscles of his leg through the thin denim. She slid her hand up until she found the bulge of his cock. It was straining against the tight material and she thought that if it grew much more it might split the material. It was a lovely thought, that she excited him so much that his prick might just rip straight through the denim to get at her. She slid her hand round to find the fullness of his balls and she squeezed them gently, then harder. He moaned at her caresses and their kisses deepened. He slid off the sofa and knelt between her legs and pushed her skirt up around her waist, pulled her panties down to her ankles, then over her bare feet, and threw them across the room and plunged his tongue into the fur of her cunt. She opened her legs as wide as she could and put them over his shoulders and pushed his head down so that he almost drowned in her wetness. 'David, darling,' she moaned. 'Snog my cunt, you bastard.'

He did as she said. Licking, biting, nibbling at her cunt lips and sucking them up into his mouth, pushing his tongue as deeply into her as it would go, then sliding it down the tender flesh between her cunt and her anus and tongued her arse until she thought she'd scream with pleasure. Which is exactly what she did as she came for the first time into the mouth of her new lover.

7

Jane collapsed back onto the sofa, gasping in the stifling air. David stood up, kicked off his shoes, unzipped his jeans and pulled them over his hips in one smooth movement. She'd been right, he wasn't wearing anything underneath. She watched as his cock sprung up erect. It looked huge, just two feet in front of her face, jutting out from the thicket of black pubic hair that covered him from the top of his thighs, almost to his navel. She marvelled at the fact, that such a huge thing was going to squeeze its way into her tight little pussy. But she knew it would and the thought almost scared her. His balls were round and firm-looking and she reached out and cupped them in one hand. He closed his eyes in ecstasy as she squeezed them between her fingers.

'They're beautiful,' she said and squeezed them tighter. He bit his lip as she did so. 'Don't worry,' she whispered. 'I wouldn't hurt them. They're too gorgeous.'

He sat down next to her, and they began to kiss and stroke each other again. She ran her fingers up the length of his shaft, then began to gently massage the tool. She licked her fingers and coated the knob of it with her warm saliva, rubbed the end and ran her fingernail around the edge of the opening. Their kisses became more passionate and he kneaded her breasts gently. 'Shag me,' she said suddenly. 'Shag me now.'

He pushed her back onto the sofa and she opened her legs. She kept her left foot on the carpet, then put her right leg up, knee bent, and braced that foot on the arm of the chair. David put one arm on each side of her and lowered himself until the swollen glans of his knob dipped into the wet crack between her legs. She guided him inside and he pushed himself into her as far as he could go. She felt as if her insides were going to burst and she began to push him away. Then, as she felt herself adjust to him, she pulled him closer. 'Christ,' she said, 'you're big.'

'All the better to fuck you with,' he said and began to move inside her. She felt her breasts flush as she neared another orgasm. Faster he pumped, and faster still, until the heat built up in her and she came again. On his cock where it belonged. She screamed as her cunt muscles gripped him tightly. As she cried out, she felt him stiffen and cry out too and shoot into her. She felt his come spray the inside of her womb in a hot shower that seemed to last for hours and she screamed again and he collapsed on top of her.

They lay there for a few minutes, then David rolled off and lay next to her. He was breathing heavily and laughing and he found her hand and held it tightly. 'I'm going to a gig tonight. Want to come?' he asked.

'Where?'

'Blaises.'

'Great. Course I'll come. But first I've got to have a shower. I'm sure I stink. Come and help me.'

She got up, tottered slightly, pulled him up after her and led him into the bathroom. She could feel his come juice running out of her cunt and down her legs in a sticky stream as she went.

The shower cabinet was in one corner of the room and she reached in and turned on the water. She let it run hot, then added cold until it was exactly the same temperature as that of her body. She stepped inside and pulled David in after her. They embraced and kissed as the water beat down on them and ran between their bodies like a tropical rainstorm. The feel of it on his skin, and her slick breasts rubbing on his chest, quickly made him hard again. Jane got the soap and lathered her hands and began to soap him. She massaged his nipples and watched as the suds washed down his body. His cock reared up between them, bobbing against the bottoms of her breasts. She knelt down and took the end in her mouth. It was so hard she almost needed two hands to straighten it and, as she let it slide between her lips and down her throat, she was afraid she might choke. She pushed it in and out, tonguing the end and milking his balls. She wanted his hot sperm in her mouth. To taste it and swallow it down so that it would be in her belly all night.

He gripped two handfuls of her wet hair and pushed his knob further down her throat. She felt as if she was going to choke again but refused to let it go. She held his buttocks and he began to spasm and shot his come into her mouth. She swallowed it greedily, feeling its warmth coating her throat. She sucked until she had every drop inside her, then reluctantly let it go and lay back against the side of the shower and looked up at him through the water that fell onto her face.

8

Sly and Nancy had fallen asleep in each other's arms and didn't wake up again until almost three in the afternoon. Nancy wanted a replay, but Sly was due at his mother's house in the East End of London for one of his infrequent visits and asked for a raincheck.

Nancy was not best pleased, but after Sly put on his cockney charm to the maximum she let him go on the proviso he called her the next day. He agreed and took her number. Then he pulled on last night's clothes, ran his fingers through his hair, kissed her gooey lips and left. He hailed a black cab at Hyde Park Corner and gave the driver his mother's address in Walthamstow.

He arrived at the door of the small council flat at three forty-five and rang the doorbell.

The door was opened by his sister-in-law, Sharon, carrying her young baby. 'Hello, Sharon,' he said to her. 'Hello, Keith,' to the baby, who regarded him solemnly. 'How's my favourite nephew?'

'You're late,' said Sharon, and turned on her heel and walked back into the flat.

Sly crossed the threshold, closed the door behind him, and followed her into the kitchen. She sat at the table and he sat opposite her.

'Where's Mum?' he asked.

'She waited for you, but had to go out. She'll be back in about an hour. She said that if you're here, she'll make you some tea,' replied Sharon, a slatternly bottle blonde with an inch of black at the roots of her hair. Sly gave her the once-over as she spoke. She was wearing a short-sleeved white blouse and a black skirt, slightly longer than was fashionable. Her legs were bare. She was still rather chubby from her pregnancy, but retained a certain brassy prettiness. Her hair was drawn back in a ponytail but wisps of it had escaped and hung round her ears.

'Great,' said Sly. 'Want a cuppa?'

'Don't mind if I do,' replied Sharon.

Sly got up, fetched the kettle, filled it at the sink and put it back on the stove. He lit the gas and leaned against one of the kitchen cupboards and looked at Sharon again.

She was in her middle twenties and had been married to Sly's brother Wayne, a merchant seaman, for three years. Sharon had never got on with her brother-in-law, but now he was a pop star she grudgingly talked to him.

'You're doing well,' she said. 'I saw you on TV the other night.'

'Not bad,' admitted Sly. 'Not bad at all.'

'Better than us.'

'If you're short . . .' said Sly.

'It's not that. But thanks anyway. It's just that Wayne's away such a lot.'

'When's he coming back?' asked Sly.

'Two months time.'

'Where is he?'

'The China Sea.'

'It's all right for some.'

'It's all right for him,' she said bitterly. 'It's me that's left here on me own with the baby.'

'Could be worse,' said Sly and as the kettle boiled he turned away to prepare the tea.

When he turned back Sharon had slipped her blouse off her shoulders, undone the nursing bra she was wearing and attached Keith to one breast. Sly watched curiously as the baby suckled at her nipple. Her breasts were large, white and blue-veined, and the sight of them made Sly go hard between his legs. Previously he had never had any carnal thoughts about Sharon, but witnessing the intimacy between mother and baby roused him.

'He looks like he's enjoying that,' he said as he poured out two cups of tea.

'Same as all men. Give them a tit and they're happy.'

Sly grinned, took the cups to the table, put one in front of Sharon, one in front of his own place, and resumed his seat. The kitchen was warm and silent except for the noises made by Keith's mouth on his mother's breast.

After a few moments she transferred Keith to her other tit. Sly saw the suck marks on her flesh, and a drop of milk trembled at the end of her nipple.

'I wonder what it tastes like?' said Sly.

'Ain't you never had none?' asked Sharon. 'A big boy like you.' Her face was flushed and a drop of sweat was caught in the loose hairs by her ear.

Sly shook his head. 'Not since I was a nipper.'

Sharon put her hand under the breast that Keith had recently vacated, lifted it and offered it to Sly. 'Go on

51

then, have a drop. But don't bite.'

Sly didn't need to be asked twice. He left his seat, went round the table, knelt by Sharon's chair and attached his mouth to her breast. Her milk was sweet on his lips, and as he sucked to get more she bit down on her bottom lip. Soon the room was full of the sound of two mouths feeding on one woman's milk.

After a minute Sharon said, 'Let me put him down.'

Reluctantly Sly let go of the pap at which he was sucking and Sharon got up and left the room. She returned a minute later without Keith. 'He'll sleep for an hour now,' she said and sat down again.

Sly resumed feeding off her and as he did her legs opened. Sly moved from one breast to the other and Sharon began to stroke his hair. As he continued, her legs opened wider and her skirt slid up her pale thighs. Sly ran his hands up the inside of them until he found the crotch of her knickers which were soaking with lubricant from her cunt.

Sly stood up and pulled her to her feet, then sat where she had been sitting. He undid his fly and freed his tool. She smiled at the sight of it. 'It's bigger than Wayne's,' she said.

'It always has been,' said Sly. 'It pisses him right off.'

Sharon pulled up her skirt, took down the white knickers she was wearing, straddled Sly, facing him, and slid onto his knob.

'Is it all right?' asked Sly, thinking of the fact that she'd recently given birth.

'Course it is,' said Sharon. 'It's tight enough for you, isn't it?'

Sly nodded, it was. Lovely and tight, as it happened. Sharon began to move up and down on his rod, slowly at first, then more frantically as she neared a climax.

'I ain't been fucked for months,' she said through gritted teeth. 'That sod's more interested in spending his money down the pub.'

More fool him, thought Sly. Leaving a horny cow like this at home. It was just a matter of time before some randy bugger caught hold of her and gave her a good seeing-to. At least he was keeping it in the family.

Sly massaged the great weight of her breasts as she worked herself off on his prick. He put his mouth to each one in turn, tasting her milk again as she rode him. The combination of her breasts being sucked and his cock inside her, drove her to a screaming orgasm and Sly felt his own juice bubble into her hungry womb as she came.

Sharon slumped down on him, covering his face and neck in hungry kisses. 'That was good, Sly,' she said. 'I haven't had one like that for years.'

'That's nice, Sharon,' he whispered in her ear. 'But now you'd better get off me, there's a good girl. Mum'll be home soon and I don't think she'd understand.'

9

The dinner that the Willoughbys laid on was indeed as terrific a spread as Alistair had promised. The party sat down to king prawns in mayonnaise, a crown roast of lamb, pink and juicy, with all the trimmings, followed by strawberries and cream. All served by the maid who had showed Jud to his room, and a liveried footman.

There were four or five different wines with the meal, including champagne to celebrate Fiona's birthday, and liqueurs with coffee.

Fiona drank sparingly, but the rest of the dinner party were more than merry by the time they left the table.

It was a warm evening and as soon as they were back in the drawing room, Fiona said, 'I want to go for a walk around the garden. Will you come with me, Jud?'

'It's dark outside, darling,' said her mother.

'We'll stay close to the house. And it's only twilight. Say you'll come, Jud.'

'Of course,' said the drummer. 'I haven't been outside yet.'

Fiona fetched a light jacket, and she and Jud went through the french windows, across the paved area outside, down some stone steps and onto the lawn that stretched for three hundred yards or more, until it met a line of trees that were all but invisible in the gloom.

Fiona took Jud's arm. He was very aware of her perfume. It mixed in his head with the alcohol he had consumed and made him feel slightly dizzy.

They crossed the lawn together and Fiona chatted about the presents she had received for her birthday, how much she wanted to go to a Getaways' concert, and all the other groups she liked. Jud was only aware of the weight of her on his arm, the growing erection in his tightly cut velvet trousers, and how glad he was that it was dark so that she couldn't see it.

'Do you want to see the lake?' asked Fiona.

'Sure,' said Jud.

'It's just through the trees. Be careful you don't trip over anything.'

She led him through the bank of trees and he saw the black surface of what seemed to him to be a stretch of water as large as the English Channel. A few yards from where they emerged from the copse was a wooden building and a short jetty.

'Let's go into the boathouse,' said Fiona. 'There's a light in there.'

'OK,' said Jud and she led him over to the building, opened a door in the side of it, leant in, found a switch and illuminated the interior.

Jud followed her inside and found himself on a wooden platform over the water. Fiona shut the door behind them, grinned wickedly at him, reached between her breasts and brought out a crumpled joint.

'You do smoke, don't you?' she asked.

Jud nodded. 'But I didn't think you would,' he said.

'Why not? All the girls at school do. Mind you,

Mummy and Daddy would go mad if they knew. You must promise not to tell. Not even Alistair. Have you got a light?'

Jud took his lighter from his trouser pocket, Fiona put the joint between her lips and he lit it for her. She sucked smoke in deeply, held it in her lungs, and exhaled. 'Lovely,' she said and passed the joint to Jud. 'Let's sit down.'

She led him over to a rowing boat that stood on the platform. She hitched up her skirt high enough to show off the tops of her nylons, stepped into the boat, and sat on one of the cushioned seats. She slipped out of her jacket and threw it towards the front of the boat, then patted the material next to her. 'Come on, Jud, join me, and we'll get stoned.'

Jud did as she said. He handed her the joint, then got into the boat and sat next to her. She looked up at him and said, 'Do you get many groupies in your band?'

'What?' said Jud.

'Groupies. Girls who want to have sex with you.'

'A few. Why?'

'Just interested. That's what a couple of the girls at school and I are.'

'What?' he said again, disbelievingly.

'When a band comes to town, we dress up, bunk out of school and go and see them.'

She saw him look at her dress.

'Not like this, silly. This is just for Mummy and Daddy's benefit. We wear all the latest gear.'

'What bands?' said Jud.

She told him the names of several of The Getaways' contemporaries.

'What do you do?' he asked.

57

'What do you think?'

'I don't know.'

'Shall I show you?' And, without waiting for a reply, she put her hand down to his groin and unzipped his fly.

Jud couldn't believe what was going on as she put her hand inside and eased his erect prick through the gap in the material.

'That's a pretty one,' she said and leaned down, opened her mouth and breathed a hot breath onto the tip of it.

After the drink and the dope, Jud was really horny, and the feel of her soft fingertips along his cock and the warm, damp exhalation from her lungs made his penis jump and almost come.

'You are eager,' she whispered. 'Don't be too quick.'

Fiona shot her little hot tongue out of her mouth and caressed the knob of his cock with it. Jud moaned and leant back against the padding of the seat behind him. Fiona looked up quickly and smiled. 'That's right,' she said. 'Relax and enjoy it.'

Jud did just that as her tongue continued over the rim of his foreskin and down the length of the shaft. She undid the top button of his trousers to allow her to get to his balls, which she kissed and licked, and ran her tongue gently through his pubic hair until he thought he'd explode.

After about five minutes of this attention, Jud could stand no more. He put his hand into the thickness of her hair and pulled her head back and up, until he could reach her lips with his.

They kissed each other's mouths and Jud pulled Fiona onto his lap. Her skirt slid up her legs as he did so and he put his hand between her knees. She wriggled about, so that her skirt slid higher, and he found her stocking tops and the plumpness of the flesh above them. He pushed it up further and found the material of her knickers. Between her legs her skin was hot and damp.

She was kissing his face and biting at his lips as he wrestled with her clothes until, eventually, her skirt was up round her waist and he could see the whole length of her legs.

They were beautiful. Long and slim, sheathed in dark nylon with a darker band around the tops, white suspenders and white, lacy, hipster knickers.

'Unzip me,' she breathed into his ear, between kisses.

Jud reached round her back, found the zip in her dress and pulled it down. Underneath the strapless top she was wearing a white strapless bra. Jud wrestled with the fastener and Fiona giggled into his ear.

'Here, let me,' she said and reached awkwardly behind her, found the hook and eye and expertly undid it. Her bra dropped off her breasts and they stood proudly under Jud's lustful eyes. He began to kiss and suck at them, and Fiona moaned at the attention he was giving the twin beauties.

She opened her legs, hitched them over his, and closed them again with his rod between the steamy meat of her thighs. He was in ecstasy. Tonight he was sure he was going to lose his cherry with this beautiful teenage girl.

They continued kissing and caressing, with Fiona playing with the knob of his cock that stuck out obscenely between her thighs.

As they wrestled on the narrow seat of the rowing boat, with Fiona's dress bunched around her waist and Jud's trousers around his thighs, Jud went for the home run. He began to pull her panties down over her suspenders and stocking tops, exposing the darker blonde triangle between her legs. She was wet with lubricant and he could smell the heavenly scent of her womanhood. With her knickers around her knees, he forced his face into the mass of crinkly hair that protected the entrance to what, to him, was paradise.

He pushed her panties down further and her legs opened so that he could see the tiny pucker of her anus in the crack of her cheeks. He tongued the skin between her quim and her arsehole and she held his head tightly into her.

By that time he was kneeling on the bottom of the boat and she was stretched out along the seat. It was now or never, he knew, and he moved between her legs in preparation to entering her.

She sensed what he was about to do. 'No,' she hissed. 'Stop it, Jud.'

He couldn't believe his ears, and moved back in surprise as she rescued her knickers from around her ankles and pulled them up to imprison the delights of her cunt.

'What?' he said.

'You can't fuck me. Sorry.'

Sorry, he thought. *Sorry*. What's with sorry?

'I don't understand.'

She pulled down the skirt of her dress, smoothing out the creases in the material as she did so, and pulled up the bodice to cover the alabaster beauty of her breasts.

'I'm a virgin,' she said. 'I'm saving myself for my

husband. I'll do anything else you want but you can't fuck me.'

'I thought you were a groupie?'

'I am. We are. But we're all virgins too.'

'Shit,' said Jud, and realising the ridiculousness of his position pulled up his trousers.

'But you liked what we did, didn't you?' asked Fiona.

'Yes. But . . .'

'So did I. Are you going to be playing near Bournemouth soon?'

'Maybe. I don't know,' he said, confused at the path the conversation was taking.

'Will you get us tickets and backstage passes?'

'Yes, if I can.'

'Oh, Jud, you are sweet. But we'd better go back now or Mummy will get worried.'

'*Go back!*'

'Yes,' said Fiona and rescued her jacket, which she put on over her crumpled dress and buttoned it up tight, then stuffed her bra into one pocket. 'Do I look all right?'

'You look fucking gorgeous,' said Jud. 'Can't we stay here a little longer?'

'No. I'll see you again though, won't I? Either in Bournemouth or when I come up to London. I will, won't I? Promise.'

Jud promised, and with that they made their way back to the house where Fiona vanished to repair her damaged make-up and Jud was forced to face her family.

Not that they noticed anything, being all well pissed by then.

Fiona went to bed about midnight and Jud sat up with the rest until, just after one, they all retired to their separate bedrooms.

10

Jud went miserably upstairs, undressed, and took his aching balls to bed.

He lay in the darkness, feeling well pissed off. He thought about wanking but he was so angry that he couldn't be bothered. Once again he was amazed at his own ineptitude. There he'd been, with a warm, wet and willing girl, and once again he'd blown it.

Another virgin. Who would credit it?

He'd been laying between the covers, half asleep for about ten minutes, when there was a tapping on the door. He sat up in bed with the bedclothes round his waist and wondered if he'd imagined the noise. Then once again he heard a gentle knocking at the door.

His first thought was that Fiona had reconsidered. That he'd made her so hot for him that she had to come to his bed in the middle of the night.

He grinned. 'Come in,' he said.

The door opened and, to his surprise, who was standing in the doorway but Caroline Willoughby. She was wearing something diaphanous and, as she stood at the threshold of Jud's darkened room backlit by the glow from the hall outside, he could clearly see every curve of her figure through the thin material.

'Caroline,' he said in surprise and leant over and switched on the bedside lamp. The light from it immediately transformed her negligee from transparent to translucent.

She came into the room and gently closed the door behind her. When Jud's eyes became used to the light, he saw that her nightdress was not quite so translucent as he had thought. The material moulded to the shape and dark hue of her nipples, and a darker cloud was visible between her legs.

He realised that he was naked from the waist up and pulled the bedclothes tighter round him.

'I couldn't sleep,' Caroline explained, standing on the carpet in front of the door about four yards from the bed. 'Sometimes I take a walk around the house when I can't. I find it settles the mind. I wondered if you were comfortable.'

'I am,' said Jud.

'Have you got a cigarette?' she asked.

'Yes,' replied Jud, about to get out of bed to find them when he realised he was naked under the covers. 'In my jacket pocket.'

She went over to where he had thrown the garment over the back of a chair, and with every move another part of her body pressed against the inside of her negligee and became clearly visible to him. As she bent over the jacket, the material tightened across her buttocks and, for the second time that evening, Jud clearly saw the crack between a pair of shapely female buttocks.

As he watched her, he felt the blood rush into his penis again. Within a few seconds he was so hard he thought the veins would burst from the pressure and he'd die there, lying in that bed, from loss of blood.

Caroline found the cigarettes and lighter, turned and came towards Jud, holding them. She perched on the edge of the mattress, now only a foot or so away from him, and crossed her legs.

'Do you want one?' she asked,

He nodded to disguise his confusion, accepted a cigarette and Caroline lit it for him. It was such an intimate gesture, in the privacy of his bedroom, that he blushed.

She sat on the edge of the bed looking at him closely. 'You're a very handsome boy, Jud,' she said. 'I envy girls these days going out with men who look like you, dress like you and wear their hair like you. It was very different in my day. Men were so formal then.'

She reached over to get the ashtray from the bedside table and the front of her nightdress fell open and Jud saw her breasts swing free for a moment. He thought he'd never seen anything more desirable before in his life. They were bigger than her daughter's, with puckered brown nipples in the centre of maroon aureoles. As she sat back they vanished, but Jud knew that she knew he had seen them and she didn't care one bit.

'Is it chilly in here?' she asked. 'Or is it me?'

Jud, who had rarely been less chilly in his life, said, 'I'm fine.'

'Do you mind if I slip under the covers with you? I should have worn something else over this for my midnight stroll.'

'No, of course not,' said Jud, ever the gentlemen.

Caroline got up and, hardly disturbing the bed-clothes, slid under them, next to the drummer.

'Isn't this cosy?' she said. 'We can have a lovely chat

now. Or are you too sleepy?'

'No, I'm not,' said Jud, sleep being the farthest thing from his mind.

Caroline moved slightly and he felt the length of her leg from hip to ankle, next to his. The material of the negligee she wore being so thin, they might almost have been naked together. He could smell her perfume, sweet and heavy, in the room, her flesh was warm against his, and he felt an almost imperceptible pressure from it against his body. They finished their cigarettes and stubbed them out, and Caroline returned the ashtray to the bedside table and plumped the pillows behind them as if being in bed with a man young enough to be her son was a nightly occurrence.

They lay back on the thick feathers behind them and looked at each other. 'Did you enjoy yourself tonight?' asked Caroline.

'Very much.'

'You must come again some time.'

'I'd like that,' said Jud.

'Do you drive?'

Jud nodded, wondering where this particular conversational gambit was leading. He didn't have to wait long.

'You could come down one weekend when my husband's away. I get very lonely.'

'Do you?'

'Yes. *Businessmen.*' As if that explained everything. 'Will you?'

Jud nodded and Caroline reached out one hand and with the nail of her forefinger ran a circle round his nipple. 'You are so handsome,' she said. 'Can I kiss you?'

Jud's mouth was so dry that he only nodded in reply.

She leant over and kissed the side of his mouth, he turned and she was in his arms so naturally that he hardly noticed. Their mouths met again, their lips parted and their tongues touched. Her hand went under the covers and straight to his root. She pulled away. 'God, you're *immense*, darling,' she whispered and they kissed again fervently. She plastered her body to his and he could feel every inch of her womanliness against him.

She pushed back the bedclothes and admired his body. 'Beautiful,' she whispered. 'So young and so beautiful.' Then she picked up the hem of her night-dress and pulled it over her head and lay back, exposing every inch of her body to his gaze.

It was Jud's turn to marvel at the beauty of another body. Her figure was perfect, even after bearing two children. Her breasts were as pert as Fiona's had been. They stood proud of her chest like twin peaks of pure sex. Her waist was narrow, then curved out into luscious hips and legs that seemed to stretch for ever. Between her legs was an ash-blonde thicket over her mound of Venus.

'Do you like me?' she asked.

'I love you,' whispered Jud.

'Then love me, darling. Love me until you can't love me any more.'

He kissed her forehead, her eyes, her cheeks, lingered at the sweetness of her mouth, slid his lips round to her ears and neck, went lower to those breasts that he already considered belonged to just him. Ran his mouth down her belly and licked at her navel. Then worked his way down to the beautiful bush between her thighs.

She called his name repeatedly as his mouth explored her cunt. To Jud, she tasted as sweet as sugar in that special part of her. He rolled her over, parted the cheeks of her arse and found her brown hole with his tongue. Then he kissed her thighs, the back of her knees and finally bit at her toes.

'You're the most beautiful man, I've ever met,' she said. 'Lie on your back.'

He did as he was told and she raised herself above him, then lowered her honeypot onto his mouth. 'Lick me out,' she said vulgarly as she sat on his face.

He watched the beauty of her cunt descend on him. Her pubic hair was soaked and her labia open. She balanced herself over him and he lapped at the hairy skin between her legs like a man dying of thirst who had found a stream of fresh, cool water.

Her breathing became faster as he licked, sucked and kissed her. She bore down on him and he thought she'd suffocate him, but he kept his tongue moving inside her private parts.

Suddenly, with a scream, she stiffened and came into his mouth. He'd never tasted such heaven, as the juices of her orgasm flooded into his mouth. She slid wetly down his chest and looked into his face.

'Now it's your turn,' she said and rose up, manipulated his cock and eased herself onto the knob. She held herself up over him and teased him by sliding on and off the end of it, as if her cunt was kissing his erection.

'Please,' he implored.

'All right, my love,' she said and finally slid right down the length of his tool.

Jud had never known such pleasure as her hot insides gripped his prick.

'You're part of me now, darling,' she whispered, looking him straight in the eye. 'Give me your seed.'

Jud knew that she wouldn't have to wait long. After the night he'd had, and now actually being inside a woman's snatch, he was amazed that he'd been able to hold his come as long as he had. Caroline moved up and down the length of him, once, twice and he couldn't stand it any longer. With a cry of pure delight he came into the womb of the woman who had taken his virginity.

As he shot his load, she stiffened and took a second orgasm off the young man.

When Jud had spasmed again and again, with spurts of semen that felt like liquid fire, she collapsed on top of him in a sweaty heap.

They lay like death together, for a few minutes, until much to Jud's surprise and Caroline's joy he began to harden again.

'You wonderful man,' she said. 'I do envy your girlfriends.'

'I haven't got any,' he said.

'Nonsense.'

'I haven't. You're the first woman I've ever made love to.'

'Are you telling me the truth?'

'I promise.'

She looked him in the face. 'I don't believe it,' she said.

'It's true.'

'Then I'm flattered, and you'll love me forever, won't you?'

Jud nodded agreement and felt himself totally hard again.

Caroline slid off him and turned, sticking her bare arse into his face and began to lick his soaking prick. She purred as she licked their come off it. Jud reached out and began to finger her pussy. She stopped her ministrations and looked over her shoulder. 'Lick me out again,' she said. 'Give me a good tonguing.' Jud moved until his mouth was plastered to her cunt, his face in the cleft of her arse, and his nose in her arsehole. He loved the smell of her and happily drank his own come mixed with hers.

She suckled at his penis until he knew he must come again and, without a word, he wrestled her round and once more plunged into the depths of her. 'Come on then,' she cried. 'Fuck me, you little bastard. Give me more of that lovely juice you make between your legs.'

And once again Jud obeyed the orders of the older woman.

When they'd had their second fuck, Caroline lay back next to him in the wreckage of his bed and looked at her watch. 'I'd better go to *my* room,' she said. 'The servants will be about soon.' She got out of bed and, ignoring the come that dribbled down her thighs, she pulled on her negligee. Dawn was just breaking as she kissed Jud on the mouth and left his room with a wave.

He snuggled down under the bedclothes, feeling the cold soup of their mutual come that Caroline had left on the sheets, and as he fell asleep with the smell of her perfume in his nostrils and the taste of her sex on his lips, he smiled to himself and thought, 'I did it.'

11

At the same time as Jud was losing his virginity in Surrey, the rest of The Getaways were gathered round the bar of Blaises, a well-known in-crowd hangout in west London.

Sly and Tony had come alone. David had brought his new conquest, Jane. She was at present in the ladies with a couple of her friends who also happened to be at the club, leaving the boys in the band free to discuss their Saturday over three glasses of Scotch and Coke.

'You fucked your *sister-in-law*?' said David to Sly above the sound of Geno Washington over the in-house PA system. 'Man, that's sick.'

'No sicker than screwing Nancy Goldstein,' said Tony. 'The woman is the size of a house.'

'Fucking great,' said Sly. 'Nancy was great. Sharon was great. I've got an open invitation to pop round and see my nephew Keith any time.'

'I bet you have,' said David. 'What was old Nancy like on the job, anyway?'

'T'riffic,' said Sly. 'You wouldn't believe what she looks like with her kit off.'

'Big,' said Tony.

'But a great fuck,' insisted Sly. 'Like a big hot water

71

bottle and an eiderdown all rolled into one. Soft and hot. Lovely.'

'I'll take your word for it,' said Tony.

'Are you going to see her again?' asked David.

'Try and keep me away. She wants to do spread on us in *Tiger Beat*.'

'Does she, by Christ?' said Tony. 'You keep on the right side of her. Don't mess her around. At least not until she's done it.'

'As if I would,' said Sly. 'Anyway, what have you two been up to?'

'You wouldn't believe it,' said Tony.

'I would,' said Sly. 'This last couple of months I'd believe anything.'

'I saw two lesbians whipping each other.'

'Yeah?' said Sly. 'Fucking great. Can I come and watch next time?'

'Who says there's going to be a next time?' asked Tony.

The other two laughed.

'OK, I can't see why not.'

'What about you, Dave?' said Sly.

'Nothing much. Jade went off to Paris and I spent the day with Jane.'

'She works for Zenith, don't she?' said Sly, referring to The Getaways' record label.

'That's right. She works for us.'

'I wouldn't mind her working for me,' remarked Sly.

'You keep your hands off her.'

'Is it love?' asked Sly.

'Bollocks. When I've had enough, you're welcome.'

'That means next Tuesday if past form's anything to go by.'

'Funny,' said David.

'So where's our drummer?' asked Tony, of no one in particular.

'He's down at Alistair's,' replied David. 'It's his sister's birthday and she wanted a famous pop star at her party.'

'What, Fiona?' asked Tony.

'S'right,' said David.

'She's lethal,' Tony went on. 'I was round his flat one night last year. She comes in all decked out in her school uniform. Up for a visit, you know. She was a bit pimply, but by Christ she was willing.'

'What happened?' asked Sly.

'We had a sixty-nine.'

'How old is she?'

'She was just sixteen then. Or at least I think she was.'

'Do you think she'll get hold of Jud?' asked David.

'I wouldn't be at all surprised,' said Tony.

'Think he'll lose it tonight?'

'What?' said Sly.

'His virginity,' said David.

'He ain't, is he?' said Sly.

'Course he is,' said David.

'How d'you know?' asked Tony.

'I just do. Intuition,' replied David.

'He never mentioned it,' said Sly in an amazed tone.

'Well he wouldn't, would he?' said David.

'Do you think the wicked Fiona will get it then?' Tony again.

David shrugged. 'We'll find out,' he said.

'Christ,' said Sly. 'Who would've believed it?'

'I thought you'd believe anything,' said Tony.

At that juncture Jane reappeared with the two friends she had met in the ladies room. She introduced them to David, Tony and Sly. The first was a German radio journalist named Marsha. She was tall, blonde and Teutonic-looking, wearing a silver minidress, silver tights and silver shoes. The other was Judy, who also worked at Zenith, in the art department. She was a tiny redhead, dressed in blue jeans and a sparkley jacket over a low-cut blouse.

Sly nudged David. 'Reckon she's the same colour down below?'

'Only one way to find out, son.'

Sly immediately zeroed in on the redhead, dragging her onto the floor to dance to an Otis Redding tune.

David found a table, and he and the other three sat down and ordered two bottles of wine. He sat next to Jane, and Tony next to Marsha.

'So where do you come from, Marsha?' asked Tony.

'Dortmund.'

'Where the beer comes from.'

'You know it.'

'I know the beer. We've been there. Did a gig last year as a matter of fact.'

'I have not been there for two years. I live now in London. Permanently,' said Marsha.

'Working for a radio station.'

'Yes. I do pop group interviews on Radio Baden-Baden.'

'You haven't interviewed us.'

'I want to very much. I will speak with your manager.'

'Don't worry about him,' said Tony. 'I'm the man to see about radio interviews.'

74

'Is that right?' asked Marsha, all of a sudden more than interested, which was exactly what Tony wanted. He winked at David and said, 'Right as rain. Where are you living these days?'

'In Kensington.'

'Ideal,' said Tony. 'Alone?'

'Yes.'

'Then it's all back to yours for a party after. Right?'

'If you want.'

'Hear that, Dave?' said Tony. 'Marsha's throwing us a party. Got plenty of booze, Marsh?'

'I have schnapps.'

'Then we're your men,' said Tony. 'Let's get Sly off the floor and get gone.'

It took a further quarter of an hour to convince Sly of the wisdom of the move, but when Judy agreed that a party sounded good he soon acquiesced and all six of them set off to Marsha's apartment. Luckily it was just round the corner, a top-floor flat in a purpose-built block.

It was expensively furnished with a lot of blond wood and the latest lines in TV and stereo equipment. Marsha went straight to the record player and slapped on The Getaways' single.

'A number one,' she said, as the needle hit the groove.

'I'll drink to that,' said Sly. 'And talking of drinking . . .'

Marsha went out of the living room and returned, pushing a trolley that contained six tiny glasses and three bottles. Tony picked them up one by one. The bottles contained peppermint, strawberry and regular-flavoured schnapps.

Marsha opened all three and said, 'Help yourselves. My father sends me these. He thinks that a girl should be able to hold her liquor.'

'By the ears,' said Sly.

Marsha looked puzzled, so Tony explained the joke and she giggled loudly. 'You English pop groups are so naughty,' she said.

'You ain't seen nothing yet,' he retorted.

Everyone took a drink of the variously flavoured liquors and toasted themselves and each other and The Getaways' success. On Marsha's instructions, they knocked the drinks back in one.

Judy almost choked. Jane wasn't far behind. David, Tony and Sly, who were more used to alcohol, did a fair job of disguising the fact that neat schnapps is lethal. But Marsha gave the appearance of someone drinking tap water and was already into her second glass before any of the rest had downed the first.

Tony looked at her, impressed. 'You're used to this stuff?' he said.

'My father owns the company that makes it.'

Tony shook his head sadly and wondered if he'd be able to keep up with the German fraulein.

By this time Sly was on the sofa with Judy, groping her all over, and David and Jane had gone out onto the balcony that looked out over the darkness of Hyde Park and were in a passionate embrace.

Marsha and Tony refilled their glasses and knocked them back. 'Show me round,' he said.

'There is not much to see.'

'Amaze me.'

Marsha took him into the kitchen, which was tiny and spotlessly clean, then the bathroom, which was the same, and finally into her bedroom which was a little bigger and contained a three-quarter size bed, a chest and a set of wardrobes behind floor-length mirrors.

Tony admired his and Marsha's reflections. Then he sat on the bed. He patted the covers next to him. 'Sit down,' he invited. 'Let's talk about interviews.'

Marsha smiled seductively. 'What kind of interviews?' she asked.

'Sit down and I'll tell you.'

'In a moment. Now I must go to the loo.'

Tony grabbed her wrist.

'Take off your dress,' he said.

'I don't know you.'

'You will.'

She smiled again and lifted the hem of her dress and pulled it over her head. Then she kicked off her silver shoes and pulled down her tights. She was wearing nothing underneath. She was very thin, with tiny breasts, bony hips and long coltish legs. Her pubic hair was the colour of butter.

'You must let me go,' she insisted.

'I will. Come on.' Tony grabbed her and took her into the bathroom and locked the door behind them. He undressed in a second and sat on the side of the bath.

'I want to watch,' he said.

'No. That is unhygenic.'

'But sexy. Go on.'

She sat on the toilet seat and he could see her hesitate, then relax. Finally she relaxed completely and emptied her bladder, sending it tinkling into the bowl.

'You're dirty,' she said.

'Let's have a bath,' he said.

'Good idea,' said Marsha, who stood up then bent down to put the plug into the hole and gave Tony a beautiful view of the one in her bottom as she did so, with the tiny tuft of yellow curls peeking out from between her legs.

'Do you like bubbles?' she asked.

'The more the merrier,' he replied, and she turned on the taps and picked up a plastic bottle and sprayed blue into the swirl of water, which immediately began to form a thick foam.

The room filled up with steam and Marsha tested the water and adjusted the flow from the taps. 'Groovy,' she said.

Tony picked her up and stepped into the bath. She beat at his chest. 'No,' she cried. 'Put me down.'

He did exactly as he was told and dunked her into the warm water, then slid down to face her across the length of the bath.

Marsha's tiny breasts floated on the top of the water and her nipples played peek-a-boo in the foam. He grabbed her hands and pulled her close and kissed her. She kissed him back enthusiastically. He ran his hands down her flanks and between her legs and found the hair that surrounded her honeypot. He pushed two fingers gently inside her and began to explore the hot cave within. She opened her legs wider to allow him access and he pushed in two more fingers to widen her crack.

'That's lovely, Tony,' she said. 'Open me up more.'

He did just that. Her cunt felt like elastic as he pushed in his thumb and widened the orifice even more. He worked his whole hand in and out of her and she rubbed her arse on the bottom of the bath. Blindly she felt for his cock under the water and began to wank him in the same rhythm as he was wanking her.

He moved faster and so did she and his whole hand seemed to be inside her. Their movements got faster still and her hand was splashing water up the walls, when he felt his orgasm building and he stiffened and she lifted the tip of his cock out of the water and sprayed his semen over her hair, face and neck. As the boiling liquid hit her skin she stiffened and, with a wail like an air-raid siren, came onto Tony's fingers.

They both dropped back into the water and Marsha searched for any come in reach of her tongue and licked it greedily into her mouth.

Tony lay back and watched her. He could feel the sweat running down his face and he splashed water onto it, then reached over for a towel and dabbed it dry.

'Gimme,' said Marsha, and he passed her the towel and she dried her own face and hair, rubbing the semen from his balls into it. 'Protein,' she explained. 'Good for shininess and condition.'

'I'm glad to have been of some use,' he said.

'You were,' she replied. 'Are we getting out now?'

'We'd better,' he replied, and pushed himself up and out of the bath and onto the mat by the side of it. He reached for another towel and began to dry himself.

Marsha emerged from the water like a fair-haired sea goddess, dripping water and bubbles, and Tony wrapped her in the towel and began to pat her dry. 'I suppose we'd better go and find the others,' he said.

12

When they went back into the bedroom, two of the others were on top of Marsha's bed. Tony and Marsha stood in the doorway to watch.

David was lying on the bed cover with his head between Jane's legs, licking at her pussy. They were both naked, their clothes strewn across the room. Tony and Marsha listened to the slurping sound of David's tongue at Jane's cunt lips and smelt her sex in the warm June night.

They continued watching as David turned Jane onto her front and she pulled her buttocks apart for him to see her arsehole. He examined it for a moment, then put his face into the cleft of her bottom and kissed it.

Jane pushed her arse up into his face and he bit at the orbs of her bottom until she rolled away from him and caught sight of Tony and Marsha watching.

'David,' she said and pulled the bed cover over her nakedness.

David looked round and grinned.

'Sorry,' he said without a trace of shame. 'We didn't think you'd mind.'

'I don't,' replied Marsha.

'Didn't think you would.'

Jane was still clutching the bed cover across her breasts and hadn't noticed that it didn't cover her damp pubic mound. Tony smiled at the sight.

'We'd better leave these two alone,' he said to Marsha. 'Let's go and see what Sly's up to.'

They turned and left the room and went back to the living room where Sly and Judy were hard at it on the sofa, and from the brief glimpses that Tony caught, he saw that Judy was indeed a natural redhead.

'You boys are so randy,' whispered Marsha.

'We're just making the most of it,' replied Tony equally softly. 'You never know when it's all going to end.'

'Not so soon for you, I think,' said the German girl. 'I believe you are going to be very popular for a long time.'

'I'll drink to that,' said David. 'Have you got a spare room where we can crash out?'

Marsha nodded, and led him through to another bedroom no bigger than a box room which contained a single bed which they both climbed into and fell asleep.

And so Saturday turned to Sunday, which eventually became Monday, which was the day of The Getaways' gig in Norwich.

13

The band rendezvoused at Sly's flat that morning at ten a.m., where they were picked up by their manager, Dominic Edwards, in his Bentley Continental, for the long drive to Norwich where they were playing at the Odeon Cinema, supported by two local bands.

The equipment had left earlier in a hired truck accompanied by The Getaways' two roadies, Donkey and Derek.

Dominic took the A12 to Colchester where they stopped for lunch and they arrived at the venue at four o'clock in the afternoon.

There were already fifty or so fans waiting at the front doors, although the show wasn't due to start until seven thirty, and Dominic drove his car around the back to avoid them, dropped off the band at the stage door and parked the limousine in the car park.

When he got back he met the cinema manager who showed him to the dressing room where the four Getaways were waiting for their sound check.

'How goes it, boys?' said Dominic as he entered the room. He was a large, florid man of about forty who loved the good things in life. Flashy cars, good food and wine, and his beautiful wife, Anya, in roughly that

order. He was an old Etonian who had worked for a
bank in the city since leaving Cambridge University,
and had seen so many fortunes made in the pop
business with the money he loaned out that he had
decided to get in on the act himself. He'd managed to
get a job as assistant to a promoter who was one of the
bank's best customers and had given himself a crash
course in group management, with particular reference
to the way Brian Epstein ran his stable of acts, and
kept his eye out for a likely looking band to manage.
One night he'd seen The Getaways perform in a
club in London and had been impressed with the songs
that Tony had written for the group and had
approached them. At the time, the band had just
sacked their previous manager and in fact were on
the point of breaking up because of the lack of
interest being shown in them by the rest of the music
business.

Dominic had convinced them to stay together, had
borrowed a substantial amount of money from the
bank he had previously worked for and with his con-
tacts had got them signed to Zenith almost immediately. He also convinced them to get rid of their
drummer, who was always so drunk he could hardly
keep in time, which they did.

And now, less than a year later, with new member
Jud, they had notched up three hits and as far as
Dominic was concerned the sky was the limit for all
concerned. In fact, on that particular Monday afternoon, he was a very happy man indeed and intended to
break some extremely good news to the band over the
dinner table.

'Not bad, Dom,' replied Tony. 'The roadies have

gone out for some beers and sandwiches. How are the ticket sales going?'

'Sold out days ago,' said Dominic gleefully. 'Over fifteen hundred tickets gone and I hope there won't be a dry seat in the house by the time you come off stage tonight.'

'Not a chance,' said Sly. 'I've got a new pair of hipsters to wear and they're so tight I can hardly sit down in them.'

'Wrap a sock round your dick and the little chicks will be coming into their knickers,' said David.

'I don't need no sock,' retorted Sly. 'My prick's big enough already.'

'Just ask Nancy Goldstein if you don't believe him,' said David to the rest of the room, with a laugh.

'Nancy Goldstein,' said Dominic. His ears pricking up at her name. 'What about Nancy Goldstein?'

Sly smiled. 'I fucked her the other night.'

'Did you?' asked Jud. 'It's the first I've heard of it.'

'You were too busy down in Surrey, from what I've heard,' said Tony.

Jud blushed crimson and Tony smiled triumphantly at David.

'It won't be the last though,' said Sly, temporarily saving Jud from further embarrassment. 'She wants us for a spread in *Tiger Beat*.'

'Spread. That's a good word for it, if all I've heard is true,' said David.

'When did it happen?' interrupted Dominic. This could be most interesting.'

'Friday,' said Sly, buffing his nails on his shirt, and with a smug look at the rest of the band. 'And don't worry, lads, I didn't let the good name of the band down. She was very satisfied with my performance. She'll be back for seconds this week.'

'I want to meet her,' said Dominic. 'And don't mess her about. She's a very important woman.'

'And a very big woman,' said Sly. 'In all the important places.'

At that moment they were interrupted when the roadies came into the room carrying boxes full of cold bottles of beer and packets of sandwiches which the cinema manager had laid on for the band. Donkey, a giant of a man, led the way, and Derek, who looked like he should be in a band himself with his long hair tied back in a ponytail, followed.

'Grub up, boys,' said Donkey, and he and Derek put the boxes on the rickety table in the middle of the dressing room.

Everyone dived in and the room was silent for a few minutes.

'Where we staying tonight?' asked Jud eventually through a mouthful of a cold chicken sandwich.

'The Grand,' replied Dominic. 'There's got to be some compensation for driving up here into the sticks. I've heard the chef is excellent.'

'Don't you ever think of anything else but your stomach, Dom?' asked David.

'You can't live on sandwiches,' said Dominic, gingerly examining the contents of his own snack.

'You should have been with us on some of our gigs before you took over,' said Tony. 'Sometimes we only ate once a week.'

'But now, only the best for my boys,' said Dominic with a smile. 'You lot are going to be bigger than The Beatles.'

'We need hits in America for that,' said David seriously.

'You will have, I promise,' said Dominic. 'Some *extremely* big things are about to happen, I promise. The new single's going to be number one soon over here . . .' He hesitated, then grinned, and decided he couldn't keep his secret to himself a moment longer. 'And I'd like to take this opportunity to announce that it will be released by Capitol Records in the USA in two weeks time, with a big publicity campaign, and the chance of a major tour this autumn.'

The rest of the young men gathered in the room looked thunderstruck.

'Capitol! That's great,' said Sly, breaking the silence. 'The Beatles and The Beachboys label. I don't believe it. That's fantastic, Dominic. How the hell did you manage it?'

Dominic touched his forefinger to the side of his nose conspiratorially. 'A coup, dear boy. A coup.' He beamed proudly.

'What happened to Neptune?' asked David, referring to the label that had released the band's previous two singles in America, where they'd barely managed to dent the *Billboard* Hot Hundred.

'Owing to some astute negotiations on my part, and the impact of the three singles you've released over here on the British charts, Capitol have taken over your contract from Neptune, and when the new single is a hit they intend to rerelease the previous two. Remember what they did with The Beatles in sixty-four?'

'Course we remember,' said David. 'You don't forget something like that in a hurry. They had most of the top ten one week. And if I remember rightly we were freezing our balls off doing a tour of scout huts in Scotland at the time.'

'No more scout huts, I promise,' said Dominic. 'Neptune were never up to it, promotionwise. But Capitol have almost guaranteed me a top-ten hit first time out. They're pulling out all the stops. And then the album. . . .' He paused for effect. 'We could all be millionaires this time next year. I intended to tell you later at the hotel and break open the champers, but with the news of Sly's latest conquest and the fact that she's on our side . . .' He paused again. 'It's like a good omen and I'm afraid we'll have to do with this rather muddy beer that's the best that Norwich can supply for now. But later . . .'

'Later!' The band and the roadies chorused, and all raised their beer bottles in a toast to their manager and shouted out their congratulations and hugged each other in anticipation of the fame and fortune that was to follow.

14

After all the excitement of the news that their manager had given them, The Getaways went on stage and ran through a few songs to get a sound balance. Not that they really needed to worry, as the PA system in the cinema was well past its best, and from previous experience they knew that the volume of the screaming from the fifteen hundred or so fans that would soon pack the place out would prevent anyone hearing what they were playing anyway. But, being pros, the band wanted the sound to be the best possible, if only for the benefit of the road crew, various cinema staff, and the members of the local bands who were sitting in the stalls listening in awe to their hit-making cousins who had come up from the big city to show them how it should be done.

In fact, The Getaways had never sounded better and came off stage after four songs to genuine applause from the small crowd that had gathered to listen.

They returned to the small room that would be their home for the next few hours in high spirits, and when the roadies came in with more drinks and some ready-rolled joints, their spirits became even higher.

Dominic, who had been to the hotel to check

everyone in, returned to the cinema at about seven. He reported an hysterical reaction from fans at the sight of his car, and rubbed his hands gleefully at the thought of the profit for the night and the anticipated increase of sales of the single in the local record shops that he'd checked on by phone from the hotel.

The first local band went on at seven thirty sharp to boos from the fans that packed the auditorium. They played for twenty minutes, then there was a short break before the second band took the stage. They'd had a record released on a tiny local label and had a few fans in the audience and went down slightly better than the first band. They too played for twenty minutes and came off at about eight thirty.

The Getaways were due on at eight forty-five and as that time arrived the band, still waiting in the dressing room, stage clothes immaculate, three guitars tuned to perfection and Jud beating out rapid drum rolls on every available surface with his sticks, were full of anticipation for a big night as they heard the roar from the hall where they were about to play.

'Let 'em wait,' said Dominic, when Derek tapped his watch.

'They'll wreck the place,' said the roadie.

'Good job,' said Dominic in reply. 'It'll be great publicity if they do.'

The cinema manager came looking for the band, obviously as worried about the fate of his cinema as Derek was.

'Be right with you,' Dominic reassured him. 'Sorry about all this. Slight problem with a guitar string.'

'As quick as you can,' said the manager, a balding fifty-year-old who would obviously much rather be presiding over a pensioners' matinee of *The Sound of Music* than the potential hazards of a pop concert.

'Go on then, lads,' said Dominic, 'mustn't keep the paying customers waiting,' and the four musicians left the dressing room with Derek in front, holding a torch to show them the way through the maze of dark corridors and stairways that led up to the stage.

The closer they got to it, the louder the roar from the audience became and, by the time they arrived and the guitarists plugged their instruments into the amplifiers and Jud got behind his kit, it was like the sound that a tidal wave makes as it is about to break onto dry land.

Derek signalled to the the stage hand who was waiting by the lever that raised the curtains and, as they began to rise and Tony hit the opening chord of their first song, 'Memphis Tennessee', a rain of jelly babies, gonks, underwear and other presents from the fans to the band began to rain down on the stage.

From that chord onwards, throughout their half-hour set, the loudest noise in the auditorium was that of the fans going crazy. The band ran through their three hits, a couple of new songs from the LP, and several rock and roll standards, but as they already knew they might just as well have sung nursery rhymes for all anyone, including themselves, could hear.

The hail of missiles never stopped and the band spent as much time avoiding them as concentrating on their act. But, as Dominic was to say later, 'That's showbiz,' and indeed it was.

As David bounced around the stage, dodging the pressies that all seemed to be aimed at his head, he noticed two girls together in one of the side aisles. They were dancing in tandem, dressed identically, and their long blonde hair seemed to catch the light like two beacons beckoning to him. He squinted through the spots aimed at the stage and it suddenly clicked that they were twins. They were shouting and waving, and he instinctively knew that the shouts and waves were aimed at him alone. He smiled at the knowledge and waved back, hoping that they realised he was acknowledging them only, then boogied over to the side of the stage and screamed in Derek's ear that he wanted the roadie to go out front after the show and tell the two girls where the band was staying and invite them round for a drink with David.

Derek nodded. It wasn't the first time he'd had such a request from one of the band and he knew it wouldn't be the last.

As the band tumbled off stage after their last number and made a run right through the back of the cinema to Dominic's waiting Bentley, the roadie made his way into the auditorium to look for the two girls that David had pointed out to him.

15

The short ride back to the hotel was made in high good spirits even though, as Sly remarked, 'We might as well have been playing with ourselves out there tonight for all any of those silly little cunts could hear.'

But when Dominic pointed out how much the receipts for the show had bolstered the band's bank account, they all agreed that the trip out to the sticks had been well worthwhile.

When they entered the staid confines of The Grand Hotel, Dominic made straight for the restaurant with Sly, Jud and Tony right behind him, but David told the other four that he wanted to get something from his room and that they should start without him. The rest of the band exchanged knowing looks as he went to the reception desk and collected his key and climbed the broad staircase to the first floor where it was located.

After he let himself into the large, comfortable double room, he took a quick look round, switched on the television, sat on the bed and made himself comfortable, whilst he waited to find out if Derek had managed to connect with the twins back at the cinema.

He wasn't to be disappointed. Within ten minutes there was a call from reception that he had visitors. The receptionist made it quite clear by the tone of her voice that two young girls calling on a lone male guest after nine p.m. was frowned upon but David ignored her, knowing that the amount of money that the band would have spent in the hotel by the time they left far outweighed any moral argument from the management. Besides it was 1966. It was time the swinging sixties arrived in Norwich.

'Ask them to come up,' he said and put the phone down on the disapproving member of staff.

Two minutes later there was a knock on the door. 'Hi,' said David to the identical twins when he opened it. 'I'm glad you could make it. Sit down.'

The two girls sat on the bed together. One either side, with their backs against the headrest and their legs dangling over the sides.

'Did you like the show?' The bass guitarist asked.

They both nodded. 'It was great,' said the twin on the right.

'You like the band?'

'We think you're great,' the twin on the right again. 'We've got all your records. We couldn't believe it when that man said you wanted to see us. We thought it was a joke. We almost didn't come.'

'I'm glad you did. What are your names?' asked David.

The one on the left said, 'Betty and Hettie.'

He smiled. 'Which one is which?'

The one on the left shrugged.

'Is there any way to tell you apart?'

The girls nodded.

'What?'

'One of us has a birthmark.'

94

'Where?'

'Somewhere personal.'

'Can I see it?'

'Maybe. If you're *very* lucky.'

'How old are you?'

'Sixteen. Last week,' said the girl on the right. 'Geminis. Isn't that perfect? Twins, you see.'

'Perfect,' agreed Dave. 'Do you always dress alike?' They both nodded.

'And underneath?' said Dave.

The twins looked at each other and giggled, then nodded again. 'It's easier,' said the one on the left. 'That way we can share.'

'What else do you do together?' he asked.

The girls grinned. 'Everything. We bathe together. Go to the loo together.'

'Do you sleep together?'

'Sometimes,' said the twin on the right.

'And what do you get up to?'

'Wouldn't you like to know?' said the one on the left coyly.

David nodded.

'Shall we tell him?' said the twin on the right.

The other one nodded and said, 'No. Let's show him.'

She leant over and kissed her twin on the lips. They moved closer together as the kiss continued.

David could hardly believe his eyes as the girls caressed each other's bodies through their identical dresses.

The two sisters broke apart. They were both flushed when they looked at him. The girl on the right spoke. Her voice was breathy and sexy. '*That's* what we do.'

'What else?' asked David.

'Everything.'

'Are you lesbians?' He said.

'Don't be silly,' said the twin on the right. 'We've both got loads of boyfriends. We just do it to each other when we're on our own and feeling randy. When we were kids we learnt how to make ourselves come together. We've been doing it ever since.'

'Are you randy now?' asked David.

The girls looked at each other and smiled. They nodded in unison again.

'Can I watch?' he asked.

'If you want,' said the girl on the right. 'I thought you might join in.'

'I might,' said David.

The twins stood up and helped each other out of their dresses. Underneath they were wearing matching, ice-blue lingerie. Brief bra-and-panty sets. One girl unhooked the other's bra, gently eased her breasts out of the cups, and threw the garment onto the dressing table. Then vice versa. They didn't seem in the least bit shy or self-conscious as they stripped each other. Their breasts were round, upright and firm. Each one tipped by a rosy red nipple. They both got back onto the bed and sat close to one another.

'Well?' said David, feeling randy himself at the sight of their fresh young bodies.

'Well, yourself,' said the girl on the left.

'Do you want a drink? A joint?'

'Both,' said the girl on the right.

David went over to the ice bucket that the management had delivered to the room whilst the band were at the gig. Inside were four bottles of champagne. Clustered round the bucket were half a dozen glasses. Dave opened one of the bottles and filled three glasses. He took two over to the twins who accepted them with a smile each. He reached into his jacket and pulled out two ready-rolled joints that Derek had given him at the hall and lit one. He took a deep drag and held the smoke in his lungs before he passed the joint to the girl on the right.

'Do you want a blowback?' She asked her sister, who replied with a nod.

The girl on the right put the lit end of the cigarette into her mouth, then leaned over, and her sister took the unlit end and the first girl blew smoke deep into her lungs until they both went almost cross-eyed.

'That's strong,' said the girl on the left.

'So which one of you's which?' said Dave when he had the joint back in his hand.

'Hettie has got a birthmark on her bum,' said the twin on the right. 'See.' She nudged her sister, who pulled her knickers down to show a small strawberry mark on her buttock.

'Hello, Hettie,' said David.

'Hello, David,' said Hettie.

'And I haven't,' said Betty, who pulled down her panties, so as not to be left out of the act. The pink-and-white cheek of her arse was blemish-free.

'Come and sit between us,' said Hettie. 'And let's have some more of that joint. It's making me horny.'

Dave did as she said and they all clinked glasses in a toast. 'What are we drinking to?' he said.

'Sex,' said Hettie. 'The best thing in the world.'

The other two raised their glasses again and David planted a kiss on each of the girls' mouths.

'So?' he said.

'He wants to watch us, Hettie,' said Betty.

'Better let him then. Go and sit down and we'll put on a show.'

David slid off the bed and sat in the armchair in the corner. The girls put their arms around each other and began to kiss. They kissed each other's mouths and ears and eyes and Hettie went down to Betty's breasts and tried to swallow each of them whole. Then she moved lower and slid her sister's panties off and buried her head in her plump blonde pudenda. Betty opened her legs wide as her sister's tongue penetrated her minge. She reached down and pushed Hettie's head deeper and looked over at David.

'Let me see your cock,' she panted.

David stood up and took off his shirt and trousers. His prick was hard and Betty smiled.

'Come here,' she said.

He went over to the bed and she reached up and took his balls in her hand. 'Closer,' she said.

He knelt over her and she began to lick and suck at his penis.

After a few moments in paradise, she looked up and said, 'Fuck Hettie. I want to see her being screwed.'

David moved to the end of the bed and gently eased Hettie's ice-blue panties over her hips. The birthmark on her left buttock was flaming red. He felt her pussy, which was hot and wet, and gently eased himself inside her, doggie-fashion. She hardly seemed to notice, so busy was she drinking from her twin's honeypot, but when he began to move inside her she pushed back to get the full experience of his hard rod at her soft fanny. The harder he fucked her, the harder she sucked at her sister until Betty was crying out with delight at the treatment she was getting.

David moved faster and faster, deep inside one sister and watching the satisfied face of the other. Before he came, he pulled out and pushed Hettie's head away from Betty's snatch and plunged into the hot wetness.

'Yes,' cried Betty. 'Give it to me.'

He was so excited he only took two or three strokes before he came into her. They rolled over as he painted her insides with his seed and lay together at the side of the bed.

'That's not fair,' complained Hettie. 'What about me?'

'Give him a cold blow-job,' said Betty. 'That'll get him hard again.'

Betty flashed a smile and went over to the ice bucket. She dug into the water and pulled out two pieces of ice which she put into her mouth. Then, returning to the bed, she knelt at one side of it and took David's wet, wilting cock into her mouth.

He cried out, almost in pain at the sensation. The ice in her mouth felt like fire on his prick. Almost immediately blood rushed into his member and he felt himself getting rigid again. Hettie ran the ice and her tongue over his penis, then climbed up and manipulated it into her cunt and began to ride David as if her life depended on it.

Her breasts wobbled over him and he reached up and held one and squeezed it hard. She yelped in delight and rode him harder and harder.

Betty lay and watched them perform the act of sex. Hettie was beating at his groin with hers and he felt the first tickle of his orgasm. He found her buttocks and dug his fingernails into the soft, warm flesh, and she cried out in pain and pleasure as she took her orgasm off his stiff dick. Then David felt the hot rush of semen from his balls and he injected the fluid up into Hettie's womb and she slumped down on top of him, gasping for breath.

'That was good,' she said when she regained her composure. 'Douche me Betty.'

Betty fetched an unopened bottle of champagne. She shook it, took off the gold paper and the metal seal and eased out the cork. It popped off with a bang. As it did so, Hettie opened her cunt with her fingers to expose her pink, wet insides, and Betty put the neck of the bottle between her cunt lips so that the cold fizz washed out her pussy. Then Hettie took the bottle off her sister, shook it and returned the compliment. David looked on, amazed.

'We'd better be going,' said Betty and pulled on the first bra and panties she saw and slipped into one of the blue dresses. 'We'll be in terrible trouble at home if we're too late.'

As she spoke, her sister found the rest of their clothes and dressed herself too.

'Thanks for the drinks and the dope and the fuck,' said Betty, 'we'll *definitely* buy the LP.'

Both girls kissed David and, blowing more kisses, left the room.

16

Meanwhile, down in the hotel restaurant, the rest of the band and Dominic had been joined by an unexpected guest. Judy Carter, star columnist from *Disc* magazine, had arrived after driving up from London to see the gig.

Judy. Twenty-three years old. Tall. Beautiful. With a mane of wild, dark hair, tied up in bunches, was dressed in the height of London fashion. She wore white slingback, low-heeled shoes, white tights, and a blue dress that hardly covered the swell of her buttocks at the back or the crotch of her panties at the front. She had already caused a furore by her appearance amongst the other, more staid guests and staff in the foyer, and walked into the dining room unannounced, much to everyone's surprise. Especially Dominic's, who had sent tickets, an itinerary and a handwritten invitation to her at the paper but, having heard nothing, had assumed she was busy elsewhere.

In fact she had thought she was going to be. An American band had been due to fly into London that afternoon but one of the guitarists – the very one she thought she'd be fucking that night had been busted for drugs at Los Angeles airport, so they'd had to delay their departure until he could be bailed out.

At the news Judy, being bored, lonely, horny and definitely at a loose end in London and having already had a brief fling with David the previous spring, had decided on a whim to travel to Norwich alone and take up her invitation. She knew that if he wasn't available some other member of the band probably would be. And Judy, a dedicated groupie, had decided a long time ago that she only slept with the members of successful bands.

'Judy,' Dominic boomed and rose to his feet like a real gentleman as she walked across to the corner table where he and the rest of The Getaways, minus David, were waiting for their aperitifs to arrive. 'What a pleasant surprise. We weren't expecting you.'

'I'll say,' said Sly and giggled. He knew about Judy and David's affair and, having also sussed out the reason for the latter's absence from the dinner table, realised this was the perfect chance for a wind-up.

Dominic shot him a warning glance. He knew what had gone on too, but didn't want to upset this doyen of the pop press.

'I thought I'd sneak up and see what you guys get up to out of town,' she replied.

'Not a lot, as you can see,' replied Dominic, always the diplomat.

'Sez you,' said Sly and giggled again.

Dominic shot Sly another withering look then, regaining his smile of welcome, said to Judy. 'Will you join us for a drink? Dinner?'

'I thought you'd never ask, Dominic. Both, if you don't mind. I'm booked into this dump and ready to rock.'

She looked hungrily at the three young men sitting at the table. 'Where's David?' she asked.

'Otherwise engaged, I'm afraid,' said Dominic. 'But I'm sure he'll be down later.'

'And I bet he'll be surprised to see you,' said Sly innocently. Before Judy could reply, a waiter brought another chair and Judy sat to the right of Dominic, with Jud on her left.

'You were saying?' she said to Sly as she sat down.

'Nothing,' interrupted Dominic, when he'd resumed his seat. 'It's a gin and tonic for you, isn't it?'

Judy agreed that it was and, after Dominic had ordered the drink from the waiter, he asked, 'What did you think of the gig?'

'Fab. What I could hear of it,' replied Judy. 'Those chicks were going apeshit. They really love you.'

'It's crazy,' said Tony. 'We can't hear a damn thing on stage. I mean, where's it going to end? I hear The Beatles aren't going to do many more live shows.'

'It's true,' said Judy conspiratorially. 'I spoke to John the other day. He said their new American tour will be their last.'

'Never,' said Sly. 'What are they going to do?'

'Spend their money,' replied Judy. 'Make some experimental records, and . . .' She paused. She loved a good gossip. Almost as much as she loved a good fuck. Then she went on, 'Now this is strictly between us and these four walls. I hear they're going to start up some kind of business co-op.'

'Do what?' Said Sly.

'It's true. They're going to call it Apple, or Orange or something.'

'I'll believe it when I see it,' said the rhythm guitarist.

'Well, you heard it here first. So what's cooking with you guys? I need some gossip for the column.'

'Tons,' interjected Dominic, in his position as spokesman for the band. ' "Here We Go" looks like a certain number one. And as I told the boys earlier, Capitol are releasing it in the states in a fortnight, with a probable re-release of the first two singles. The new album is out shortly. And we're probably going to the States ourselves in the autumn. We're back in the studio soon to cut a new single to come out in August, and Nancy Goldstein from *Tiger Beat* wants to run a big article on the boys.'

'I'm impressed,' said Judy as her drink arrived and she sank half of it in one swallow. 'But you'd better not give that Goldstein bitch anything you won't give me. Remember who wrote about you first in the UK.'

The rest of the party looked hard at Sly at that comment and he had the good grace to blush slightly. A fact that Judy Carter didn't miss and noted down for future reference.

Dominic cut into the gap she left in the conversation.

'Judy,' he said with as much sincerity as he could muster. 'Believe me. And I know I speak for the rest of the boys when I say this. We don't, I repeat *don't*, ever forget our old friends. Not of course that I'm suggesting for a moment that you're old,' he added with an ingratiating smile. 'when it comes to the press, you're second to none. If there's an exclusive on The Getaways, you'll get it first every time. Trust me.'

Somewhat placated by Dominic's earnestness, Judy said, 'Thanks, Dominic. It's brilliant news about Capitol. They're just the kind of label you need

Stateside to bust the band wide open. Can I use the story next week?'

'Of course you can,' replied Dominic. 'No one else has got it. And they won't, I promise. It's all yours. I was going to phone you tomorrow anyway. And I couldn't agree more about Capitol. It was just what I was saying to the chaps earlier. In fact, we're all overjoyed at the news. Aren't we?' He looked round at the nodding heads of the band. Then, remembering his duty as a host, he said to Judy, 'Would you care to order?'

The waiter reappeared as if by magic and Dominic smiled smugly. All five diners ordered, and Dominic chose the wine and they settled back in anticipation of the meal to follow.

As the waiter left, the roadies appeared at the doorway of the dining room.

'Oh Lord,' said Dominic, 'the hired help's here.'

'Don't be such a snob,' said Tony, and beckoned Donkey and Derek over. 'You stopping?' Tony asked and Dominic pulled a face.

'No,' said Derek, spotting Judy. 'More's the pity. It could get interesting later.' Especially, he thought, if David turns up for dinner with a blonde twin on each arm. Because the roadie too, knew of the brief liaison between the bass player and the beautiful journalist. 'This is too posh for us,' he went on. 'We're getting back to London. If we hurry, we can be down The Speak for a nosh-up before it closes. Mind you, I'd love to stay. I enjoy fireworks.'

'Fireworks?' said Judy. 'Are there going to be fireworks?'

'You never know,' said Derek innocently.

'I love fireworks too,' she said, suddenly getting the joke. 'When are they going to start?'

'Are you boys all right for cash?' interrupted Dominic quickly, to change the subject and get rid of the road crew.

'We could do with a bob or two,' replied Derek. 'As we're not staying over.'

Dominic took a fistful of fivers out of his pocket, counted off a few, and handed them over. 'Have a good evening,' he said.

Derek grinned and plucked the rest of the money from Dominic's hand. 'Don't be tight. Otherwise the fireworks might start sooner than you think,' he said, as he rifled through the cash.

'As if,' said Dominic with a dagger-filled look. 'Now, why don't you two get going. It's a long drive back to town and you don't want to be too late, do you?'

'Too true, Dom,' said Derek, winking at Judy. 'Thanks for this.' He held up the money. 'We'll give your regards to Mario.' And with that, the two dusty roadies said goodbye all round and left.

'Those two,' said Dominic. 'They'll be the death of me.'

'They're great guys,' said Sly. 'You leave 'em alone. They're the ones who keep us going.'

'All right, Sly,' said Dominic. 'I know your plebeian views of old.'

'Is that some kind of VD?' asked Sly innocently and the table erupted with laughter.

'So what *is* David up to?' asked Judy.

When there was no reply, she said, 'As if I didn't know. You lot don't have to worry. I know what life is like on the road. It's not as if we had an arrangement.

I'm just here to have a good time at your expense. I'm sure I can find some other pleasant diversion whilst I'm here. What do you say, Jud?' And she smiled at the young drummer sitting next to her.

Jud was amazed at being asked. He blushed and stammered an incomprehensible reply as the rest of the table burst into laughter again. He didn't know if Judy was serious or taking the rise out of him. He'd always fancied the young woman and the way she had spoken to him almost reduced him to jelly. When she placed her hand on his thigh under the table he blushed even more furiously and buried his face in his glass to hide his embarrassment.

'I love shy men,' said Judy. 'I find they're so much more of a challenge.' And she moved her hand higher up Jud's thigh towards the hard bulge that his blood-filled cock was making in his trousers. Her fingers just brushed the top of it and satisfied that she was making the required impression on him, she withdrew her hand.

By then, her words and the slight caress had Jud's face almost the same colour as the claret that Dominic had ordered from the wine waiter.

'Maybe we can find something to do together later, Jud,' said Judy.

Sly caught Tony's eye and said, 'I just bet you can,' and everyone at the table, except for Jud, burst out laughing for a third time.

Halfway through the meal, David made his entrance into the restaurant. When he saw Judy sitting with the rest of the entourage, he stopped in mid-stride.

'Hello, David,' she said. 'Been having a good time?'

'I was tired,' he said. 'Went up to my room . . .'

'And had a nice lie down,' interjected Sly, with another of his knowing looks.

'Something like that,' said David, then to Judy: 'I didn't know you were coming.'

'Obviously,' she replied. 'But don't worry. The rest of the boys and Dominic have been looking after me. Jud and I are going out later to see what delights this one-horse town has to offer. Aren't we, Jud?'

'Er . . . Yes, if you want,' stammered Jud in reply.

'Oh,' said David in surprise. 'Are you sure you don't want to do something with me?'

'I think you've done enough already,' said Judy with a smile. 'Why don't you sit down and have something to eat? You need to keep your strength up, don't you?'

After the meal was over, the party went en masse to the bar. David had no doubt that he could persuade Judy to spend the rest of the evening with him and was very surprised that, after one drink, she grabbed Jud and said to the rest of the gathering:

'We're off to sample the fleshpots that beautiful Norwich has to offer. Anyone else coming?'

Sly and Tony looked at each other and Sly said, 'We're going to stay here for a few, but there's a club called Ronnie's that stays open late according to the barman here. We're going to pop down later. About twelve. We'll meet you there, all right?'

David said nothing, just sat and sulked quietly, and Dominic opted to have an early night.

'He's going to count the profits,' said Sly teasingly.

'Well, we're off then,' said Judy. 'We'll see you later, Sly. Tony. Good night, David. Sweet dreams,' and she jumped up from her seat, yanked Jud up from his, tucked his arm under hers and the pair of them left.

David pulled a sour face at their retreating backs to raucous laughter from Sly and Tony and a rueful grin from Dominic.

'Nice arse she's got,' said Sly. 'Real nice. And they make such a lovely couple, don't you think? Who would have believed it? He's a real dark horse that Jud.'

'He's coming along,' agreed Tony.

'A right one of the lads, eh David?' said Sly, enjoying rubbing the bass player's nose in it.

'Fuck right off,' said David and went up to the bar to get another drink.

'Touchy,' said Sly and laughed again.

Outside the front entrance of the hotel in the warm summer darkness, Judy said to Jud, 'What's it to be then?'

'Dunno,' said Jud, almost lost for words at being alone for the first time with the beautiful woman he'd fancied from afar for so long.

'My car's over there. Fancy a run out in the country? It's beautiful round here. The pubs are probably shut by now, but we can take a ride. It's a lovely night. Then we can find that club later. The porter said it's just round the corner. It's open 'til two. With you lot in there, we might get them to stay open even later.'

Jud nodded, and he and Judy walked together in the direction of her car.

It was a big, pale blue Vauxhall Victor, brand new. She unlocked the driver's door, got in and leant over and opened the passenger door for Jud. He joined her on the bench seat and Judy started the engine, put the car into gear, switched on the lights and pulled away.

Within a few minutes they were on the outskirts of the town and a few minutes after that the car was running along the main arterial road out of Norwich towards the coast. Judy took the first B-road off it and switched on the main headlight beam as the street lights became fewer and further apart, before they vanished altogether, and the couple were in the country proper.

'Light me a cigarette, will you, Jud,' she asked and he took out a packet, lit two and passed one to her. Their fingers touched as he handed it to her and he felt a shiver of excitement run up his arm.

After they passed through a tiny village, Judy saw a turn off and swung the car into it, pulled it well off the road and stopped.

She killed the lights and switched off the engine and the only sounds inside the car were the ticking of cooling metal and their breathing.

'Want some music?' she asked. 'Or shall we take a walk.'

'Let's walk,' he said and they both got out of the car.

It was very dark by the side of the road and Jud could only tell where Judy was standing by the tiny red coal of her cigarette.

'Where are you?' she asked as he got close and she grabbed onto his hand for support. 'Don't let go. I don't want to end up in a ditch.'

'I won't,' he whispered. In fact he would sooner have died just at that moment than to break the contact of her hand in his.

'Look at those stars,' said Judy.

Jud looked up. The sky was ablaze with myriad pinpoints of light.

'What a shame the moon's not full. Then there'd be

plenty of light,' she continued.

Jud disagreed but said nothing. If there'd been enough light to see, he reckoned he wouldn't be holding onto the beautiful creature next to him.

They walked across the deserted road and found a hummock of soft, sweet-smelling grass. Judy sat down and Jud joined her. He lit two more cigarettes, an intimate gesture that he was beginning to enjoy. Especially when he thought that the cigarette that was touching her lips had so recently been touching his.

'This grass is so soft and cool,' whispered Judy. 'I want to feel it all over me.'

As Jud's eyes became accustomed to the darkness he saw that she was undressing. She took off her dress, her bra, shoes, tights and panties.

As he strained to see in the darkness he could just make out the alabaster whiteness of her skin, broken only by the dark shadow of pubic hair between her legs, against the darkness of the grass.

'It feels wonderful,' she exclaimed. 'So erotic. Take your clothes off, Jud, and feel it.'

He didn't have to be asked twice. He tore off his clothes and threw them on top of hers. The night air was still warm but by the time he was completely naked he could feel goose bumps of excitement breaking out all over his body.

When he lay on the grass it was cool and luxurious on his back.

'Isn't it gorgeous?' said Judy.

'Gorgeous,' he echoed.

'Come closer, I can't hear you.'

He moved towards the whiteness of her body and felt for her hand again. When they touched, he felt goose pimples on top of his goose pimples and his already engorged penis became harder and heavier between his legs.

'This is so wonderful,' said Judy. 'I'm so glad we came.'

'So am I,' said Jud.

'You're not as shy as I thought, are you?'

He didn't reply.

'Aren't you going to kiss me then, Jud?' she asked coyly.

Jud was in heaven. Once again, he didn't have to be asked twice. He pulled Judy's naked body towards him, placed his other hand behind her head and drew her mouth towards his. Their kiss was long and wet and luscious, and suddenly her naked body was in his arms and he was caressing her all over.

Her warm hand found his cock and started wanking it gently as he laid her back onto the grass and slid his mouth down from her mouth across her chin, neck, and down to her tiny, firm breasts which he tried to swallow whole, one after the other. Her nipples were hard on his tongue and he sucked at them until they became even harder.

She wanked him faster and with her other hand alternated between rubbing his back tenderly and scratching it with her nails.

When Jud tired temporarily of sucking at Judy's breasts, he pushed his head further down her body, stopping briefly to lick out her belly button which caused her to giggle in delight, before taking the final plunge and moving down to her long silky pubic hair, parting it with his tongue and invading the privacy of her oily minge.

112

Her giggles turned to sounds of joy as he parted the lips of her labia with his lips and he found the inside of her cunt with his tongue.

He mounted her body so that he could get his head deeper between her legs and, to his delight, felt her push his cock into her hot wet mouth and begin to tongue the glans.

He put his hands under her thighs and pulled her torso up to meet his mouth and slid it along the crack of her arse. As he did so he could hear her moan through her mouthful of male member, and he smiled to himself and continued to ministrate to her even harder.

After five minutes or so of *soixante-neuf*, Jud moved around so that they were head to head again and they tongued each other's mouths and he felt his cock rubbing against her cunt and suddenly, wonderfully, naturally, it was inside her.

She screamed as he entered her and he pushed down as hard as he could into her soaking, tender pussy.

She bit at his face as he fucked her and in his excitement he bit back and rode her harder and harder.

After a minute he could bear it no more. He felt way back in his balls the first feelings that relief was coming and he pumped at her even harder until, with twin cries of delight, they orgasmed together.

17

Jud rolled off Judy and lay gasping for breath on the grass, looking up at the stars.

'Was that good?' asked Judy.

'Fabulous,' replied Jud.

'Yes, it was, wasn't it?' she said. 'You're much better than David. Much nicer.'

Jud laughed and found her hand in the darkness and squeezed it tightly. 'Thanks,' he said and they lay together as their skin cooled.

After a few minutes Jud said, 'Don't you think we'd better get dressed? It's getting cold.'

'All right,' said Judy reluctantly. 'But I could stay here all night with you.'

'Me too,' agreed Jud. 'But I think we'd better go.'

Judy disengaged her hand from his and started to search around for her clothes. She put on her panties, dress and shoes and rolled her bra in her tights. Jud found his clothes, too, and dressed hurriedly and they both returned back to the car.

Judy put on the interior light and repaired her make-up. 'Do I look OK?' she asked. 'No grass stains or anything.'

Jud looked at her along the front seat. 'You look marvellous,' he assured her.

'Are we going to the club?' asked Judy.

'Why not? I fancy a drink,' said Jud.

'Do you think the others will be there?'

'Probably.'

'Do you think they'll guess?'

'Probably. Do you care?' asked Jud.

'Not if you don't.'

'I don't. Not one bit.'

Judy leaned over and kissed him.

'I like you a lot, Jud,' she said. 'Judy and Jud. Our names go well, don't they?'

'They do,' agreed the drummer.

Judy started the car, put on the lights, reversed out of the lane and started back the way they'd come towards Norwich again.

They got back to town at about twelve thirty and found Ronnie's easily. The doorman recognised Jud and let them in without charge. As they walked through the double doors into the club proper, The Stones were blasting 'Satisfaction' out of the loudspeaker system. Jud smiled secretly at Judy and she winked back.

Sly and Tony were sitting at the bar with about half a dozen young girls who had obviously recognised them, drinking and enjoying being in the limelight for the second time that night.

When they saw Jud and Judy enter, they beckoned them over. 'Come and join us,' said Sly, raising his champagne glass in a toast. 'Where've you two been?' His voice was slightly slurred and he grasped the edge of the bar to keep his balance.

'For a drive in the country,' said Judy.

'Did you ladder your tights?' asked Sly, looking down at her legs.

Judy laughed and Jud blushed again.

The girls who were standing with Sly and Tony looked puzzled.

'This, as if you didn't know is our drummer, Jud,' said Sly, by way of introduction. 'And this,' he indicated Judy, 'is a famous journalist up from London to get the lowdown on The Getaways. And by the looks of it, she's succeeded. At least with one of them. Or two now, isn't it? And two to go.'

'You'll be lucky,' replied Judy.

Sly ignored the comment and looked along the bar at the girls and shook his head as if puzzled. 'I don't know all these young ladies names, I'm afraid,' he said. 'But I'm sure I will before I get much older.'

'If you get much drunker, you won't know anything,' said Judy.

'Too true,' replied Sly. 'I think that calls for another round. Barman! More champagne.'

The barman grinned and turned and took two more bottles of Moet from the bucket behind him, opened them with a pop, produced two more glasses for Jud and Judy and filled the rest that were lined up along the bar.

Sly looked around the club. Being Monday night, it was almost empty. 'This place is a drag,' he said. 'I vote we all go back to the hotel, wake up the night porter and get down to some serious drinking. What do the rest of you say?'

'I'm game,' said Tony. 'No work tomorrow.'

'You're lucky,' said Judy, who knew that if she

stayed in the vicinity of Sly much longer, she'd end up hitting him over the head with one of his own champagne bottles. 'Some of us have. I'm going back to get some beauty sleep.'

'It looks as if you've been lying down all night,' said Sly with a drunken giggle.

Judy ignored him.

'Will you walk me back, Jud?' She asked.

'Sure,' he replied and finished his drink with one swallow. He knew of old what a night's drinking with Sly could lead to. And he was pleased enough with the way the evening had gone already to go back to his room. Maybe with Judy, with a bit of luck.

'Party poopers,' said Sly. 'What about you girls?'

Four of them reluctantly said that they also had to get off home but two, one a tall blonde called Lisa who was draped all over Tony, and the other a dumpy little raver with chubby thighs and a skirt so short that even Sly had looked twice and who answered to the name of Maureen, agreed to go back to the hotel with the two rock-and-rollers.

Sly paid the bill, leaving a good tip for the barman, and they left. Maureen had to hold onto him tightly to stop him falling over during the short walk back but they made it to the front door of the hotel without incident. Once inside, Sly rang the bell at reception and eventually an elderly party in faded green livery arrived to see what all the fuss was about.

'Champagne,' demanded Sly.

'Not at this time of night, sir,' replied the elderly party when he could drag his eyes away from Maureen's thighs.

'What you got then?' demanded Sly.

'Pale ale, Scotch whisky and soda or gin and tonic,' replied the porter.

'Got any ice?'

The elderly party scratched his head. 'There might be some left,' he said eventually.

'There'd better be, the prices we're paying here,' said Sly. 'Bring us a bottle of Scotch, the ice bucket and four glasses.'

'Sly,' warned Tony. 'You know what you get like when you mix Scotch and champagne.'

'Course I do,' replied Sly. 'And that's exactly how I feel like getting.'

Tony shrugged, the elderly party disappeared in the direction of his stash of booze, and the two musicians and the two girls made their way towards the resident's lounge.

Once inside, Sly made straight for the piano which he found to be locked.

'Got a hair pin?' he said to Maureen.

'Yeah,' she replied.

'Well, give us it then,' said Sly.

The girl pulled one from her hair and handed it over. Sly opened it and slid one end into the lock mechanism of the piano. He twisted and turned it for a few seconds, all the time with his head cocked as if listening. Finally satisfied, he tried the lid and smiled beatifically when it opened.

'Nothing to it,' he said to Maureen. 'I trained as a locksmith.'

She seemed impressed, then asked: 'Can you play it?'

'Can I?' He said and ran his fingers along the keys. 'Just listen.'

He started to play 'Yesterday' and hummed along, then began a boogie-woogie bass roll with his left hand and segued the melody into 'Blueberry Hill'. And finally stood up from the piano stool and started a raving version of 'Great Balls Of Fire'.

Tony dragged Lisa over and began to beat time on the top of the piano and joined in the chorus with Sly until, with a crash of chords, he finished the tune.

Maureen and Lisa applauded them and Sly and Tony took a bow.

As they did so, the elderly party came into the lounge carrying a tray with a Scotch bottle, a tub of ice and four glasses balanced on it.

'You can't play that,' he said. 'It's locked.'

'It was,' said Sly. 'Ain't now.'

'Where did you get the key?'

Sly winked.

'There'll be complaints.'

'No. Quiet as a mouse.'

'I could hear it right down the corridor.'

'Did you like it?' asked Tony.

'Not much. I prefer Mantovani.'

Sly sat down at the stool and began to play 'Charmaine'.

'That's better,' said the porter. 'Where shall I put these?' referring to the bottle and glasses.

'Anywhere,' said Tony. 'On the table'll do.'

The porter set the tray down and stood and listened as Sly continued. Tony loaded the glasses up with ice and whisky and handed them round. When Sly finished playing, he grabbed his glass and downed the contents in one swallow.

'*Sly,*' Tony warned him.

'No pain, mate,' he replied. 'What do you fancy next?' He asked the porter.

'You'd better stop now and let me lock up the piano,' said the elderly man.

'No,' insisted Sly. 'I'm just getting in the mood. How about some Russ Conway?' And he started playing a wobbly version of 'Sidesaddle' which got the other three young people laughing but did nothing for the porter.

'Stop it now,' he said. 'If the manager hears about this . . .'

'What?' said Sly.

'I'll be in serious trouble.'

'More than your job's worth, is it?' said Tony with a wicked grin.

'That's right,' said the porter. 'More than my job's worth.' He seemed to like the expression.

'Naah,' said Sly. 'You'll get a pay rise for keeping the guests happy. Now, why don't you just go and do whatever you should be doing and leave us to this bottle. If we need you, we'll come and find you.' And he reached into his pocket, produced a couple of pound notes and gave them to the porter. 'Put the drinks on Mr Edwards' bill. He's our manager and looks after things like that. It's more than his job's worth if he don't.' And he laughed.

The porter seemed a bit happier after he'd pocketed the cash and said, 'You'll have to sign.'

'I'll sign whatever you like,' said Sly. 'Except for a blank cheque. OK?'

'I'll go and make out the bill,' said the porter and left, closing the lounge door behind him.

'Silly old bugger,' said Sly, when he'd gone, and

poured out another large drink. 'What do you reckon, Tone? Are we on for a laugh?'

'Depends,' replied Tony warily. 'What've you got in mind?'

'We could go on manoeuvres,' said Sly.

'No, Sly,' said Tony. 'Not that.'

'Yeah,' said Sly back. 'I'll go and find us some ammo,' and with that he left the lounge.

'What's manoeuvres?' asked Lisa.

'You'll find out,' said Tony. 'Did you bring a mac?'

'No,' said the girl. 'It wasn't raining.' She looked out of the window. 'Still isn't.'

'Stick around,' said Tony. 'It soon will be.'

The three of them sat down and sipped at their drinks until Sly came back into the room struggling under the weight of four fire extinguishers. 'Got 'em,' he said triumphantly.

'What are you doing?' asked Maureen.

Sly dumped the heavy extinguishers onto a sofa where they clanged together. 'Just watch,' he said and picked up one and unravelled the hose.

'Water or foam,' asked Tony, beginning to get into the spirit of things.

'Three water, one foam. But there's plenty more where these came from,' replied Sly.

He banged the top of the extinguisher he was holding and water began to gush from the nozzle. He directed it at Lisa, who shrieked and ran to hide behind Tony.

Tony dived for a weapon of his own and shouted, 'Get armed. This bloke's a menace.'

He struggled with the extinguisher as Sly continued aiming his own at him but, luckily for Tony, the former was so drunk that his aim was well off.

Maureen grabbed an extinguisher herself and with a shout of triumph covered Sly in thick white foam.

Tony succeeded in getting his to fire and washed most of the foam off Sly and on to the carpet.

Then Lisa got into the act and took the last extinguisher from the sofa and worked the action on top. As water sprang from the hose it soaked Maureen, whose short dress quickly became transparent, showing off the shape of her large, bare breasts beneath it and the outline of her brief knickers.

Seeing what had happened, Sly aimed the remainder of his extinguisher in her direction too and she was soon as good as naked in front of the other three's eyes.

Tony turned his extinguisher on Lisa who fled the room, screaming as she went and leaving a trail of foam on the walls.

The other three followed her and Sly went running towards the back of the hotel for reinforcements to add to the arsenal.

Meanwhile Tony and Maureen chased Lisa up the main stairs of the hotel to the first floor, where they cornered her in one of the corridors and subjected her to twin torrents of water until she threw down her own extinguisher, her dress also soaked into transparency, her hair like rats' tails and mascara running down her face.

'Stop it,' she begged. 'No more.'

A door along the corridor opened and a man appeared demanding to know what was going on, but soon jumped back into the room as both Tony and Maureen aimed their giant water pistols at him in unison.

As the door slammed, Sly arrived carrying two fresh

extinguishers, one of which he threw to Lisa and the other he aimed at his fellow band member.

As Tony's extinguisher was empty, he threw it down and ran in the direction of his room, pulling his key from his pocket as he went.

He threw open the door but, before he could close it, the other three burst in after him. He dived across the bed and into the bathroom, slammed the door shut behind him, locked it, and collapsed onto the floor in a flood of hysterical laughter.

Sly and the two girls stood looking at each other and then Sly saw the cooler full of champagne, similar to the one in David's room but untouched, and said, 'Hey girls, let's have a drink.'

Soaking wet and still lathered with foam, he tore off his shirt and dried his chest with a sheet from Tony's bed, then took a bottle of champagne from the cooler. He shook it, opened it with a bang and a shower of spray, poured out three glasses and looked at Maureen and Lisa.

Both of them were soaking wet also and their underwear, or lack of it, and their full figures could be seen clearly through their wet dresses.

Sly went to the bathroom door and hammered on it.

'Truce, Tony,' he yelled. 'There's more booze out here and we need some towels.'

There was a pause, then the lock clicked and Tony stuck his grinning head round the door.

He looked at the three of them and said, 'Oh shit. You lot look like drowned rats.'

'Look at yourself,' said Sly. 'Come and have some champagne and get us those towels. It's getting chilly in here.'

Tony went back into the bathroom and came out carrying an armful of towels, warm from the rail.

Maureen unselfconsciously peeled off her sopping dress and knickers, took a large bath towel from Tony, wrapped herself in its fluffy softness, took her champagne glass and went and sat on the bed.

The other three also stripped naked and helped themselves to towels with which to cover themselves and sat together on the bed, drinking.

'Got any dope?' asked Sly.

Tony nodded. 'The roadies left me a couple of joints.'

'Great,' said Sly. 'Get them fired up.'

Tony did as he was told. He went over to the chest of drawers, opened one of them and found a couple of ready-rolled joints hidden in the folds of a T-shirt where he had stashed them earlier.

He threw one to Sly and lit the other using a book of hotel matches. He inhaled deeply and said, 'I bet Jobsworth's on our tail.'

'For sure,' agreed Sly, lighting the joint he had caught with another match, taking a couple of deep drags and passing it to Maureen. 'Let's give him a clue where we are.'

'*Sly*,' said Tony, but the former ignored him, got up, opened the window, looked out to make sure the coast was clear, picked up the TV set that was sitting on top of the chest of drawers and dropped it over the windowsill. There was a breathless silence for a moment, then the crash as the TV set hit the pavement outside.

'I hope there was nobody out there,' said Tony.

'No, mate. But I bet there will be in a minute. Now give us a hit on that joint.'

18

Tony passed the joint to Sly and dreamily he took a drag.

'Well, girls,' he said. 'What shall we do to pass the time until the police arrive?' And he doubled up with a gust of laughter in which the others joined.

'You're crazy,' said Lisa. 'Do you do this all the time?'

'When you're on the road, you get crazy,' said Sly. 'It goes with the job.'

'What else do you do?' asked Maureen.

'What else is there to do? You get stoned. Get drunk. Wreck the hotel and cap it off by getting fucked,' replied Sly. 'And I'm drunk and stoned now. I've done my best to wreck the hotel and I've even dropped the TV out of the window as an encore. So all that's left is to get fucked.'

Maureen stood up, unfastened her towel and dropped it to the floor.

'Come on then,' she said. 'I'm game.'

Sly stood and looked at her large, round breasts, with their tiny pink nipples like bullseyes in the centre of them. His eyes went down to the hint of a tummy that she had. Then to her large dimpled bottom and her short, chubby legs with a thick patch of blondish hair between them that covered her fleshy mound of Venus. And as he looked he felt his cock harden and rear up between his legs and tent the towel that was wrapped round his waist.

'I just bet you are,' he said and he undid his towel and let it drop to the floor too.

Maureen's eyes fastened on his cock and she smiled and licked her lips.

'Not on my bed,' said Tony. 'Use the bathroom.'

Sly grabbed Maureen and dragged her into the bathroom where he closed and locked the door behind them.

'On the floor,' he ordered.

Maureen got down on the thick carpet that covered the bathroom floor and Sly mounted her without any preliminaries. He didn't want to waste any time because he didn't know when some figure of authority would appear at Tony's door to demand recompense for his destruction of hotel property.

For a moment he wondered if she would be ready for him but he needn't have worried. Her cunt was warm, wet and open, just as he'd hoped it would be.

Sly's cock slid down the length of Maureen's vagina and she opened her legs wide and he pushed them up until they were around his shoulders and she was bent almost double.

'Christ,' she said breathlessly. 'That's good.'

'It's going to get better,' he said as he began to move his prick in and out of her pussy, rubbing the top of it along her clitoris.

Maureen couldn't believe the sensation she was feeling. She'd been screwed by lots of the local boys in

Norwich, but they were all wham-bam-thank-you-ma'am merchants who only cared for their own pleasure and not hers. The only way she'd come before was by herself, with her fingers or some hard object, in the privacy of her own room. But this crazy, drugged, destructive, drunken rock-and-roller from London was different. He seemed to care that she enjoyed it as much as he did. He was hot. And he was making Maureen feel hotter with his cock than all the other men she'd been fucked by put together.

She pinned his shoulders to hers with her legs and hugged his neck with her arms and ground her hips against his to get the maximum sensation.

She was laughing and crying all at the same time and she could feel the carpet burning her back and Sly's cock almost screwing her to the floor.

It felt like they'd only just started when she felt the first warmth of an orgasm in her womb and she came onto Sly's pumping organ, not once, not twice, but three times in quick succession, and her screams of delight echoed around the bathroom walls as if she was in an echo chamber.

Sly continued to ride her, until he too climaxed and rolled off her and lay gasping for breath next to the bath.

When he'd regained some composure, he said, 'Good, or what?'

'Brilliant,' she said. 'Can we do it again?'

'Next time we're in Norwich. No danger. Now we'd better go and see what's cooking next door.'

What was cooking was that Tony and Lisa were on top of Tony's bed screwing each other like crazy.

The sight of first Maureen, then Sly dropping

the towels that covered them, had got them horny too.

When the bathroom door had closed behind the couple and left Tony and Lisa alone, Tony had simply leant over and flipped Lisa's towel off too and he'd discovered that she dyed her hair and in fact was almost as dark as he was. A fact he hadn't noticed before because he'd been too busy looking at Maureen's enormous breasts.

'Two-tone,' he said.

'Do you mind?'

'Not in the least.'

'I would have dyed it too but I heard it's dangerous.'

'Could sting,' said Tony, who couldn't have cared less if she'd shaved the lot off, in fact he wouldn't have minded at all.

Lisa had very small breasts, which stood out proudly from her chest and her nipples were deep red and looked almost transparent against the paleness of her skin.

Tony had liked them from the beginning and now, naked and swollen in front of him, he liked them even more.

He reached out and gently touched one. Lisa giggled and moved away. He followed her across the bed until she was trapped up against the bedhead.

He put his hand under her right breast, cupped it and leant over and gently kissed the nipple. It felt rough and hard under his lips in contrast with the soft, smooth flesh of her breast itself.

'You're tickling,' she protested, but not with any particular vehemence.

He silenced her by kissing her on the lips. Her mouth

opened and he kissed her teeth and found her tongue with his.

He caressed her breasts again and that time she didn't protest at all, just pushed herself against his hands.

He pulled off the towel that was wrapped around his waist and her fingers explored his balls and cock. He laid her back on the bed and pushed her legs apart and kissed the dark hair on her cunt, then let his tongue explore the sweet/sour taste of the inside of it.

She began to moan and groan with pleasure and need, and he crawled up her body and inserted his hardness into her softness and began to move on top of her.

She responded with movements of her own and soon they were shagging each other hard.

As the pair of them were about to reach climax, the bathroom door opened and a naked Sly and Maureen appeared in the doorway. Maureen's back was sore and red-looking from rubbing on the carpet, as were Sly's knees and elbows.

They stood there watching as Tony hurled himself at Lisa and she responded in kind, and they were still standing there when the door to the suite was flung open by the night manager with a pass key. He was accompanied by Jobsworth, Dominic, who had been rudely dragged out of bed and still looked half asleep, and two police constables who the manager had summoned by telephone to arrest the madmen and women who were trying to destroy his hotel.

19

Slightly earlier, Jud and Judy, who had indulged in a
swift replay of their previous love-making in Jud's suite
and then had quickly fallen asleep in each other's arms,
had been wakened by the noise of the TV set exploding
in the street just under their window. Jud, who had
recognised the sound from previous experience, had
wisely decided that they should get up and get dressed.
They then followed the sound of official footsteps
upstairs and, a few minutes or so after the under
manager had opened up the room, also stuck their
heads through the doorway to see what all the excitement was about.

Inside they saw a scene of chaos.

Tony was sitting on the bed stark naked, penis still
erect and angry. Lisa was having hysterics, clutching
the edge of the bedspread around her naked body to
hide it from the prying eyes of the – as it appeared to
her – hordes of people who had burst in just as she was
about to reach a climax.

Sly was also naked but doing nothing to hide it and in
convulsions of laughter, with a champagne bottle in his
hand, guzzling from the neck. Maureen was screaming
obscenities at the two policemen as one of them tried to

cover her nakedness with his tunic – with little success, as parts of her kept popping out from between the edges of the material.

Dominic, hair sticking out from his head in all directions, and minus his usual studied cool, was remonstrating with the night manager, who was threatening to press charges first, and sue everyone in the room later, unless the band and hangers-on left the premises immediately.

The elderly porter was standing stock still in the middle of the carpet with the kind of expression on his face that said he hadn't had as much fun since VE night. And possibly not even then.

The only member of The Getaways' entourage missing was David, who was fast asleep in his suite upstairs alone until he was wakened by a phone call from Dominic and instructed to pack at once and vacate his room. Which he did with the minimum of fuss. And soon afterwards all eight of them found themselves on the main street of Norwich in various states of disarray.

Dominic gave Lisa and Maureen, who had both managed to struggle into their damp clothes, a five-pound-note each and hailed what was probably the town's only all-night cab and put them into it and sent them home. But not before Maureen had surreptitiously slipped the constable who had tried to contain her large, slippery breasts into his jacket, her phone number.

Dominic then collected the Bentley from the car park and stuck the band into it with instructions to keep very quiet, before returning to the foyer of the hotel, under police escort, to pay the bill. Plus extras for breakages etc. Plus a large tip to the under manager for any inconvenience caused and with many, profuse apologies for the behaviour of his charges.

Dominic had then pressed onto the police officers, who were still hinting darkly at unspecific but serious charges that could be brought, a large donation to the Police Benevolent Fund, at which point their attitudes changed and they went outside and got the band to autograph their notebooks, before getting into their squad car and driving back to the police station for an early breakfast and a very interesting story with which to regale their colleagues for months to come.

Finally Dominic, who had at last run out of people to say sorry to, or bribe, or both, gave Jobsworth, who had hardly left his side in the past half-hour, yet another fiver – why, he wasn't quite sure – before getting into the car and preparing for the long drive back to London.

Meanwhile, Judy had gone to her own room and packed the small bag she had brought with her and was about to follow the Bentley in her car. But before she went, to the accompaniment of catcalls from the other band members, she had leant into the limousine, kissed Jud on the lips and asked him to call her soon.

Dominic had apologised profusely to the journalist for what had happened, but Judy brushed the apologies off and told him she hadn't enjoyed herself so much for ages and he should look out for a censored version of the story in the paper in the very next issue.

So that was more or less that, and the small convoy left Norwich in the direction of London as the first hint of dawn appeared on the horizon and another successful, if rather expensive, out-of-town gig for The Getaways came to a satisfactory conclusion.

20

Tuesday passed quietly, with all concerned recovering from their adventures in Norwich.

In the evening, Dominic got a call to tell him that the single had moved up to second position in the charts and that sales were increasing daily – so much so, that the record company was having to lease out extra pressing facilities to meet demand. And also that, the next night, *Top of the Pops* were going to rerun the clip of 'Here We Go' from the band's previous appearance on the show – which would not only save them the trip to Manchester, where the programme was shot, but would almost certainly push the record to number one the following week.

Dominic was jubilant, and in his triumphant phone calls to the band he promised them the biggest party of their lives if they reached the pole position.

On Wednesday morning the music papers appeared in London and everyone rushed into town to secure copies and see the evidence in black and white.

That afternoon Dominic telephoned Tony and asked him to call at his flat in Highgate the following day at four p.m. for a meeting about the new single to be recorded later that summer.

Tony agreed and went back to the piano, where he had been doodling with a few ideas, and tried with only moderate success to get a couple of decent songs finished before the next day.

He watched *Top of the Pops*, where Alan Freeman introduced the clip, and he too prophesied a number one for The Getaways. Feeling well pleased with that at least, Tony phoned the rest of the band to make sure they'd also been watching, which they had and, after mutual congratulations, he sat up late, still fiddling with the songs, but inspiration wouldn't come and he sloped off to bed in the small hours with very little to show for the day's work.

The next morning he got up late and went to the King's Road for brunch. After he'd eaten, he went back to the flat to put in a couple more hours work, but to little effect again. Just before three thirty he got into his car and drove to Highgate to keep his appointment.

Dominic's wife, Anya, answered the door. 'Hello, Tony,' she said. 'What brings you here?'

'I'm supposed to be meeting Dominic.' He replied. 'A business meeting.'

'I'm afraid he's not here. He got called into the office.'

'Do you know when he'll be back?'

She shrugged. 'God knows,' she said. 'Do you want to come in and wait?'

'If that's OK.'

'It's always OK for one of Dom's stars to visit. It's you that pays the rent, after all.' She opened the door fully and he went into the flat. 'Come on through,' she said. 'I'm in the conservatory.'

Tony followed her through the living room into the

warmth of the glass extension that looked out over London. She picked a drink off the bar and took a mouthful. 'Want one?' she asked.

Suddenly he realised she was drunk. 'Sure,' he replied.

'I'm drinking gin and tonic. I always have a couple of belts about this time. Will you join me?'

A couple of belts, thought Tony, more like a bottle and a half. 'Sure,' he said. 'Whatever's easiest.'

'Sit down,' she said. 'Make yourself comfortable.'

He did as she said, choosing a cane armchair with a flower-patterned cushion on the seat and watched her as she made his drink.

Although they'd met before, on social occasions, she didn't have much to do with the business and this was the first time they'd ever been alone. The only thing he knew for sure about her was that she used to be an actress but not a very successful one. He guessed she was a year or two younger than Dominic. But well preserved, Dominic's money saw to that. She had a thick head of blue-black hair. Her figure was full, but youthful and firm-looking. Her breasts were large, as were her hips and buttocks, but she had a small waist, accentuated by the outfit she was wearing, and she obviously believed in keeping in shape. She was dressed in a two-piece suit of navy blue material. The skirt was slightly longer than the latest fashion. It came to just above the knee but was very tight over her arse and accentuated every curve under it. On her legs she was wearing dark nylons, with seams, and her feet were shod in high-heeled, pointed-toed leather shoes that threw her slightly forward as she stood, into a sexually provocative pose.

Her legs were very good and he felt a faint stirring in his crotch at the sight of them. The jacket of the suit was single-breasted and tight-waisted to give her a perfect hour-glass figure. Her neck and the top of her chest was bare and he'd seen an inch and a half of shadowy cleavage as she'd welcomed him.

She brought him his drink and, as she bent down to put it on the table next to him, her jacket fell away and he was presented with a good deal more than cleavage as her breasts bobbed into sight. She was wearing a low-cut black bra under her jacket. She did nothing to hide the view, just looked up from under her thick fringe of hair and smiled at him. She straightened up after a moment, went back to the bar to get her drink, and sat in a matching cane chair opposite him. As she sat down her skirt rode up her thighs and he saw the darker band of stocking tops beneath the hem of her skirt.

Stockings. Tony loved stockings, always had done. They reminded him of the forbidden glimpses of female lingerie on his female relatives and their friends from his childhood. He hated tights, even though he knew that the micro-minis coming into style dictated that they be worn. He thought they were the least sexy garments he'd ever seen, with their ugly gussets and seams.

'So how's it going?' asked Anya.

'Pretty good,' Tony replied. 'The new record looks like a certain number one.'

'I know. Dominic is very happy.'

'It was touch and go,' said Tony, 'but the pirates gave us a lot of plays.'

Anya crossed her legs and her skirt rode up even further. Tony thought that he could see an inch of creamy thigh above her stocking tops and wondered if her knickers matched her bra. He would have bet half a year's royalties that they did. Once again he felt a stirring in his groin and hoped that Dominic didn't hurry back.

'How's your girlfriend?' asked Anya.

'Which one?' he asked guilelessly.

'I suppose you're fighting them off these days.'

'You could say that. It's a joke. A year ago I had to work hard to get a girl to go out with me. And now . . .'

'Yes?'

'Like you say, I'm fighting them off. There's always at least half a dozen hanging around outside the flat and I even find them hiding in closets when we go on the road.'

'And what do you do with them?'

'Fuck them usually,' said Tony boldly. After all, he thought, that's what she wants me to say.

She squirmed in the chair, managing to show off even more white thigh. 'How?' she asked.

'Any way they want it?'

'Up the arse?'

'Sometimes.'

'I love being fucked up the arse,' she said.

'Do you?' He could feel his cock getting harder in his jeans and he knew that she knew the effect she was having on him.

'Yes. Do you think I've got a nice one?'

'It looks pretty good to me.'

'Does it, Tony? Does it really?'

'It does,' he said and his voice sounded husky in his ears.

141

'Just *pretty* good? Or very good. I've been told lots of times that it's very good.'

'Yes,' he agreed. 'Very good.'

'Or even better.'

Christ, but he was getting hot. 'Better,' he said. 'Much better. The best arse I've ever seen.'

'Would you like to see it up close?'

'Yes.'

She put her drink down, stood up in front of him and turned round, then pulled up her skirt slowly. She turned her head to see his reaction. The material travelled up the meat of her thighs, revealing her seamed stockings, the band of darker material at the top and the fastenings of her suspenders at the back. Then he saw creamy white skin. She smiled and gathered the material over her hips. Slowly, more of her thighs were revealed.

Tony licked his lips and tasted sweat. Inch by inch, her skirt travelled higher. Her skin was flawless and the black straps of her suspenders seemed to make it even whiter and more perfect. Then he saw the first swell of her buttocks and the cleft of her arse deep in shadow. Higher still her skirt went and he saw she was wearing a tiny pair of black panties. Almost a G-string, like the strippers used to wear on the Reep in Hamburg, in those far off days when the band had had to play twelve hours a night for money for food and drink and drugs.

The material was pulled tightly up in her crack and for all of her flesh that it concealed she might as well not have been wearing anything under her skirt. She eased the garment up to her waist and turned round. At the front her knickers were just a tiny triangle of lace and black pubic hair escaped from around the elasticised edges. Her suspender belt was just a lacy froth, fastened tightly round her waist. She turned again, even more slowly, and Tony was sure that her arse was in fact the best he'd ever seen.

'What do you think?' she asked and her voice sounded as husky as his had been a minute or two before.

'Beautiful,' he breathed.

She fiddled with the fastening of the skirt and pushed it over her hips, let it fall to the floor, and stepped out of it. She undid her jacket, shrugged it off and tossed it over the chair she'd been sitting in. Her breasts stood up boldly in the black bra that confined them. In one smooth motion she pushed her panties down her legs and kicked them in his direction. Her bush of black hair was thick and oily and he could see the glint of moisture deep inside it and could smell her femininity in the close air of the conservatory.

She turned around again so that he had to look at her backside. She put one hand on each buttock and pulled them apart to reveal her anus. He looked at the puckered little star of dark skin that surrounded the hole and saw that her thick pubic hair grew almost up to it. 'There,' she said. 'No secrets, Tony.'

For the first time he moved. He got up out of his chair and walked towards where she was standing. He knelt down behind her and pushed his face against her hot skin. He licked the cleft between her buttocks and forced his tongue into her anus. She moaned and pushed herself hard back against him. He ran his hands up her legs, loving the contrast between the nylon of her stockings and the smoothness of her skin, and round to her pubic hair. It was stiff and crisp and he tugged at the curls gently, then slid his fingers into the wetness between her legs. She opened them to allow him easy access and stood astride as his hands wandered over her most intimate parts. She rolled her hips, reaching back to put her fingers into his long hair and pull his head even deeper into the crevice of her bottom.

After a couple of minutes Tony stood up, turned her round and began to kiss her. Their mouths opened and their tongues met in an orgy of passion. They nibbled each other's lips and slid their tongues around each other's teeth. Their kissing became frenzied and they started licking each other's faces like animals. Tony tore at the fastening of her bra and ripped it off and dropped it on the floor. Her breasts were luscious and full with dark aureoles and nipples made even darker by the blood that hardened them until they were like two tiny buttons.

She pushed him backwards until he felt the seat of the chair behind his legs and he fell back into it. She stood above him, then bent until her breasts were in front of his face.

'Suck,' she ordered and pushed the right one into his mouth. He took the nipple between his lips and did as she told him. He tongued and sucked it until it became even harder, impossible as that seemed.

'Now the other one,' she said and moved round so that her left breast was in his mouth. Once again he obeyed. He liked the feeling that she was in control. She moved again, making him lick and suck first one breast then the other.

As she straddled him, he slid his hand into her cunt again. She was dripping juice and he smeared it under her crotch to her arsehole. He used her pussy lubrication to moisten her anus and pushed first his little finger into the hole and, as it opened, his forefinger. Her face was a mask of ecstasy. 'God, that's good,' she said.

As the hole opened even further under his ministrations, he forced first two, then three fingers into it. She was panting and moaning as he did so. 'Fuck me, Tony,' she said. 'Fuck me now.'

He stood up in order to let her sit, so that he could kneel between her legs and shaft her, but she said, 'Not in my cunt. My cunt's for my husband. In my arse, like I said.'

She bent over the cane chair so that her bottom was sticking up in the air. Tony tore off his shoes and jeans, thankful he no longer wore underpants and, still wearing his shirt, he pushed his erection into her crack. She guided him to the entrance to her arse. 'Push,' she cried. 'Push, you bastard.'

At first he thought she would be too tight for his engorged member, but her hole was slippery with the juice he'd used for lubrication for his fingers and all at once it opened and allowed the tip of his prick inside. He pushed harder and she screamed once, and he felt his knob end open the cavity and suddenly his cock was all the way inside and being gripped tightly by her flesh.

'Yes,' she screamed again. 'Yes, you fucker. Do me. Shag me, you cunt.'

Tony grinned at her profanity and wondered if she shouted like that when old Dominic fucked her. He doubted it. No wonder she wanted a young man to service her needs.

He began to move inside her. Her muscles were strong and he had to push and pull hard to get the required friction going. As he moved, she called out more profanity, urging him on. 'Do it, you bastard. Fuck me harder. I can hardly feel it.'

He pushed deeper inside her, wanting her to beg him to stop. That he was hurting her. But she just urged him on. Faster and faster, he moved as her arse became used to the intrusion of his prick. They were both sweating with the exertion of the fuck and Tony was gritting his teeth as he felt his orgasm coming closer. He saw that her hands were gripping the arms of the chair so hard that they were white and bloodless. The sight of them drove him to even harder thrusts. He put one hand beneath her and tugged at her pubic hair, wanting and needing to hurt her. His fingers found her clitoris in the folds of skin protected by her bush and he massaged the tiny piece of engorged tissue.

'More,' she begged. 'Do it more.' And suddenly she stiffened and let out a scream that he thought would shatter the glass in the walls and roof of the conservatory. She came with more screams and the sound of them heightened his passion until he climaxed, too, deep inside her, with hot spurts of come that he thought would never stop. But stop they did and he slumped down over her supine body.

After a minute he freed himself from her and they collapsed together onto the cushion of the armchair. She curled up in his arms and they lay, stuck together by their sweat for what seemed like hours, without speaking.

Eventually she extricated herself from his embrace and got up. As she did so, a car door slammed below. 'Christ,' she said, looking at her watch, 'that sounds like Dominic. Quick, get dressed. I must look a mess.'

She grabbed her clothes, and ran out of the room.

Tony quickly scrambled into his jeans and shoes, took his empty glass and made himself another drink. He walked over and looked at the mirror by the door. His face showed no sign of what he'd been doing and he pushed his long hair into some semblance of neatness before Anya came back, with Dominic close behind. She too was dressed and her lipstick was fresh.

'Tony, dear boy,' boomed his manager. 'Sorry I was delayed. I hope Anya's been entertaining you in my absence.'

Tony looked at Anya, who winked at him slyly. 'Sure, Dom,' he replied. 'We hardly noticed that you weren't here.'

21

The meeting went smoothly except, as far as Tony was concerned, for the disconcerting presence of Anya, who supplied them with drinks and the offer of food as the afternoon turned into the evening.

Finally, about seven, with Dominic in a fine mood, Tony took his leave.

Anya showed him to the door and kissed him on the cheek. 'Do pop round any time, Tony,' she said. 'You know you're always welcome here.'

Tony grinned. 'Thanks,' he said. 'I might take you up on that.'

He went back to his car and drove into town. He stopped at Sly's flat in Chelsea and found his friend getting ready to go out.

'Where you off to?' he asked.

'Got a date with old Nancy Goldstein. What are you up to?'

'Nothing.'

'Come along then. We're going to eat, then see what's happening. Fancy it?'

'Sure,' said Tony. 'As long as she won't mind.'

'Course not. The more the merrier. She's dying to meet you. She's such an old groupie. Just keep your hands to yourself. Mind you, there's more than enough to go round with old Nance. We'll see if we can get that interview with *Tiger Beat* organised. Now we're on Capitol in the good old USA. And now that Alan Freeman says we're going to be number one. ''Ere didn't I look pretty on telly last night?'

'We all did,' said Tony. 'Don't go getting *too* big-headed.'

'What, me?' said Sly. 'No chance. So, you coming or not?'

'Course I am,' said Tony and they left the flat.

'What have you been up to?' asked Sly, once they were in Tony's car and heading in the direction of Hyde Park.

'Had a meeting with Dominic about the new single,' replied Tony. 'Nothing much else.' He didn't tell Sly what had occurred with Anya. He decided to keep that a secret for the present.

'Got any new masterpieces?' asked Sly.

'A couple of things. Nothing finished.'

'There's plenty of time,' said Sly. 'Don't worry about it. You came up with all the songs for the album double quick, remember? I've got faith in you, Tony me old mate.'

'I wish I was as confident.'

'Come round one night. Bring what you've got. We'll get Dave and Jud in and get something finished.'

'Good idea,' said Tony.

'Yeah. And I fancy some of those song-writing royalties too. I'm spending dough like it's going out of fashion.'

'No problem,' said Tony. 'We're going to be number one. It's a cert. You watch. We'll all be loaded soon.'

'Nice thought, ain't it,' said Sly. 'I could do with some of that. Slow down, we're nearly there. Next on the left and pull in anywhere.'

Tony did as he was told, and they went up to Nancy's flat where she was waiting, watching TV in her black beatnik regalia.

She was delighted to meet Tony and full of congratulations for the band's achievement.

'Looks like the big one next week, boys,' she said. 'I saw you on *Top of the Pops* last night. You looked *so* cool.'

'Told you, Tone,' said Sly, preening himself in front of the mirror.

'*All* of you,' said Nancy. 'Especially that groovy little drummer of yours.'

'You trying to make me jealous, Nance?' said Sly, winking at Tony.

'No. But I gotta meet that guy,' said Nancy.

'He's scoring well at the moment,' said Sly. 'I'll have to watch him.' The rhythm guitarist fluffed up his hair. 'Number one. I can't believe it.'

'Great stuff,' said Nancy.

'And we're signed to Capitol in America,' said Sly proudly. 'Got the news a couple of days ago. "Here We Go" is coming out in a couple of weeks. And they're putting all their muscle behind it. Dominic reckons we could be number one there too.'

Nancy hugged him. 'Then you're *definitely* on for a feature in the paper. Maybe even a front cover. I'm going to Germany for a week, on Saturday, then back to the States for a few days. I'll suss out what's happening over there. I'm going out to the coast. I'll check out some buddies of mine at Capitol. Get the big word from them, then twist my editor's arm until she lets me give you guys the biggest spread in the paper's history. I want to be known as the girl who broke The Getaways Stateside.

'As big as *your* spread,' said Sly lasciviously.

'Sly! Don't be so disgusting,' said Nancy. But she smiled at the memory of what they'd done together and what she hoped they'd do again before the night was out.

'You'll miss our party,' said Sly.

'What party?'

'When we get to *numero uno*. Dominic's promised us an orgy.'

'Sounds good,' said Nancy. 'There's nothing I like better than a good old-fashioned orgy. It's a shame you'll have to take someone else, Sly.'

'Not me,' said Sly. 'You're the only woman in the world I care about.'

'Don't shit me, Sly,' said Nancy. But she smiled again, even if she didn't believe a word he was saying.

'Tony's coming with us tonight,' said Sly. 'He's at a loose end. Don't mind, do you?'

'Mind? Me?' replied Nancy. 'A night out with two members of the hottest band in the country? The other girls will be wetting their knickers.'

'Just as long as you do too,' said Sly.

'How do you know I'm wearing any?' asked Nancy coyly.

'I'll find out later,' said Sly confidently. 'Where we going to eat?'

'There's a new place just round the corner,' said Nancy. 'That actor guy's just opened it. What's his name? You know.' She mentioned the name of the British star of that summer's hit film. 'It's *tres* groovee. Everyone's talking about it. And *so* exclusive. It's impossible to get a table. They don't even answer the phone for reservations.'

'How are we going to get in then?' asked Sly.

'Don't worry,' replied Nancy. 'I have my methods.'

'I know that,' said Sly. 'But how are we going to get inside this place to eat?'

'Funny,' said Nancy.

'I try to be,' replied Sly. 'But how are we going to get in?'

'Wait and see,' said Nancy.

The three of them went downstairs into the street and after a short walk they arrived at the restaurant, which was called Les Maisons Alfie.

There was a crowd outside but Nancy led the way and pushed through to the front door which was guarded by a big bruiser in a dinner suit.

'Nancy Goldstein,' she announced, 'plus friends. We're expected.'

The bruiser looked at her and she looked right back.

'Come on then, asshole,' she said. 'Shake a leg. We're starving. Your boss won't like it if I tell him you kept some very important people waiting outside in the street.'

The bruiser scowled, then allowed them into the foyer where they waited under the watchful eye of another bruiser who was sitting at the reception desk, buffing his nails and ignoring the phone that was ringing off the hook beside him, as the first one vanished further back into the restaurant.

'Shithead,' said Nancy.

The second bruiser gave her a dirty look which she ignored.

Within a few minutes the first bruiser was back, accompanied by a fey-looking boy in a see-through shirt and black trousers so tight that it seemed impossible that he could sit down in them.

'Miss Goldstein,' he fluted, 'I *do* apologise for the delay. Your table is ready. Please come this way. Unless you'd prefer a drink in the bar first.'

'*I* would,' said Sly.

'The bar it is then,' said Nancy, and the fey boy took them down a corridor lined with smoked mirrors into a large cocktail bar full of more mirrors, exotic plants, low glass-topped tables, leather sofas and at one end a long mahogany bar with at least a thousand bottles stacked up behind it on glass shelves.

Between the bar and the bottles stood two more equally fey-looking boys in white shirts and black trousers covered with long aprons.

The room itself was populated with half a dozen or so beautiful people, dressed in the latest California hippy style, draped over the various pieces of furniture, chatting and drinking.

The first boy saw Nancy, Sly and Tony to a table, and took their orders.

Nancy ordered a martini cocktail, seven to one, with an olive. Tony requested a Scotch and Coke and Sly asked for a pint of best bitter.

The fey boy did his best to smile and told him that they did not serve beer.

Sly smiled back and told him that he thought they probably didn't and that he'd settle for the same as Tony.

The fey boy took their order to the bar, where one of the barman got mixing.

'Fuck me,' said Sly. 'What a bleedin' place.'

'Exclusive,' said Nancy.

'Bleedin' right,' said Sly. 'So bleedin' exclusive you can't even get in.'

'You're only pissed off because no one recognised you,' said Tony.

'Too right,' replied Sly. 'What's the point of being number one, if no one knows who the hell you are?'

'We're not number one yet,' corrected Tony.

'So next week I get in with no trouble. Right,' said Sly.

'Maybe,' said Tony. 'Wait and see.'

'So what's the food like?' asked Sly. 'Do they do chips?'

'You're such an inverted snob,' said Nancy. 'Bitter indeed. I suppose you wanted it served warm.'

'A pillock, more like,' said Tony.

Sly grinned. 'You know me,' he said. 'I just hate all this poncey, swinging London bollocks.'

'Except when you make money out of it,' said Tony.

'Right again,' said Sly. 'Here come the drinks. I'll be better in a minute.'

And he was.

After they'd finished their cocktails, the fey boy returned and showed the trio into the restaurant itself.

It was a dimly lit dream of even more smoked mirrors, chrome, pink linen tablecloths and heavy silver cutlery.

The menu was in French and after more messing around from Sly, who demanded translations of everything, they put in their order for food and the wine waiter brought them a bottle of some ridiculously expensive white Burgundy that was older than any of them.

'Now, this is the business,' said Sly when he tasted from his glass. 'I do like a glass of good plonk. We'd better get the waiter to put another couple of bottles in the fridge for later.'

'Shut up, Sly,' said Nancy. 'Just enjoy the good life. You've earned it.'

'Haven't I just,' agreed Sly.

The food arrived a few minutes later and they all tucked into what even Sly had to agree was a delicious meal.

With the dessert, the famous actor, Alfie Smith, a curly, blonde-headed East Ender who had lent his name to the restaurant, arrived to meet and greet his customers.

When he realised who Sly and Tony were and that Sly had been born and bred just a short bus ride from his own home, he called for a magnum of champagne to celebrate meeting a fellow cockney and to the success of the band.

This was much more up Sly's street and he basked in the admiration of Alfie, the staff and the other diners.

Alfie stayed at the table, chatting, and when the first bottle of bubbly was finished Sly called for another, so by midnight all four of them were extremely drunk, and when Alfie suggested that they head for a club, the other three readily agreed.

They cabbed round to a place that Alfie knew, not far from the restaurant, and from there he called his girlfriend who turned up with another friend for Tony.

They turned out to be a pair of indistinguishable,

silken blonde-haired, skinny models named Anthea and Cleo, who looked even skinnier next to Nancy's bulk. But who turned out to be able to match the bigger girl's capacity for alcohol, glass for glass.

By three o'clock in the morning all six of them were totally out of control and, when the lights in the club came on and the Hoovers came out, Nancy invited everyone back to her place for a nightcap.

They all fell into another cab and within minutes were back at Hyde Park Mansions where Nancy stuck the new Beach Boys album on the stereo and made a pot of coffee and fetched out the brandy bottle whilst Sly rolled up a couple of joints from the stash she always kept handy.

22

From where he was sitting, cross-legged on the floor, rolling up the joints on the back of a Gerry and the Pacemakers' album which he considered the only thing it was good for, Sly looked round the room at his companions.

Alfie was sitting on the sofa with his hand up either Anthea or Cleo's skirt, Sly couldn't figure which was which, him being so drunk. Not that it seemed to particularly matter. And as Anthea/Cleo's skirt was so short that it barely covered the brief white panties that she was wearing, that hardly seemed to matter either.

Tony was sitting on the armchair, which was the only other furniture in the room, with the other model on his lap. They were kissing passionately and it made Sly horny just to look at them.

He finished rolling the first joint and tossed it to Alfie, who lit it with a gold lighter and gave the girl he was with a blowback, then began kissing her too, which made Sly even hornier.

He began rolling the second joint and Nancy came into the room from the kitchen carrying a tray containing the coffee pot, milk, sugar, and cups and saucers.

She dumped it onto the carpet next to Sly and said,

159

'Come on, guys. Coffee's up.'

'Where's that brandy you promised?' asked Alfie, temporarily letting go of his blonde and passing the joint he was holding to Tony.

'I'll get it,' said Nancy, the perfect hostess, and went back to the kitchen for the bottle and six glasses.

When she returned Alfie was pouring the coffee and she put the booze tray on the carpet next to him and poured out half a dozen hefty tots of brandy.

'Come and get it,' she called and everyone gathered round to get their drinks.

Sly grabbed Nancy. 'What we gonna do?' he asked.

'Who knows, handsome,' she said.

'I fancy a fuck,' he said.

'You're not the only one by the looks of it,' she replied.

'Soon,' he said. 'Otherwise I think I'm going to crash out.'

'Not with me, boy,' she said. 'I won't be seeing you for a while and I want something to remember you by.'

'So?' said Sly taking a drag on the second joint he'd rolled.

'So, I'll shoo this lot out and we can get down to some serious fucking.'

'Sounds good to me,' said Sly.

Ten minutes passed and Nancy was as good as her word. She made a big deal out of yawning a couple of gigantic yawns, which in a girl her size was a bit like an earthquake on one of the continental land masses.

'Gee, guys, but I'm tired,' she said. 'I hate to break up the party, but . . .'

She didn't finish the sentence.

Tony looked at Sly, who winked at him.

'Yeah,' said Tony. 'I think we should let these people get to bed. How about the rest of you coming back to my place? I've got the car outside. I think we'll all squeeze in.

He was thinking particularly of squeezing Anthea, who was the model who had been sitting on his knee earlier.

Reluctantly Alfie and Cleo got up to leave.

'Sly,' said Alfie. 'Any time you're around, call into the restaurant. I'm usually about, or they know where to find me. Unless I'm on location, that is,' he added with a self-deprecating smile.

'I'll do that, Alfie,' said Sly. 'It's been great to meet you. We must do a pub crawl round the old neighbourhood soon.'

'Nothing would suit me better,' replied Alfie and with much kissing and promising to keep in touch, the four of them left and Nancy and Sly were alone.

'Nice bloke,' said Sly.

'Terrific,' agreed Nancy. 'Now what was that about a fuck?'

'Let's go,' said Sly, who was already unbuttoning his shirt. 'I want to know the truth about the state of your knickers.'

Nancy came over to him and they embraced. She smelled of gin and patchouli oil, and the mixture filled Sly's nostrils like an aphrodisiac.

He began pulling at her sweater, tugging it out of her skirt and up over her head, sending the shades she was still wearing flying across the room.

'Calm down, boy,' she said laughingly. 'Those glasses cost me fifty bucks.'

Sly ignored her protests and found the zip at the back

of her skirt and pulled it down, then pushed the garment over her wide hips until it dropped to the floor.

Just as he had guessed, she wasn't wearing any knickers, and the scent of her cunt mixed with the perfume and booze was almost too much for Sly to bear.

He grabbed her hand and dragged her into the bedroom and flung her onto the bed. She lay there, legs open, dressed only in black stockings, a suspender belt and a black bra, which was low cut and barely contained the fullness of her huge breasts.

Sly looked at her greedily as he tore off his clothes, then dived onto the bed next to her.

'Is that a pistol, honey, or are you just glad to see me?' she said, referring to his engorged penis that swung between his legs as he did so.

'It's a pistol,' he said. 'And it's aimed at you.' And rolled her round so that he could get at the fastenings of her bra.

He undid them and slid the straps off her shoulders to allow her breasts their freedom. They dropped down to her belly. Huge, fat and white. The raspberry-coloured nipples that tipped them, as big as saucers.

'I love your tits,' he said.

'They're a bit bigger than the ones on those two diddy models tonight.'

'But you're a real woman,' he said.

'Come here and prove it, lover,' she replied and reached for Sly.

She wrapped him in a huge bear-hug that almost prevented him from breathing and covered his face with kisses. Their lips met and he poked his tongue into her mouth until he found hers.

Sly closed his eyes and felt the room spin slowly round him. His hands went to her breasts and he squeezed and kneaded them like a baker preparing raw dough for the oven.

They filled his hands with their soft warmth and he thrilled at the sensation.

'I want to come over them,' he said between kisses.

'I want you to come inside me.'

'Later,' he said feverishly. 'I've gotta come over your tits. I've just gotta.'

'Be my guest then, honey. If you want to so bad,' said Nancy.

Sly pushed her back onto the coverlet and mounted the roundness of her belly. He put his cock in between her breasts and lifted them until they almost hid his tool, then began to move himself between them. They were damp with sweat and his prick slid easily and pleasurably against the soft, wet skin.

Nancy put her hands over his, to push her breasts even tighter over his cock, and he moved one hand behind him and into the dampness of her pubic hair.

Her cunt was dripping with lubrication, and the tops of her thighs were wet with it.

'You horny cow,' he said. 'You're soaking.'

'I've been watching you all night and my pussy was wet for you all the time. I wanted to take you into the ladies in that restaurant and have you over the sink.'

'You should have said,' said Sly. 'I'd've been game. I'd've been game to have you over the table with everyone else watching.'

Nancy closed her eyes and bit down on her lower lip at the thought and her legs opened wider and her cunt seemed to suck his searching fingers even deeper until he found her clitoris and she gasped and she rubbed her breasts even harder over his cock.

From his position above her, Sly looked down at the flesh covering his prick, with only the knob, dark with blood, showing at the top of her cleavage. She had pushed her tits so hard together that the aureoles of her nipples seemed to meld together into one huge, swollen pink mass. His hand moved to cover them and, as he did so, he felt his cock jump and he shot a thick jet of semen up over her neck and face and hair.

She screamed as the hot wetness sprayed across her face and she licked at her chin and lips, sucking what she could reach with her tongue into her mouth and swallowing it greedily.

Sly dropped down onto her and kissed her face, tasting his come, still warm on her skin, and felt it matting his hair against hers.

'That was fucking great,' he gasped.

'Oh Sly, darlin',' said Nancy. 'I could go for you in a big way.'

'Me too, Doll,' he said.

'You going to make me come?' she said.

Sly lifted his head and grinned down at her. 'I thought I'd leave you horny. Tease you a bit.'

'No, Sly,' she begged. 'It's not fair. I won't be able to sleep.'

Sly's grin widened, then he relented and slid down the length of her until his head was deep into the hot wetness of her cunt. He licked at her clitoris which was still standing proud after his previous ministrations.

He felt her wriggle and gasp, and her hands found his damp hair and pushed his face deeper between her thighs. He felt unable to breath but kept licking and sucking at the hairy opening until he felt her excitement mounting and he grabbed a breath and stuck his long tongue as deeply into her as he could until she screamed again. A long wail, like a banshee, and she beat her heels on the bed as she orgasmed. Sly rolled off her and lay breathless, with one hand gently playing with her pubic hair.

'Christ,' she said after a minute. 'I love you, baby.'

But by then Sly had fallen asleep and didn't hear a word.

23

The rest of the week passed quickly for the band and its
entourage. Nancy left London for Germany and her
trip back to the States and, by the following Tuesday, it
was confirmed that 'Here We Go' was indeed number
one on the British charts. The band had never seen
such a constant party. They were summoned to a
meeting in Dominic's office in Regent Street on that
afternoon. It was the same day as Jade was due back
from her modelling assignment in Paris and David was
on tenterhooks to meet his girlfriend, but Dominic
insisted that the meeting was vital. 'Business before
pleasure,' he said and, reluctantly, David agreed. He
telephoned Jade at her hotel in the morning and told
her that he'd meet her back at home, just as soon as the
meeting was concluded.

Tony was the first to arrive. As songwriter and
unofficial leader of the band he usually had an informal
half-hour chat with Dominic before the other members
showed up.

Marsha, Dominic's secretary, showed Tony into
Dominic's office with its panoramic view of Piccadilly
and the band's manager leapt up from his chair behind
the huge, empty desk where he conducted his business.

He shook Tony's hand warmly.

'Congratulations, dear boy. Now that it's official. Just think about it.' He gestured at the street outside, silent behind the double-glazing. 'You and the rest of the boys have the most popular record in the country as we speak. Name me one young man on that pavement who wouldn't wish to be in your shoes at this moment.'

Tony grinned broadly. 'We could never have done it without you, Dominic,' he replied.

'Nonsense,' said the older man. 'But thanks for the thought. I appreciate it.'

Tony sat in one of the four armchairs dotted around the room and took out his cigarettes and lit one.

'Coffee?' asked Dominic.

'Why not?'

'And a brandy, I think,' said his manager and spoke through the intercom to his secretary.

Within minutes she delivered a tray of refreshments and Dominic played mother and gave Tony a china cup and saucer and a balloon glass half full of amber spirit, and than resumed his seat behind his desk.

'I hear you and Anya got something going the other afternoon,' he said conversationally after a sip at his coffee.

Tony froze.

'Do what?' he asked after a moment.

Dominic saw the look on his face and smiled. 'Come now, Tony,' he said. 'Don't be coy. She told me all about it after you'd gone.'

'I . . . I . . .' Tony stuttered.

'Don't worry. Anya and I have an arrangement. We have a very modern marriage. Here, let me show you.'

He took his briefcase from the floor beside him, laid

it on the desk and opened it. 'Come and look.'

Tony, who half expected Dominic to take a loaded pistol from the case and shoot him, stood up nervously and went over to the desk. Inside the briefcase were a couple of spools of eight millimetre film and a sheaf of ten by eight black-and-white photographs. Dominic threw them onto the top of the desk and Tony picked them up. They were all pictures of Anya, screwing and being screwed in every position imaginable by a succession of young men and women.

'Fucking hell,' said Tony, rifling through them, suddenly not nervous at all. 'This is hot stuff. Did you get any of me?'

'Unfortunately not. Not this time. Neither were you captured in living colour.' He tapped the spools of film. 'You must come over one night and let me show you some home movies. They are most edifying I assure you.'

'I just bet they are,' said Tony and laughed out loud. 'Is this how you two get off? Fuck me, Dominic, but you're a case.'

'Aren't I just? And yes, this is how we "get off", as you so delicately put it. It's harmless and we both enjoy it. Anyway, when I told Anya you were coming over the other day, she asked me to make myself scarce for a while. She couldn't wait to be alone with you. She's expressed great admiration for you for a very long time.'

Tony was amazed at the direction the conversation had taken. 'Is that right?' he asked.

'One hundred percent. I trust you enjoyed yourself as much as she did?'

Tony grinned. What the fuck? he thought. 'Yes, Dominic, I did,' he said. 'I think I probably did,' and he raised his brandy glass in a toast to his manager. 'You're amazing, mate,' he said. 'And the more I know you, the more amazing you become.'

On the plane back from France, Jade Dollar was sitting next to Gerry Preston, the hottest and most handsome photographer in London, with whom she had spent most of her free time over the last ten days in Paris.

'Is your boyfriend going to meet you at the airport?' asked Gerry.

Jade pulled a face. 'No. He's got to go to a business meeting with the rest of the band and his manager and he hasn't got time. He phoned me this morning to tell me.'

'It's a tough life at the top,' said the photographer, who had heard about the band's arrival at number one from Jade, after a phone call from David the previous day.

'Too tough to meet me obviously,' she said bitterly.

'It doesn't matter,' said Gerry. 'My car's at the airport. I'll give you a lift home.'

Jade, who had been secretly wishing that he would say exactly that since they'd taken off, smiled her beautiful smile at him. 'Thanks, Gerry,' she said. 'I couldn't face a cab in this heat.'

As she spoke, the seat belt and 'No Smoking' signs flashed on and, after a few words from the pilot, the plane banked into its final turn towards London airport, and Jade turned to face the seat in front and thought about Gerry.

They hadn't consummated an affair, although things had got pretty steamy a couple of times during their stay in Paris. She desperately wanted to get the photographer into bed but, on the other hand, she knew his reputation with women, especially models, who he was reputed to treat like cattle once he'd fucked them. And of course her current boyfriend was a very big star right now. But still, she thought, what the eyes doesn't see . . .

Also, she knew that David himself was far from a faithful lover and she wondered what he had been up to himself over the last ten hot London days and nights, especially now he'd finally got what he and the rest of the band had been working towards for months, if not years.

It was a dilemma, but a delicious one, and as she stole a glance at Gerry's beautiful profile, topped with his thick mop of dark brown hair, against the opposite window of the plane, she knew that if she could get him, she would.

The plane touched down with a shriek from the rubber of its tyres and Gerry turned to her and said, '*Vogue* want me to go to Berlin this weekend. Take some of the winter collection and get a few shots against the wall. It's a bit old hat, I know, but the money's good. I'm looking for a model. Fancy it? It'll just be the two of us. Well, apart from the hairdresser and make-up and the fashion editor from the mag and anyone else who can get in on the jaunt. But you know what I mean.' And he smiled warmly at Jade.

'Do I want to go to Berlin for *Vogue*?' said Jade. 'Just try and stop me.'

'It's only that you've just been away and David might want you to himself for a while.'

'Business before pleasure,' she said, using Dominic's words exactly.

'You don't want to think about it?' asked Gerry.

Jade shook her head emphatically.

'Right. There'll be a ticket waiting for you at the *Vogue* office tomorrow afternoon,' said Gerry. 'And we're booked into the best hotel in town for three nights. Friday, Saturday and Sunday, all expenses paid naturally. Sorry if it's a bit short notice. But that's the fashion business.'

'Not at all,' said Jade. 'It sounds dreamy,'

'All the dreamier for you being there,' replied the photographer and he smiled at her again.

Back at Dominic's office the rest of the band had arrived and were lounging in the armchairs drinking Dominic's brandy, smoking cigarettes, teasing Dominic and Marsha when she was in the room, and generally having a good time. Except for David who was still a little miffed at not being able to see Jade as soon as she arrived but, as the brandies went down his throat, he was becoming less concerned by the minute.

Dominic clapped his hands and the band looked up. 'Right lads,' he said. 'Let's get down to business. Firstly, *Top of the Pops* this week. You're there and you're on. And I can't tell you how important this slot is. But I'm sure you know. Nuff said?' He looked round the room but no one spoke. 'Right. You're booked on the morning plane to Manchester tomorrow. You'll do your spot after lunch and you'll be back in time for supper. All right?'

'Beautifully organised as always,' said Tony, and the rest of the band applauded. 'But it sounds like you're not coming.'

'I'm not.' He saw the band's faces fall as one.

172

Dominic had always gone everywhere of importance with them up until then. 'Now, don't worry. I'm glad you mentioned organisation, Tony. There's someone I'd like you to meet.' He pressed down the switch on his intercom and said, 'Marsha, darling, has Malcolm arrived yet?'

The box squawked something unintelligible back and Dominic said, 'Show him in then, would you?'

The members of the band looked perplexed as well as worried now, but Dominic smiled reassuringly and a moment later the door opened and Marsha ushered in a truly massive individual dressed in a navy blue suit.

'Boys, meet Big Malcolm,' said Dominic. 'Malcolm, these are The Getaways.'

Big Malcolm stood in the doorway and grinned broadly at the people inside the room. 'Good afternoon,' he said, 'pleased to meet you all.'

'Come in and sit down, Malcolm, while I explain,' said Dominic.

Malcolm did as he was told and walked his massive frame over to the window, where he perched on the windowsill, and his shadow darkened the room almost as much as if the curtains had been drawn tightly against the afternoon light.

'I've decided that from now on, I can't travel with you everywhere,' said Dominic. 'This whole thing is getting too big. And, besides, after the other night I'm in fear for my Bentley. So, I've decided that you lot need a professional driver and bodyguard. And after making extensive enquiries I've decided that Big Malcolm here is just the man for the job. Ex-SAS. Ex-Metropolitan Police. Black belt in judo. Firearms expert. And before you start moaning, he's also a

Rolls-Royce trained chauffeur and I've just done a very good deal on your behalf for a second-hand Silver Cloud. So you won't be suffering, comfort-wise, and it leaves me time to make enough money to pay for the thing.'

The band looked at each other and finally Sly asked, 'Can he roll decent joints?'

Big Mal smiled. 'Rolls-Royce trained,' he said, which seemed to break the ice and everyone in the room laughed.

'Malcolm's first assignment is to get you to Manchester and back tomorrow,' said Dominic. 'And I trust you'll all be co-operative, or I'll want to know the reason why.'

'Seems fair,' said Tony. 'We'll break him in, Dom. Don't fret.'

After they'd collected their luggage, Gerry and Jade went to the long-term car park at the airport, where his Aston Martin was parked.

'What a lovely car,' said Jade, admiring its dark blue paintwork and white leather interior.

'It's a car,' said Gerry. 'Hop in.'

He took the main road into London and once they were on their way, he said, 'You live in Parson's Green, don't you?'

Jade agreed that she did.

'What time is David getting home from his meeting?'

'Christ knows.'

'Do you fancy a drink at my place first?'

'Where do you live?'

'Hammersmith.'

'It's on the way.'

'Isn't it just? So, is that a yes?'

She nodded. 'Sure it is,' she said.

At three o'clock, Gerry steered the car into the garage of a block of flats overlooking the bridge, got his stuff, left Jade's in the boot of the car, and took her upstairs to his penthouse apartment.

As he made a jug of Bloody Marys, she opened the french door that led out onto the balcony and went outside.

'What a beautiful view,' she called back over her shoulder.

'Isn't it?' He said as he joined her, a glass in each hand, and gave one to her.

'You are lucky to live in a place like this,' said Jade.

'The way you're going, you'll be in a mansion in the country soon. Isn't that what all pop stars want?'

'I don't know, Gerry,' she replied. 'It's not what I expected it to be.'

'What?'

'Going out with a pop star. If you really want to know, it's drag number one. Being chased down the street by stupid little girls. Never being able to go anywhere and be alone.'

'You sound like someone about to make a big decision about her life.'

'I think I am. It's all so serious. I want some fun.'

'I'm available,' he said. 'Fun is my speciality.'

'But I heard you're a bastard.'

'Who isn't? Jade, listen. I'll tell you once and I won't tell you again. What you see is what you get. Like it or not, that's the truth.'

'I wouldn't mind getting you, I must admit. I think I like what I see.'

'I do too,' he said. 'Just say the word.'

'The word,' she said.

He took her glass from her hand and led her by the arm through the flat to the bedroom, which was deliciously cool after the heat outside. 'You can change your mind,' he said when they were inside the room.

She shook her head.

'Come here then,' he said and gathered her up in his arms and kissed her on the lips.

She held him tightly as they explored each other's mouths with their lips and tongues.

God, she thought, he's so handsome, and she felt her insides melt as his hand caressed her back and sides and she pressed her breasts into the hardness of his chest.

Gerry pulled her over to the double bed in the centre of the room. 'There's still time,' he said. 'We can stop now and I'll take you home.'

'No,' cried Jade. 'No. I want you. I want you so badly.'

'And I want you.'

'So take me.'

Gerry laid her on the bed and undressed down to his underpants. She watched as he exposed his hard muscled body and with every fresh inch of naked flesh she saw she wanted him more.

He knelt beside the bed and she leaned over and kissed him, and as their mouths were glued together he undressed her expertly.

She hardly felt the clothes leave her body under his touch and it was only when she looked down at herself that she realised she was completely naked.

She luxuriated in the feeling and knowing that his eyes were hungrily devouring the sight of her.

'Do you like me?' She asked.

'I never realised you were so beautiful,' he whispered.

'You must have seen me changing at the shoot.'

'It's different there. It's just flesh. Here, it's not the same. It's you. Just you and me.'

'You say the most beautiful things,' she said.

'And I mean them.'

'You'll forget all about me within a week.'

'I doubt that, Jade. I really do. That boyfriend of yours doesn't know what he's got. Or had.'

She smiled and put her finger on his lips. 'Not so fast,' she said. 'This is all so sudden.'

'Not to me, it's not. I've been dreaming of this moment ever since I first saw your photo months ago.'

'A secret admirer.'

'Not so secret now,' he said, looking down at the bulge in his briefs.

'Take them off,' she whispered. 'I want to see you naked too.'

He stood up and did as she had asked and revealed his long, hard, fleshy cock.

'That's lovely,' breathed Jade. 'So lovely. I can't wait to have it inside me.'

'Not so fast yourself,' he teased. 'I want this to last. To be the best memory of your life.'

'Oh Gerry,' she said. 'What am I going to do with a romantic boy like you?'

'Fall in love with me, I hope.'

'Maybe,' she said. 'But first I'm going to fuck you.' She clapped her hand to her mouth. 'What *am* I saying? Gerry. What you must think of me.'

'I love it. Say it again.'

'I can't.'

'Say it.'

She hid her burning face in her hands.

'Come on, darling,' he said. 'Say it for me.'

'But first I'm going to fuck you,' she said obediently and grinned like a naughty schoolgirl.

'That's the best offer I've had for months,' he replied.

'It had better be.'

Gerry rejoined Jade on the bed. Gently they kissed, teasing each other's mouths open and touching the tips of their tongues together. Then their kisses became more passionate and they began to stroke and fondle each other's naked bodies. Jade made Gerry lie on his back whilst she worshipped his manhood. His cock reared up into her face and she kissed, sucked, stroked and licked it to a hardness he was sure he'd never known before. She tongued down between his legs and made him lift his buttocks slightly so that she could find his hairy arsehole. As she kissed and licked him he made her move so that he could stroke her long legs and push his hand up to the tuft of sooty pubic hair between her legs. She wriggled happily as his fingers found the opening of her cunt and pushed into the wetness there.

'You're dripping,' he said.

'I'm not surprised. You're turning me on.'

'Suck me while I wank you,' he said.

She was more than happy to oblige and slurped away enthusiastically at his hot knob as he moved first one, then two, then three fingers around the hot inside of her.

'I want to come in your mouth,' he said.

In reply, she sucked him harder, massaging his cock with one hand and playing with his balls with the other, until he could hardly bear the ecstasy he was feeling.

'I'm going to come, Jade,' he cried.

She sucked even harder, if that was possible, until she felt his whole body jerk and come surged up through his penis and splashed her lips and tongue and the back of her throat in an explosion of hot, salty, thick, creamy semen.

She swallowed thirstily, sucking the last drop out of him and into her mouth.

Gerry lay back moaning softly and Jade collapsed on top of him in a sweaty heap. 'God, that tasted good,' she said.

'It was wonderful,' he gasped. 'I've never come like that. Ever.'

'Do the same to me,' she begged. 'Make me come with your mouth.'

He was more than eager. He made Jade lie flat on her back, lifted her legs over his shoulders and lay with his head between them. He started to kiss and caress her fanny with his lips and tongue. She *was* soaking. Her lubrication smeared her thighs and dripped down onto the bedspread. His saliva made her wetter still and he was frightened he was going to drown in the hot gloop between her legs.

She was moaning and crying as he worked on her, clutching the bedspread in her fingers and tossing her head from side to side. Gerry kept on sucking at her cunt, the hair wet and scratchy on his face, until with a scream of pent-up feeling she climaxed into his face.

He lay on his side, his head cushioned on her damp

thighs and looked up at her. Her face was beatific. Radiant after her release.

'Beautiful,' was all she could say, repeating the word time after time.

'So are you,' he said.

'Come and kiss me.'

He did as she said and she licked her own juices off his lips and chin.

As she did it, Gerry felt himself responding again and soon he was as hard as before.

'Someone likes me,' she whispered feeling his cock pushing at her thigh.

'Someone does,' he confirmed.

'Does someone want to go inside me.'

He nodded.

'And do what?'

'Plant my seed.'

'That's such a lovely thing to say,' she said. 'No one's ever said anything like that to me before. I think I'm falling in love with you.'

'I've loved you since the first day I saw you in Paris,' said Gerry.

'Why didn't you tell me?'

'I was scared to. I knew about David. Everyone does. I didn't realise you didn't like what was happening.'

'I like being with you.'

'I like being on you,' and so saying he climbed gently onto her body and she accepted his prick into her pussy for the first time. As it slid the length of her she closed her eyes in delight.

'That feels so beautiful,' she said. 'Your cock seems to go on forever.'

'I wish it did,' he said and began to move gently inside her. 'How does that feel?' he asked.

'For the first time ever I feel like a complete woman. You've filled the hole in me. You're part of me and I never want to let you go.'

'Now who's being romantic?'

'Me. And I like it. I can never talk like this to . . .' She stopped. 'Sorry. I shouldn't talk about another man when we're making love.'

'Talk about what you like. Tell me your fantasy.'

'Two men. One in my mouth, one in my cunt.' He looked down at her and she blushed again. 'Oh Gerry,' she said, 'that's rude. I've never told anyone about that before. I don't want to *really*. It is just a fantasy. I'm a one-man woman, although I'm not behaving like that much today. I'm confused. I don't know what to think. One moment I want to be loving and gentle, the next I want to be so rude. I keep thinking about so many things.'

'That's all right. I understand.'

'Do you?'

'Sure I do. As long as you keep thinking about me, I don't care what else you think about.'

'You're so good.'

He smiled down at her.

'Don't stop,' she said. 'I love that feeling when you move inside me.'

Gerry started to fuck her again. He tried to keep moving slowly but soon he felt a tickle in his balls and he began to move faster and faster. Jade kept up with him, undulating her hips in perfect time to the thrusting of his pelvis. Faster and faster they went until the sweat broke out on their bodies and they clenched their teeth in concentration of the ultimate goal. A mutual orgasm. Still faster they went until, with two cries that sounded like one, they came together and Gerry fell on top of Jade's body.

While Jade and Gerry were engaged in carnal delight at Gerry's flat in Hammersmith, back at the office Dominic had a second announcement to make.

'I promised you a party if the record got to number one?' he said. 'And a party you shall have. The party of the year, in fact. I've hired Lambert House in Sussex for the do. Malcolm, Marsha and I have organised the catering and entertainment and the invitations went out by messenger yesterday. We've been phoning round to catch people and, believe me, this *does* look like being the bash of the year, if not the decade. People are cancelling their own weddings to come. It's all been rather a rush, but the party happens on Friday night. Marsha has instructions on how to get there on her desk. Please take one each when you leave.'

'Great,' said Sly. 'A real thrash.'

'Sounds excellent,' said Tony.

'Well done, Dom,' said David.

'Yes,' agreed Jud. 'Well done.'

'And with that, gentlemen, I declare this meeting over,' declared Dominic. 'Itineraries for tomorrow are waiting with the details of the party. Apart from those two dates, the rest of the week is your own. Enjoy.'

Big Malcolm got up from his seat by the window. 'There's a drinking club just round the corner, off Shaftesbury Avenue,' He said. 'Denman Street. The Tudor, it's called. They serve booze all afternoon. I'm a member. I'll be buying in ten minutes. Just say Big

Mal sent you. Anybody interested?'

The band looked at each other and nodded as one, and left the room to collect their itineraries and then head for the bar.

When David dragged himself away from the impromptu party and got back to Parson's Green it was almost eight, and Jade was not at home.

He was more than half drunk and rampaged through the flat calling her name.

She arrived half an hour later.

'Where the hell have you been?' he demanded.

She bit her lip. She'd made love to Gerry twice more and then they'd fallen asleep together. She'd woken up in a blind panic twenty minutes earlier, dressed, and had Gerry drop her off on the corner of the street.

'I was with Gerry Preston,' she replied truthfully.

'That poofy photographer. What the hell were you doing with him?'

Poofy, she thought. If that's poofy, show me some more. 'Talking,' she lied.

'Talking. You should have been here five hours ago. What the fuck were you talking about?'

'A job he wants me to go on with him.'

'What job?'

'A shoot in Berlin. For *Vogue* magazine.'

'Who cares about that? We're number one. And I want you here. I haven't seen you for nearly a fortnight, and I've got to go to Manchester tomorrow to do *Top of the Pops*.'

'I care about it,' she said defiantly.

'You don't *need* to do this modelling shit,' said

David. 'You're wasting time. *I* want you here. I want you with me.'

'I need to do it, David,' Jade said calmly. 'I'm not your wife. I have my own career to think about.'

'Well, anyway,' said David, sensing he was heading into dangerous waters, 'forget Berlin for now. We'll talk about it later. We're having a big party at the weekend to celebrate getting to the top of the charts. It's at a big country house. It's going to be amazing.'

Jade's face fell. 'This Friday?' she asked.

'Yes. Have you got a problem with that?'

'I've agreed to go to Berlin this Friday. The shoot's this weekend.'

'With Gerry Preston?'

'That's right.'

'Are you sure you were only talking this afternoon?'

Jade knew she must look guilty, and the gusset of her knickers was wet with her and Gerry's secretions. And she only hoped that David didn't want to get inside them. Mind you, she thought, the mood he's in at the moment, and the way he's talking, he'd be very lucky to get anywhere near me.

'Yes,' she said.

'Are you quite sure?'

'Course I am. You're the one who said he's a poof, don't forget. If he is, you've got nothing to worry about, have you?'

'You're not going,' declared David. 'And that's that. I don't like any of this.'

'I *am*.'

'If you do, we're through.'

'Don't be silly.'

'And don't call me silly.' he retorted angrily.

'Sorry, David. But Friday morning I go to Berlin. I pick up the ticket tomorrow. Now I'm going to unpack.' And with that she turned on her heel and lugged her bags into the bedroom and shut the door behind her.

David shrugged. Bollocks to her. She'd be sorry. Plenty more fish in the sea, he thought, as he fetched his address book and dialled a number.

The phone at the other end was answered almost immediately.

'Jane,' he said. 'It's David. Get your best dress ironed. You're going to a party with me on Friday.'

PART TWO

24

The E-Type swished up the drive of Lambert House on the following Friday afternoon. As Tony turned and winked at Mandy, the dashboard clock read four o'clock. 'Just in time for the fun and games,' he said.

The space outside the house was jammed with cars. Rolls-Royces, Bentleys, including Dominic's, Ferraris, Alfa Romeos, more E-Types, Aston Martins, every kind of flash motor that the successful player in the pop game could wish for. And in the middle of the parking lot, dusty and incongruous, a rented Avis three-ton Ford truck.

Tony parked behind a pink Cadillac convertible with the top down and jumped out. Mandy got out of the passenger's side.

'Who's here?' she asked. 'Anyone we know?'

Tony looked at the cars. 'Looks like the rest of the boys are here and the roadies. Dominic, of course.' Then he reeled off the names of several DJs from the pirate ships, a few more pop-group members and several other high-flyers in the music business. 'Looks like it's going to be quite a party.'

He went to the back of the car and lifted out their cases. Then they walked together up to the imposing front door. He pulled the old-fashioned bell and heard it clang inside. Within twenty seconds the door was opened by Big Malcolm, dressed in butler's livery.

'Hello Mal,' said Tony with a big grin. 'What's with the monkey suit?'

'Hello, Tony,' replied Big Malcolm. 'The boss reckoned I should look the part.'

'Mandy,' said Tony, 'this is Malcolm, our new driver and bodyguard. He looked after us great in Manchester this week. Mal, this is my friend Mandy.'

'Pleased to meet you, Mandy,' said Malcolm.

'Aren't you going to join in?' asked Tony.

Mal's face broke into a grin. 'Later. Now, where are you?' he picked up a clipboard on the table next to the door and referred to it. 'Oh yeah. The West Wing. I'll have your maid show you the way.' He turned and shouted. 'Gloria. Get your arse out here. Now.'

One of the doors off the hall opened immediately and a portly, grey-haired man of about fifty appeared. He was dressed only in a leather apron, a leather dog-collar with a long silver chain attached and a leather domino mask that covered his eyes.

'This is Gloria,' said Mal. 'He's your personal maid for the weekend. He'll do whatever you ask without question. Won't you, Gloria?' The way he put it, it wasn't a question, but an order.

'It will be my pleasure,' said the man. 'If I do not satisfy, I expect to be punished. Severely.'

Mal looked to the sky. 'Tony and Mandy are in the West Wing. The Blue Room. Show them the way.'

Tony bent to pick up his and Mandy's cases. 'Gloria will carry them,' said Mal.

Gloria immediately obeyed and picked up the two cases and turned towards the staircase. 'This way, sir, madam,' he said. As he did so the pair saw that he was naked under the apron, the big pink cheeks of his buttocks completely visible.

'If he's bad, kick him up the jacksie,' said Mal. 'He'll like that.'

Gloria took them up the stairs, along what seemed like a mile of corridor to their room. Both Tony and Mandy got the uncontrollable giggles as they watched his cheeks swaying as he walked but Gloria ignored them. Eventually he stopped outside a door painted Wedgwood blue. Gloria put down the cases and took a key-ring from the pocket of his apron and opened the door, then stood back to allow Tony and Mandy to enter. They walked inside. It was a beautiful room with a double four-poster bed, a three-piece suite, TV set and record player. The afternoon sun poured through the open french windows that led out onto a balcony that overlooked the grounds at the side of the house. There was a door in the wall directly to their right. Gloria opened it.

'En suite bathroom,' he said, then pointed to a bell push by the bed. 'If you need anything night or day, please ring.' He handed the door key to Tony. 'Can I be of further assistance?'

'No,' said Tony. 'If we need you we'll let you know.'

'Very good, sir, madam. Mr Edwards is downstairs. Cocktails will be served at six in the drawing room. Dinner is at seven thirty.'

'Thanks,' said Tony.

'May I go now?' asked Gloria.

'Yes,' said Tony.

Gloria backed out of the room, closing the door behind him.

'He's incredible,' said Mandy.

'So are you,' said Tony and pushed her over to the bed. 'We've got nearly an hour.'

'And what can we do in a hour?' she asked.

Tony pushed her onto the bed cover. 'I'll show you,' he said.

'There's a mirror,' exclaimed Mandy. 'Up there.'

Tony looked up at the ceiling. 'All the better to see yourself,' he said, and pushed up her skirt.

Her tiny pink knickers were wet at the crotch and almost transparent.

'What's this?' said Tony.

She blushed to almost the same colour as her underwear.

'Seeing that old bastard's bare bum got you at it, didn't it?' he said.

She blushed an even deeper pink.

'It did, you dirty little cow.'

'I can't help it if older men turn me on,' she said.

'We'll have to see if we can find you one later.'

'That *would* be nice.'

'But for now we'll have to see if this young man can satisfy you,' he said and roughly pulled her knickers down and buried his face into her wet, hairy pussy.

She moaned as his tongue found the lips of her box and opened the folds of skin and entered the hot, fragrant flesh.

She grabbed two handfuls of his long hair and pushed him deeper until he could hardly breathe.

He found her clitoris with his teeth and nibbled at it until it was hard. She was breathing heavily and crying out his name as he tongued and bit at it.

'Harder,' she panted. 'Hurt me, hurt me.'

He bit at her roughly until her body stiffened and she came, pushing her pubis into his face, then sagged back onto the counterpane.

Tony stood up and ripped at his clothes, then pushed her legs wide and, cock erect, shoved himself into her. Their mouths met and she sucked her own juices off his lips and chin. He pounded at her in his excitement. She found his rhythm and they fucked until he could hold back no longer and he came into her hard, then dropped down onto her body.

They were both soaked with sweat and laughing at their own exertions. Tony pushed his damp fringe out of his eyes and looked at her. 'That was fucking good,' he said.

'Great,' she agreed. 'What were you thinking about?'

'You.'

'Me? Doing what?'

He didn't answer.

'Tell me.'

He smiled secretly to himself.

'Tony!'

He shook his head.

'Tell me,' she demanded again.

'Nothing.'

'Liar.'

He laughed out loud at that.

'Go on, Tony, tell me,' she wheedled.

At that he gave in. 'You being fucked by Gloria,' he admitted.

'Do you want me to be?'

'Yes.'

'Then ring the bell.'

'Are you serious?'

'Course I am.'

He leant over and did as she said, then got up and pulled on his clothes.

She tossed her knickers into the corner and tugged her skirt down over her thighs.

Within two minutes there was a gentle knock at the door. 'Come in,' said Tony.

The door opened and Gloria appeared, dressed exactly as before. 'Is there something you want?' he asked.

'I need a bath before dinner,' said Mandy. 'I want you to run it.'

'As madam wishes,' said Gloria, and went into the bathroom, and they heard water running. Then he reappeared. 'Does madam wish the oil in the bath or bubbles?'

'Bubbles,' replied Mandy.

Gloria bowed his head and disappeared back into the bathroom.

Mandy got up off the bed and stood in the middle of the room facing Tony. 'Gloria,' she called.

Once again Gloria appeared in the doorway.

'Unzip me,' ordered Mandy and turned her back to him.

Gloria walked over and pulled down the long zip at the back of Mandy's dress. She shrugged it over her shoulders, let it fall to the carpet and stepped out of it. She stood naked, with Tony's come running down her thighs and winked at him, then turned to face Gloria. She looked beautiful standing there in a band of sunshine from the window that reflected from the wetness between her legs.

'I'm all messy,' she said. 'I want you to lick me clean.'

Tony could see that Gloria had an erection under his apron. His hard prick pushed at the leather. He knelt down on the carpet and began to lick the semen off Mandy's thighs. She opened her legs wide to allow him access to her cunt and threw her head back in ecstasy as the second tongue of the day found the sensitive skin around the entrance.

Tony watched entranced as his girlfriend rode Gloria's face while his mouth sucked at her cunt lips. 'That's good, Gloria,' she gasped. 'Go deeper. Get it all out. Drink my lover's come.'

Gloria did as she ordered and the sound of his tongue lapping at her honeypot was the only sound in the room.

After a few minutes Mandy said, 'Stop.' Gloria did so straight away. 'Stand up.' Gloria did as he was told again. Mandy pulled the leather apron to one side. Gloria's penis stood at attention from his thatch of grey pubic hair. It was long, thick and red, with a circumcised knob at the end that was blue with blood.

'You're so big,' said Mandy, 'and hard.'

There was a drop of come hanging from his cock hole by a thread. Mandy touched it with her fingertip, then transferred it to her mouth. 'Delicious,' she said. 'Now fuck me, like a dog.'

She knelt down on the carpet facing Tony with her legs apart. Gloria knelt behind her, then entered her cunt from behind. Tony watched as she closed her eyes in pleasure as Gloria's huge prick entered her body.

She pushed herself backwards until the cock was in as deep as it could go, then she started to work herself off on it. Gloria stayed perfectly still. 'Screw me,' she shouted. 'Come on you fucker, do it to me.' Gloria obeyed as he had obeyed every previous order, without question. He moved back and forward into Mandy, pleasuring her as she desired.

They moved faster together and Tony heard Gloria's belly slapping against Mandy's buttocks. She opened her eyes, looked straight at Tony and smiled a euphoric smile. Then she came with a scream, not once but twice.

'Come,' she shouted. 'Come, you bastard. Give me your sperm. I want it all.' And Gloria obeyed again with a grunt, then laid his head on her back.

Mandy wriggled off his cock which hung limply down between his legs now he had shot his load.

'Get out now, Gloria,' she said. 'I want my bath. I'll ring if I need you again.'

Gloria got to his feet without a word, straightened his apron, nodded to Mandy and Tony and left the room. Mandy smiled. 'Was that what you wanted?' she asked.

'Just what I wanted,' he said.

'Well, I'm going to have my bath, I'll see you in a minute.' And she ran into the bathroom and slammed the door behind her.

25

Mandy came out of the bathroom ten minutes later with a towel wrapped around her. 'Your turn,' she said.

'Is there any hot water left?' asked Tony.

'Tons. Wait a minute.' She opened her case, pulled out a red minidress decorated with ruby-coloured beads and shook it out. 'Take this in with you,' she said. 'Hang it up. The steam will get the creases out.'

'Wow!' said Tony. 'That's some dress. Where did you get it?'

'Mary Quant, yesterday. It cost me a week's wages.'

'It was worth it,' said Tony and took it with him into the bathroom.

When he came back, also with a towel wrapped around his waist, carrying the dress, Mandy was sitting at the dressing table sticking on a set of false eyelashes. 'Looking good, babe,' he said.

'Feeling good, babe,' she replied. 'All over. Is my dress wrinkle-free?'

'Just like your face,' he said, picking up her comb and running it through his wet hair, and began to unpack his own bag. He put on a flowered shirt, tight blue jeans with a slight flare, Anello & Davide Beatle boots and a black dinner-jacket from Mr Fish.

'You look lovely,' said Mandy. 'I could almost fancy you myself.'

'I could almost fancy myself, myself,' he replied.

She stood up, dropped the towel and pulled on a minuscule pair of red knickers and stepped into the red dress. 'Zip me up,' she said.

He did as she asked. 'I wonder who'll be unzipping this later?' he said.

'Who knows?' she grinned at him shamelessly. 'Are we going down for a drink?'

'Why not?' He looked at his watch. 'Let's see who's about.'

Mandy took Tony's arm and they left the room and walked along the corridor and down the main staircase to the drawing room. Quite a crowd had gathered already. The Getaways' album was on the record player. Dominic was at the centre of the action, standing next to Anya, who was wearing a tight black satin dress which showed off her ample figure to perfection. Tony looked at her nipples, clearly visible through the thin material, and wondered if before the night was over he might have a replay of their afternoon in the conservatory.

Mandy saw him looking. 'Down boy,' she said.

'I can look, can't I?'

'So can I,' said Mandy. 'From what I hear, she goes both ways.'

'Well, you should know if anyone does.' Tony grabbed two glasses of champagne off a tray carried by a passing waiter.

'That's so true,' said Mandy, taking one from him.

At that point Dominic noticed their entrance. 'Tony,' he cried at the top of his voice, making for them

and scattering other guests behind him in his wake.
'One of our stars. Welcome.'

'Hello, Dom,' said Tony. 'How's tricks?'

'Wonderful. And congratulations again on writing
the number-one tune in the nation.' Dominic grabbed
Tony's hand and pumped it hard. Over his shoulder
Tony saw Anya giving him a hooded-eyed look.

He nodded to her and she smiled.

'Who is this now?' Dominic asked, referring to
Mandy.

'A friend,' said Tony. 'Mandy Prentiss.'

'Mandy,' said Dominic and grabbed her hand and
kissed it.

'Welcome to our little circle. Let me introduce you to
a few people. Excuse us, Tony.' Dominic took her arm
and propelled her away from Tony, who sipped at his
champagne and looked round the room.

Derek was sitting on a sofa by the window. He
looked uncharacteristically spruce. His long hair was
clean and hung loose around his shoulders. He was
wearing a white shirt, black leather trousers and black
low-heeled boots. He was holding a champagne glass
and gazing through the window at the grounds outside.

Tony went over to the roadie. 'Derek,' he said,
'how's it going?'

'Not bad,' he replied.

'You're looking very smart today.'

Derek looked down at his clothes, then back at
Tony. 'Day off,' he said, 'party time. I hope you don't
begrudge your loyal and dedicated crew a rest. Or are
you getting too bigtime to mix with the likes of us?'

'Bollocks,' replied Tony.

Derek grinned. 'How does it feel to be number one

in the nation?' he asked, cruelly mimicking Dominic's voice as he did so.

Then it was Tony's turn to smile. 'It ain't quite what I thought it was going to be,' he replied, 'but it's better than being number none. You reckon any of us'll ever be able to afford a gaff like this?'

'I doubt it,' said Derek. 'There's too many fuckers out there trying to rip you off.'

'Always the optimist, eh mate?' said Tony. 'Who are you with?'

'Some fucking scrubber. I pulled her at the Speak last night.'

'What's she like?'

'Willing.'

'What more can you ask?'

'Someone who can remember her own name. But still, can't complain. She sucked my dick all the way from Wimbledon to here. I nearly crashed the car three times.'

'Car?' said Tony. 'Didn't you come down in the truck?'

'No. Donkey drove it down. I came in Big Mal's motor.'

'Can't be too bad. Seen the rest?'

'They're about somewhere. What do you reckon's gonna happen later?'

'A lot of booze, dope and fucking.'

'Sounds reasonable. Not a bad job, being in the industry of human happiness, is it?'

'I've had worse.'

'Who's that you're with?' asked Derek.

'Mandy.'

'Where'd you find her?'

'Picked her up at a club, a couple of weeks ago.'

'Nice work. But watch it, old Dom's trying to get his fingers up her arse if I'm not much mistaken.'

'Good luck to him,' said Tony. 'I might be with her now, but later, who knows?'

'That fucking Anya's got some form,' said Derek, changing the subject.

Tony turned and looked at their manager's wife and smiled. 'You can say that again,' he said.

'What do you reckon?' asked Derek. 'You think she'd do a turn for the boys?'

'I wouldn't be at all surprised,' said Tony. 'But you shouldn't talk about your employer's wife like that.'

'I know,' replied Derek, 'but it's a lovely thought, ain't it?'

'You're a filthy swine,' said Tony. 'I'm going to look for the others. Coming?'

'Nah,' said Derek. 'I'm just going to sit here drinking this stuff, looking out at an English country garden.'

'What's the dope situation?' asked Tony.

'Impeccable. Dominic gave me a bunch of cash to score. When I can move this lazy body of mine I'll go and get it and start rolling.'

'The quicker the better.'

'Come back soon and I'll see what I can do.'

'I'll do that little thing. See you then,' said Tony.

'See ya,' said Derek. 'Don't do nothing I wouldn't.'

'Christ, Derek, that's impossible,' said Tony and went through the french windows into the garden.

He ambled across the lawn in the direction of a summerhouse that stood about two hundred and fifty yards away by a copse of trees.

As he got closer he heard voices he recognised. He

stepped up onto the wooden veranda that surrounded the place and poked his head through one of the open windows. David, Sly, Jane and another girl were sitting on deckchairs inside passing round a joint.

'Save some for me,' he said.

'Tony, how are ya?' said David. 'Come on in. Join the party.'

Tony did as he was bidden. He sat cross-legged on a pile of canvas and accepted the joint from David.

'You remember Jane?' said David.

'Course I do,' said Tony. 'All right?'

Jane nodded.

'And this is my latest flame,' said Sly. 'Sylvia. All the way from Romford without a stain on her character.'

Sylvia was a rather plump girl in a miniskirt, a plunge-neckline white jumper which showed off the tops of her ample breasts, knee-length white socks and black shoes. 'Hello, Tony,' she said. 'I love the record. Congratulations.'

'Thanks,' said Tony.

'She thinks you're fabulous,' said Sly. 'She only came here with me to meet you.'

'Don't, Sly,' protested Sylvia with a blush. 'You know that's not true.'

'Only time will tell,' said Sly, then changed the subject. 'Old Dom's on good form. He's really pushed the boat out for us.'

'At our expense, man,' said David. 'But there's plenty more where that came from. I hear the album's got two hundred thousand advance orders already.'

'And America beckons,' said Tony.

'Too bloody right it does,' agreed David.

'We're going to be rich, boys,' said Sly, retrieving the

joint, 'beyond the dreams of avarice.'

'Who's he?' said Sylvia.

'Don't you just love her?' asked Sly. 'I could eat her up.' And he grabbed Sylvia and pushed his face into her ample chest.

'Sly, stop,' she protested. 'You'll get me all hot.'

'That's the idea, baby,' said Sly in a muffled voice.

Sylvia pushed him away and adjusted the neckline of her jumper with a long look at Tony.

'See what I mean?' said Sly. 'She wants to get hold of you, son.'

Sylvia blushed an even brighter red. 'Stop it, I said.'

Sly just giggled a stoned giggle and sat back in his deckchair. 'Have you seen the swimming pool?' he asked Tony.

'No.'

'In the basement. You could sail the *Queen Mary* in it. We're all going to have a dip later, ain't we, girls?'

Jane and Sylvia said nothing.

'Skinny dippin',' said Sly triumphantly. 'I want a look at old Sylvia's tits.'

'Sly,' said Sylvia, 'I've told you before. Don't be so rude.'

'You love it, girl,' said Sly. 'Doncha?'

She didn't deny it.

'You coming swimming, Tone?' asked Sly.

'Maybe,' said Tony. 'Depends what else is on offer.'

'Plenty, I reckon,' said Sly. ''Ere. Did you have some daft old cunt dressed in a leather apron take your bags?'

Tony nodded.

'So did we. Fucking mental, if you ask me.'

Tony smiled at the memory.

'Anyway,' Sly went on, 'he said something about cocktails. I fancy some of that. How about you lot?'

They all agreed that they did and left the summer-house and headed back to the main building.

26

The five of them trooped through the french doors back into the drawing room and saw Jud talking to Dominic, who exclaimed at their entrance, 'Here's the rest now. The boys are all here.' There was a smattering of applause from the rest of the guests and Dominic beckoned Tony, Dave and Sly over to where he was standing with Jud.

Anya put the single of 'Here We Go' onto the record player. 'Now boys,' said Dom, 'it's my proud duty to announce that today your latest single – still number one by the way–' It seemed he couldn't stop talking about the fact '– has attained sales of more than a quarter of a million in this country. And our old friend – and may I say one of the original people of good taste to pick up on the band – Judy Carter from *Disc*, is here to present a silver disc to celebrate the fact.'

There was more applause. Louder this time.

'Judy, the floor is yours,' said Dominic.

Judy Carter, who had been standing in the doorway, stepped forward and smiled at Jud, who smiled back partly in surprise at her being there, partly in embarrassment because he hadn't called her and partly in pleasure as he remembered their night together in Norwich.

'Boys,' she said, 'Tony, David, Jud and Sly. The Getaways. My favourite band. I can't tell you how proud I am to present you with this silver disc on behalf of everyone in your management, record company and the paper. I hope it's only the first of many.'

She bent and retrieved a glass-fronted, framed silver record from where it had been hidden behind an overstuffed armchair and presented it to Jud, who blushed furiously.

'Don't worry,' she said. 'There's one for each of you.'

The band each kissed her on the cheek to more applause, Anya spun 'Here We Go' one more time and waiters appeared with more champagne and cocktails.

Judy grabbed Jud by the arm. 'You never called,' she said.

'I've been busy,' he replied sheepishly.

'Come outside. I want to talk.'

They slipped away from the throng and went outside.

'Let's sit in my car,' said Judy.

She led him to her Vauxhall Victor parked at the side of the house. It was unlocked. She got in the driver's side and he the passenger's. She surveyed him along the length of the big bench front seat.

'I didn't know you were going to be here tonight,' he said.

I know you didn't. 'Why didn't you call?' she asked.

Jud couldn't tell her the truth, that he'd wanted to but hadn't had the nerve, thinking she hadn't meant it when she'd asked him to.

'I'm sorry,' he said.

'Didn't you have a good time with me?'

'Course I did.'

'Then you should have phoned. We could have done it again. Lots of times.'

'I was going to. But . . .' He paused.

'You weren't afraid, were you?' she said into the silence.

Jud blushed again and Judy laughed. 'Jud and Judy,' she said. 'You should have remembered.'

'I'm sorry,' he said again.

'Don't be. I understand.'

He smiled and reached for her and she slid along the seat into his arms. They kissed long and lingeringly and her perfume was strong in his nostrils. The scent reminded him again of their night together in Norwich and he felt his penis thicken and rise. Judy put her hand onto the crotch of his trousers and laughted softly. 'You see,' she said, 'I knew you liked me really.'

'I do,' whispered Jud. 'You know I do.'

At his words, Judy felt a flood of heat in her belly and between her legs and her head spun in the warm atmosphere of the car. She couldn't ever remember being so horny and her cunt began to drip with desire inside her underpants. She knew she needed the release of a good fucking.

'Then show me,' she said throatily.

'Here?'

'Where else?'

'What happens if someone comes along?'

'Who cares? Let them. You're a star. You can do whatever you like, whenever you like. It's allowed. The gods are smiling on you at the moment. Don't waste it. You might regret it later.'

'Let's get in the back,' said Jud.

'No. I can't wait,' said Judy, and pulled her skirt up around her waist. 'Get my knickers off quick. I need a fuck real bad.'

Jud did as he was told. He pulled down the white panties she was wearing under her dress and exposed her hairy minge to his hungry eyes. 'Beautiful,' he said, as he threw her knickers into the the back of the car.

He tugged at the zip on his tight velvet trousers and pulled them and the brief underpants he was wearing down below his knees. Before he could get his trousers right off, Judy grabbed at the erect prick that jumped up under her eyes as he struggled to undress.

'Oh Jud,' she moaned, lay back, opened her legs wide, and put one foot across the steering wheel and the other over the back of the seat where she was lying. 'Give it to me. I need something hard inside me.'

Jud climbed onto her prone body and was managing with some success to grant her wish, when the foot she'd put on the steering wheel got caught up in the horn ring. With a noise that made the lovers jump almost out of their skins the klaxon on the Vauxhall screeched.

'Christ,' shouted Jud, looking round the inside of the car in panic. 'What's happening?'

'It's me,' Judy shouted back. 'I've got my foot caught. Help me.'

Jud tried to get off her but found that *his* feet had got inextricably caught in his trousers and pants and the combined weight of them had trapped his arms behind her back and, try as he might, he couldn't move.

'I'm stuck,' he replied, amazingly calmly under the

circumstances. He struggled to extricate them from their predicament but only managed to get Judy's foot jammed even harder against the steering wheel, his own legs even more twisted up in his clothes and his arms pushed even deeper into the upholstery of the seat. As far as Judy was concerned, the more he moved around the deeper his prick pushed into her pussy, which she found extremely enjoyable and began to giggle.

'Don't laugh,' said Jud. 'It's not funny.'

'It is,' said Judy, tears coming into her eyes. 'Keep going. I'm enjoying it.'

'I'm not,' said Jud.

'Shift off then,' she said.

'I can't. I told you, I'm stuck.'

The sound from the hooter went on as Jud tried to get his legs free from the material that had them bound together and Judy tried to free her foot from the horn ring but they only managed to get hotter and sweatier and more and more tangled up together. As he moved around, on and inside Judy, Jud suddenly saw a face at the window of the car. It was Donkey, with a huge, stoned grin on his face.

'Help us Donkey,' screamed Jud and the huge man tugged at the passenger door of the car. Suddenly it opened and Jud and Judy who were both leaning on it, were deposited outside onto the gravel of the drive, freeing Judy's foot from the mechanism that sounded the horn. Instantly, the noise ceased and an almost deafening silence fell upon the three of them.

As they hit the ground, Jud and Judy separated and his cock popped out of Judy's hole and sprung up red and wet between his legs.

Donkey looked down at it from where he was standing and said, 'What are you doing Jud? Showing her your paradiddle?' And he brayed a huge laugh which sounded not unlike the animal he had been named after.

Jud jumped up red-faced, collected his clothes from the car and hastily pulled them on, whilst Judy leant over the front seat and scrambled to find her knickers. Donkey craned his neck through the side window of the car to see her bare bottom bobbing up and down as she did so.

Eventually she located them and tugged them on and, properly dressed again, she joined the other two outside.

'What do you want anyway?' said Jud crossly when he zipped himself up.

'I just came to tell you that Dominic says that dinner is being served,' he said. 'He was wondering where you'd got to. Just as well, wasn't it? Otherwise everyone would have come out, the row you were making. That would have been interesting.' And he brayed with laughter again.

'Thanks, Donkey,' said Jud. 'You can scarper now. We're just coming.'

'Not from the state of you just now you weren't,' said Donkey and, with a fresh gust of laughter, he left them and made his way back to the house.

'Sorry about that,' said Jud.

'Don't be. I liked it,' replied Judy. 'Later we'll do it properly. Somewhere comfortable. All right?'

'You're on,' said Jud and leant over and kissed her. 'I really am sorry I didn't call you before.'

'Stop being sorry, Jud,' the girl said. 'You don't need

to be. Now let's go and have something to eat. I'm starving.'

She took his hand in hers and they, too, walked back to the house.

27

The dinner that was served that night was indeed a strange one.

The dining room was at the back of the house and was at least a hundred foot long; the dining table stretched for almost the full length of it. The table was covered with a snowy-white tablecloth and set with solid silver cutlery. Down the centre of the table, alternately, were vases of fresh flowers and ice sculptures depicting scenes from the *Kama Sutra*.

At each end there was clear space in the centre of the table, about six foot long.

There was a minstrel gallery at one end of the room, and set up there was a stool, a guitar on a stand, a small amplifier and a microphone. The stool was empty.

The only illumination, apart from the evening sunlight pouring through the open windows, came from three massive chandeliers that hung down from the ceiling on thick gold chains.

Dominic sat at the head of the table, Anya at the foot. David sat on Dominic's left. Sly on his right. Next to David was Jane. Next to Sly was Sylvia. Tony was seated to Anya's right, next to Mandy. The two seats on Anya's left were empty. As they entered, she beckoned to Jud and Judy, who walked the length of the room towards her. The rest of the guests were seated, alternately male and female on both sides of the table, between the members of the band. Donkey faced Derek almost exactly in the middle, sucking on a bottle of beer, and as Jud and Judy took their places he waved, then leant over to Derek and said something and they both laughed.

Dominic stood as Jud and Judy sat down.

'Ladies and gentlemen,' he said. 'Now that the guests of honour are all here, we'll begin. You've heard the album and, I'm sure, by now you know the single off by heart. All the speeches have been made. I'm not going to say anything more now . . .'

As if one, the band and roadies cheered at that and everyone else laughed.

'. . . Except to say . . .'

Boos from the band and roadies this time.

'. . . Except to say, that "Here We Go" was released in America yesterday to an advance order of almost half a million copies.'

Not a sound from anyone at that, except a few whistles and gasps of amazement. Not least from the band themselves.

'. . . No one here was aware of that. I was saving the good news for precisely this moment. In fact I've just heard from our promotion people in LA that it's expected to be the highest new entry in the *Billboard* Hot Hundred charts next week. Maybe even straight into the top five. Our new friends at Capitol Records are ecstatic. The Getaways are going places and I'm happy that you're all here today to share our good fortune with us. And with that . . .'

He clapped his hands.

'. . . On with the motley and let the fun *really* begin.'

And he sat down to a roar of applause from everyone at the table.

'Half a fucking million. Did you hear that?' said Sly to anyone who was listening. 'Dominic, whatever I've said about you being a prat in the past, I take back.'

'Thank you so much, Sly,' said Dominic. 'And anything I've said about you being a common little oik, I take that back too.'

'Fair enough,' said Sly. 'Let's drink to that.'

And they did.

As they put down their glasses, Big Mal, still dressed as a butler, led two naked girls into the room by chains attached to collars round their necks. The heads of all the diners craned at the sight. He took them to the table and picked the first one up easily and laid her in the clear space in front of Dominic at the head of the table and unbuckled her collar. Then took the second one down to the foot of the table and lifted her gently and placed her in the clear space in front of Anya.

The whole room fell silent as he did so.

Then he beckoned and Gloria, carrying a large black leather bullwhip, led in a procession of half a dozen waiters and waitresses all dressed exactly as he was, in a collar and chain and a leather apron that left their backs entirely naked. Each was masked. The first two were pushing wheeled trolleys which each supported a massive bowl of beluga caviar which they proceeded to pile upon the bodies of the naked girls.

The silence was broken as, at another signal from Mal, a strange collection of fire-eaters, jugglers, clowns, belly dancers, midgets, giants, musicians and as many other sorts of circus and fairground acts as could be imagined, burst into the room.

The guests looked on amazed as the brightly dressed performers circled the table whilst the half-naked staff served the first course off the totally naked girls who had been laid on the table before them.

'Jesus!' exclaimed Tony. 'Who's idea was this?'

'Mine,' replied Anya. 'Do you like it?'

'Like it? I love it,' replied Tony and leaned over and took a gob of caviar off the breast of the girl in front of him with his finger and put it in his mouth. 'Dig in,' he said. 'It tastes good.'

At the other end of the table, Dominic stood again and clapped his hands until the guests and entertainers fell silent.

'One final thing,' he said. 'It's my proud duty to announce that for our further entertainment tonight we have with us a new and very exciting signing to Zenith Records. His name is Craig Sinclair. And after he's eaten, he's going to sing and play his first release for us from the minstrel gallery, where some of the more observant of you among us might have noticed that a small PA system has been set up. Craig, please stand and meet your adoring public.

A young, slim black man dressed in denims and a silk shirt rose from his seat and acknowledged the polite applause from the diners.

'I hear that Craig is going to be massive,' said Dominic. 'And tonight is the first time ever that anyone outside the company has heard the record. So good luck, Craig, and I hope you have as much success as my boys.'

Craig sat down again and David leaned over to Jane

and said, 'Know this bloke?'

'I've heard about him on the grapevine. But he's not one of my acts. I'll have a word with him later.'

She looked at the black man and thought to herself that 'a word' was not all she'd like with him, and wondered how she could get him onto the roster of acts she worked on. She'd never had a black man and she'd been watching him since he arrived with more than a little interest.

The meal continued, with the waiters and waitresses serving fish, followed by roast lamb and a choice of desserts.

A different wine was served with each course and as the guests got more drunk they began to fondle the staff as they served the meal. Pretty soon the room began to resemble a Bacchanalian feast.

Even though Mal and Gloria, still armed with his whip which he used on diners and staff alike, tried to keep some control over the meal, it was quite late before coffee and liqueurs were brought in.

When they finally arrived, Dominic got unsteadily to his feet to introduce Craig Sinclair again, who smiled, left his seat and went up to the minstrel's gallery, where he plugged in his guitar and regaled the company with several of his songs.

When he'd finished, to ecstatic applause from the inebriated throng, they abandoned the dining room and went back to the drawing room where the bar had been replenished with champagne.

28

From then on, the party really reached its height, as the champagne flowed and Derek rolled up joint after joint from the stash that Dominic had asked him to bring down from London.

Anya was deep in conversation with Mandy. Jane was chatting to David but keeping one eye open for Craig Sinclair. Sylvia had been cornered by a lecherous Australian DJ from the pirate ship 'Radio England'. Dominic was trying to tie up a deal with a concert promoter, and the other guests were milling about getting more drunk and stoned by the minute. Tony had just got a drink from the bar and was looking round the room for someone to talk to, when he was button-holed by Sly.

'Hello, mate,' he said. 'What a do, eh?'

Tony had to agree.

'And what about the record in America? Amazing, ain't it? Just what we were talking about before.'

Tony nodded.

'Who's that sort you're with? I don't know her, do I?' asked Sly.

'No,' said Tony in reply. 'I met her a while back. Her name's Mandy. Works for a record company.'

'Don't they all, mate?' said Sly. 'Where'd she spring from?'

'I told you about her, remember?' said Tony.

'No,' said Sly.

'Yes I did. That night down in Blaises. When we met that German bird, Marsha. Jane's friend.'

'I was pissed, wasn't I?' said Sly.

'You're always pissed, Sly,' replied David.

'Yeah, all right. What about her? This Mandy.'

'I told you I watched two lesbians whipping each other. Remember?'

'Fuck me. Course I do. Is that one of them?' asked Sly, craning over the crowd to get a better look at Mandy.

Tony nodded.

'Is the other one here?'

Tony shook his head.

'Shame,' said Sly. 'I could have done with some of that tonight.'

'You might get your wish,' said Tony, 'the way Anya's looking at her.'

'She's not one, too, is she?' asked Sly in amazement.

'From what I've heard.'

'Who from?'

'Never you mind.'

'Blimey,' said Sly. 'Who would have thought it? Do you think Dominic knows?'

'I wouldn't be surprised,' said Tony. 'He's into all sorts too.'

'From what you've heard,' said Sly.

'From what I've heard,' agreed Tony.

'What sorts of things?' asked Sly.

'He likes to watch,' said Tony.

'What? His missus?'

'That's right.'

'Who's been telling you all this? Are you sure they're not pulling your plonker?'

'Could be, but I don't think so. It's a pretty reliable source.' Tony didn't tell Sly that it was Dominic himself.

'Who?'

'Never you mind.'

Sly pondered for a moment. 'He watches his missus. What, with other birds?'

'And men.'

'Dirty slag.'

'Who? Him or her?'

'Him. Watching.'

'You do,' said Tony.

'I ain't got a missus.'

'You crack me up, Sly,' said Tony.

'No, it's different. The sorts we meet. Groupies. All that lot. It don't matter. But your *missus*. That ain't right.'

'You fucked your sister-in-law.'

'Yeah, I know, but . . .' And Sly laughed. 'Fuck me, I don't know. Things ain't 'alf changed over the last year. Bleeding funny old world, ain't it, Tone?'

'It sure is,' replied Tony. 'But it's not too bad if you don't weaken.'

'So you reckon your sort and Dom's missus might . . .'

'They might,' said Tony.

'Fuck me. That I would like to see.'

'You just said . . .'

'Yeah, I know. I surprise myself sometimes, how

disgustin' I've got. Besides, like I said, it ain't my missus. Or yours. So it don't matter.'

'If you say so, Sly.'

'Reckon Dom'll let us watch?' asked the rhythm guitarist.

'Don't know,' replied Tony. 'Depends how much he's had to drink.'

'I hope he's a had a lot. I reckon that Anya's right tasty. And your bird, too,' he added.

'You're not the only one.'

'You'll let me know, won't you? If they do, like.'

'Course I will,' said Tony.

'I'm going to get a drink,' said Sly. 'And capture old Sylvia back from that Ozzy bastard. Those cunts on those pirate ships are sex mad. Two weeks at sea with nothing to look at but the sea gulls, and nothing to do but take drugs, drink and wank themselves. They see a half-decent bird and they're all over it before you can say knife. Look at him.'

Tony looked over to where the Australian DJ had backed Sylvia into a corner and was busy looking down the front of her dress as if he'd never seen a pair of breasts before.

'He'll climb in with her soon if I don't get over there,' said Sly. 'Cheeky sod. Just 'cos he plays our record, he thinks he can get hold of my tart.'

'You'd better go and show him different,' said Tony.

'I don't care that much if he does, as it goes,' said Sly. 'She's nothing to me. Mind you, I wouldn't mind seeing her going case with Anya and your bird. Reckon she'd join in, do ya?'

'You know her better than me.'

'That's the point. I don't know her at all. Don't even

rightly know where she sprang from. One minute I was on me own. Next minute she was there. Can't remember a thing about it. Must have pulled her at a club or something.'

'Do you think you might be taking too many drugs, son?' asked Tony.

'Christ, I hope so,' said Sly. 'See you later. Don't forget what I said. If anything interesting happens, you find me.'

'I will,' said Tony.

'See you then,' said Sly and with a wink he left Tony and weaved in and out of the crowd in the direction of the bar.

Tony laughed and weaved his way through the crowd too, in the direction of Derek who had just finished rolling a massive joint.

'Give us a hit on that spliff,' he said as he got close to the road manager.

'Cost ya,' said Derek, with a smile.

'What, from my favourite roadie?'

'Only kidding,' said Derek. 'Here you go.' And he passed the joint to Tony who took a deep drag, held it down until he was almost choking, then let out the smoke.

'Good party,' said Tony.

'Not at all bad,' agreed Derek.

'Where's the bird you came with?'

'Fuck knows,' replied Derek. 'I think she's gone off for a swim with Donkey.'

'That'll be nice for her. Seen anyone else you fancy?'

'Yeah. There's a couple of likely looking sorts who might come across.'

'You never know your luck.'

'I carry my luck with me,' replied Derek.

'What? In your trousers.'

Derek grinned in reply. 'You might say that. If I give one of them a couple of drags on one of these,' he held up the joint, 'within minutes they're putty in my hands.'

'Who are we talking about here?' asked Tony.

'Them two over there.' Derek gestured in the direction of the bar. 'See 'em? One's got a pink dress on. The other's in jeans and a flowery shirt.'

'I see them,' said Tony as his eyes found two attractive-looking girls of about twenty standing beside the bar, glasses in hand, chatting to each other and surveying the room between sips.

One had long straight brown hair, sunglasses perched on the end of a pert little nose, and an attractive open face, with a mouth that looked like it would smile easily. She was wearing a short pink cotton dress that hugged her full figure closely and exposed as neat a set of legs as Tony had seen for a long time.

The other was darker. Her hair cut into a Vidal Sassoon wedge, wearing a multi-coloured shirt with the top three buttons opened to show off her cleavage and well-faded, tight blue jeans over cuban-heeled boots. Although the outfit was simple, she made it look as if it had cost a million pounds. Tony especially noticed that the jeans were cut very tightly over her pert bottom.

'Nice,' he said. 'Which one's yours?'

'Whichever one doesn't immediately fall for the pop star,' said Derek. 'You know the way it goes. But what's your new girlfriend going to say?'

'I think she's otherwise engaged. Besides she's not

my girlfriend. And we have a very modern relationship.'

'I just bet you have,' replied Derek.

'Shall I fetch them over?' asked Tony.

'I thought you were never going to suggest it,' replied Derek. 'Tell them we've got plenty of dope.'

'No problem,' said Tony and moved away from the roadie.

On the way to the bar he stopped by Mandy and Anya, who were still engrossed in their conversation.

'All right?' he asked.

They both looked up at him.

'Never better, Tony darling,' said Anya.

'Fine,' said Mandy and she blushed.

'Great,' said Tony. Then to Mandy: 'I'm not ignoring you, love. But I've got to circulate. You know how it is?'

'Course we do,' said Anya. 'It's your party. You've got to keep the guests satisfied.'

'That's right,' said Tony. 'Can I leave Mandy with you for a little bit longer?'

'For as long as you like,' replied the older woman. 'We're having a lovely chat. Aren't we, Mandy?'

Mandy nodded.

'That's fine then,' said Tony. 'I'll catch up with you later.'

'Take as long as you like,' said Anya. 'The night is still young.'

Tony smiled and continued towards the bar and the two girls who were still standing beside it.

He ordered champagne and as he waited for the barman to fill a glass, turned in their direction. As he expected they were both staring at him. He smiled.

They smiled back. He collected his glass and moved closer.

'Hi,' he said. 'I'm Tony Parker.'

'We know who you are,' said the girl in the pink dress. 'It's your party.'

'I keep being told that. But I'm afraid I don't know everyone. Who invited you?'

'My brother,' said the girl in the flowered shirt.

'Who's he?' asked Tony.

She mentioned the name of the promoter that Dominic had been speaking to.

'Really,' said Tony. 'That's interesting. I think we might be doing a tour with him later in the year.'

'And I'm her friend,' said the girl in the pink dress.

'What are your names?' asked Tony.

'Sonja,' said the girl in the shirt.

'Vanessa,' said the girl in the pink dress.

Tony changed his glass from his right to his left hand and solemnly shook hands with each of them.

'I'm very pleased to meet you,' he said. 'What do you do?'

They both pulled faces and said, 'We're students,' simultaneously, then laughed.

'What university?' asked Tony.

'LSE,' said Sonja.

'I'm impressed,' said Tony. 'I was going to go there, until I joined the band.'

'Just like Mick Jagger,' said Sonja.

'That's right. I'd've been a year behind him. How old are you two?'

'Nineteen,' they answered in unison again.

'Babies,' said Tony with a grin.

'Not such babies as you might imagine,' said Sonja

and fixed Tony with a frank gaze.

He fixed her with a gaze of his own.

'Are you with anyone?' he asked. 'Apart from your brother, that is.'

Sonja shook her head.

'No boyfriends?' Tony expanded his gaze to take in Vanessa.

'We have so many,' said Sonja. 'We couldn't decide. So we left them all in London.'

'Wise move,' said Tony. 'Do you smoke?'

'Sometimes,' said Sonja.

'My roadie's over there. I think he'd like to meet you. He's got some very good gear.'

'A roadie,' said Sonja scornfully.

'Don't let him hear you say it like that,' said Tony, 'he's a very moody guy.'

'I like moody guys,' said Vanessa wistfully.

'My brother says that roadies are not to be trusted,' said Sonja.

'What about guitarists?' asked Tony.

'He says that they're not to be trusted either,' said Sonja and smiled up at Tony.

Tony laughed. He'd liked her straight away and was liking her more by the minute.

'He's quite right,' he said.

'I like men who are not to be trusted,' said Vanessa.

'Come on over then,' invited Tony. 'We can take a walk in the garden and get some fresh air.'

The two girls looked at each other and shrugged. 'OK,' they both said and Tony led the way back to where Derek was sitting.

As they approached he was just putting the finishing touches to another joint and he looked up and smiled.

'A successful mission, B'wana,' he said.

'Accomplished without harm to life or limb,' said Tony.

'Derek, I'd like you to meet Sonja and Vanessa. They both go to the LSE. Sonja's brother might be promoting our autumn tour. And he says that roadies and guitarists are not to be trusted.'

'He's perfectly correct,' said Derek. 'They drink, take drugs and abuse young women. But then you should meet some drummers. They're *really* bad.'

'He's right,' agreed Tony. '*They* cut young women up, cook them and eat them.'

Sonja looked at Vanessa, who looked back, then said, 'Do you two always go on like this?'

'Always,' said Derek. 'We're famous for it.'

'He's right again,' agreed Tony. Then said to Derek, 'I've suggested a walk around the grounds, just the five of us.'

'Five?' said Vanessa.

'Yes,' said Tony. 'You two girls. Us two untrustworthy and decadent rock-and-rollers, and that little number that Derek just rolled.'

'You're crazy,' said Vanessa.

'You're right. But it doesn't make us bad people. Now are you coming or not?' asked Tony.

'Course,' replied the girl. 'Try and stop us.'

They strolled out through the french windows and walked across the rolling lawns in the direction of two empty benches that had been placed close to the bank of trees at the far end.

Derek fired up the joint as they went and passed it around the small group.

★ ★ ★

At the same time, back at the party, Anya, who had been regaling Mandy with tales of her life as an actress before she met and married Dominic, finished the latest in a long line of glasses of champagne and said, 'I feel like a mess, dear. I need to freshen up. Come upstairs and we can continue our little chat whilst I change.'

Mandy agreed. She was in awe of the older woman, who seemed to have led such an interesting, jet-set style of life. And not only that. She fancied Anya like mad. And the thought of seeing her undressing excited her tremendously. Gossip around the business was that Anya was bi-sexual and Mandy was determined to find out if the gossip was true. The young girl felt a familiar fluttering of desire in her stomach as she looked at Anya's voluptuous figure clad in the black satin dress, and she hurriedly swallowed the last of her drink and followed Dominic's wife through the crowd, out of the drawing room, across the hall and up the wide flight of stairs to the first floor.

Big Mal noticed their departure, grinned to himself and went and found his boss, who had just concluded the preliminary phases of what looked like being a most lucrative deal for the headline slot on one of Sonja's brother Joseph's late-autumn package tours. The Getaways' manager was feeling very pleased with himself.

Mal tapped Dominic on the shoulder and whispered something in his ear. Dominic excused himself from Joseph for a moment and drew Mal aside. They had another short, whispered conversation, before Mal left. Dominic beamed to himself, then resumed his conversation with Sonja's brother but, after a few minutes, made the excuse of having to place an urgent telephone call and he too left the room and went upstairs.

A few minutes later he came back down, still smiling, and went back into the drawing room. He looked round, frowned, then spotted David and went over and asked him where Tony had got to.

David pointed him in the direction of the garden and Dominic also went out through the French windows.

He looked round, then saw Tony, Derek, Sonja and Vanessa seated on the benches by the trees and made his way over.

'Tony,' he said as he got close. 'I'm terribly sorry to disturb you. But I need a quick word. Can I drag you away for a moment?'

'What about?' said Tony, who was fancying Sonja more by the minute.

'Business. It won't take long.'

'Is it about the tour?' asked Tony. 'Because before you say anything, this is the promoter's sister.' He gestured in Sonja's direction.

'Yes,' lied Dominic. 'It looks like it's in the bag.'

He turned to Sonja and laid on all his public-school charm.

'So you're Joseph's sister. It's Sonja, isn't it? He told me you were here.'

He leant down and took her hand and shook it.

'I'm delighted to meet you,' he continued. 'Your brother is a charming man. And very astute. He's been twisting my arm to get the boys on one of his tours for weeks.'

'Has he succeeded?' asked Sonja.

'Almost definitely. We're going to meet up again next week to thrash out the details. That's why I need a

quick word with Tony. I promise you I won't deprive
you of his company for long.'

'I'm sure it's very important,' said Sonja. 'This is my
friend Vanessa, we're at university together. I'm afraid
we rather gatecrashed today. I insisted that Joseph
bring us down when he said who the party was for. I
hope you don't mind.'

'No problem at all,' replied Dominic, taking
Vanessa's hand and shaking it. 'Any friend or relation,
or for that matter friend of a relation of Joseph's is
more than welcome here. Now Tony, do come along,
dear boy. I promise I won't keep you long, but I've
something I'm dying for you to see.'

'Sorry,' apologised Tony. 'The pressures of life at the
top. I'll be as quick as I can. Derek, don't let these two
out of your sight till I get back.'

'Your word is my command, boss,' said Derek. 'I'd
sooner die than let you down.'

Tony grinned. Took one last drag on the joint,
passed it to Sonja, got up from the bench where he was
sitting and joined Dominic who led him back across the
lawn in the direction of the house.

'What's up?' asked Tony. 'I thought it was your job
to deal with tours.'

'It's got nothing to do with the tour,' replied
Dominic. 'But I couldn't tell you what it was in front of
them. Come with me. I've got a little surprise for you.'

29

Dominic led Tony into the house and up the stairs to the first floor and into one of the rooms along the corridor.

Inside it was dark and Tony stopped on the threshold to allow his eyesight to adjust.

'Come in, Tony,' said Dominic. 'Don't be shy. I think you'll like this.'

Tony did as he was told. He moved up behind Dominic and saw that on one wall of the room was what looked like a large colour TV screen, with a projector in front of it. Then, as he focused through the haze of alcohol and dope, he realised that it was a movie camera in front of a clear glass window into the next room, and that the reels were gently turning as they recorded what was happening there.

From where he was standing he could see a double bed covered in a raspberry-coloured satin spread. Anya and Mandy were sitting side by side on one edge of the bed. They were both holding champagne glasses. There was a magnum bottle of Moet on the bedside table, next to an ashtray, cigarettes and lighter. Mandy looked drunk. Anya less so.

Anya picked up the bottle and filled their glasses.

She gave herself noticeably less than she gave the younger girl. The noise of the bottle chinking on the glass was amplified through speakers into the room where Dominic and Tony were watching.

'All mod cons,' said Dominic. Then added, 'Don't worry, they can't hear us.'

'Is this a set up?' asked Tony.

He saw Dominic nod in the gloom. 'You don't mind, do you?'

'No. I think Mandy fancies your missus. She was talking about her before.'

'Is she that way?' asked Dominic.

'Wait and see,' said Tony and grinned to himself.

Both men watched as Mandy and Anya drained their glasses. Then Anya took Mandy's and put it, with hers, next to the champagne bottle. 'You're a very pretty girl,' she said. 'And that's a lovely dress.'

'So is yours,' said Mandy.

'Do you think so? Would you like to try it on?'

'I don't know if I've got the figure for it. I'm a bit flat up top.'

'Nonsense dear,' said Anya, who stood up and pulled the black satin dress she was wearing over her head and threw it on the bed. Underneath she was wearing nothing but a suspender belt and black seamed nylons. Tony looked at her firm, full figure and the black brush between her legs and licked his lips.

'Do you still wear stockings?' said Mandy.

'Of course. I know everyone thinks they're old-fashioned but men love them. Tights are so sexless.'

'I know. Tony hates them. That's why I'm glad it's summer and I can go bare-legged.'

'Stand up and I'll unzip you,' said Anya and held out

her hand. Mandy took it and stood up beside her, then turned to face the mirror. Tony was sure that she must be able to see him.

'Can't they see us?' he asked Dominic.

'Not a chance. The mirror was specially fitted by the owner of this place. He has similar tastes to us. It's uncanny, I know. But all she can see is a reflection of the room they're in.'

Whilst the two men had been speaking Anya had unzipped Mandy's dress and slid it off her shoulders with a touch that was more of a caress. Mandy shivered as Anya's fingers ran over her shoulders. Mandy's dress dropped to the floor and revealed the tiny red panties she was wearing. Both Tony and Dominic saw that her nipples were hard and engorged with blood.

'She's loving it,' whispered Dominic. 'We should be in for a good show.'

'You've got a beautiful figure,' said Anya, looking over Mandy's shoulder into the mirror. 'Lovely tits. Not flat at all. And your skin's so white.'

'So have you,' said Mandy, turning to face her. 'And I love tan skin. I wish I could go brown but I burn.' She touched her arm against Anya's to better show the contrast. The touch lasted longer than was necessary and Tony could feel the sexual tension between them as he watched.

'Here, slip this on,' said Anya, breaking the silence, and picked up her dress and handed it to Mandy.

Mandy slipped it over her head, then turned to admire herself in the mirror. The dress did fit, and accentuated the slim curves of her figure.

'I told you it would suit you,' said Anya and sat on the bed with her back against the headboard, filled the glasses with champagne again and lit a cigarette. She sat with her legs parted indelicately and Tony could see that her pubic hair looked damp and matted. She blew out smoke with a hiss that made the hairs on the back of Tony's neck tingle.

'Come and join me,' she said and patted the bed beside her. As Mandy moved towards her, Anya said, 'Slip the dress off, we don't want it to get creased, do we?' Mandy obeyed, and pulled it over her head and draped it across a chair, then sat next to Anya and picked up her glass.

'Here's to us,' said Anya and they touched glasses. Mandy went to take a sip and Anya said, 'No, like this.' And linked her arm around Mandy's so that when they drank they were looking into each other's eyes. They gazed at each other in silence for a moment.

'Isn't this cosy?' said Anya and stubbed out her cigarette and draped her arm casually round Mandy's shoulders. 'Just girls together. It's like being back at school.'

'A midnight feast in the dormitory,' said Mandy. 'But we never had champagne.'

'Did you ever have kisses?' Asked Anya.

'No,' said Mandy. 'We were very proper girls.'

'Not even a tiny peck?' pressed Anya.

Mandy's face blushed scarlet, and the blush spread down to her breasts and tinted her nipples rose pink. She looked down and saw the blush and covered her breasts with her arms, shyly. 'No,' she repeated in a little girl voice.

Liar. Thought Tony.

'We did,' said Anya. 'That was the best part.'

'Was it?' asked Mandy and looked into Anya's eyes,

their faces less than six inches apart.

'Yes,' said Anya softly and leant over and kissed Mandy very gently on the lips. 'You see,' she said. 'That didn't hurt did it?'

'No,' said Mandy throatily. 'It was lovely.'

Tony could feel an erection growing in his jeans and saw that Anya was very excited. There was a gleam of moisture at the centre of her pubic bush and her legs were much wider apart.

Anya pulled the younger girl gently towards her and kissed her again, for longer this time, and her hand went to Mandy's breast and began to stroke the smooth skin. The kiss went on and on and both Mandy and Anya opened their mouths. Tony watched them French-kissing, their mouths glued together for what seemed like hours. When they finally broke away, Mandy said breathlessly, 'Are you sure we should?'

'Why not, darling?' breathed Anya. 'It's perfectly natural. We're just two girlfriends learning about each other, and giving each other pleasure.'

'What happens if someone comes in?'

'The door's locked. Don't worry,' said Anya and, with that, she put her head down and found Mandy's right nipple with her mouth and began to suck and lick and kiss it. Mandy's head went back and she opened her mouth and closed her eyes at the feel of the other woman's hot wet mouth on the sensitive bud at the tip of her breast. As Anya's kissing and sucking became more urgent, Mandy began to lick her lips until they were wet with saliva. Tony imagined that her other lips were becoming similarly moist.

Anya's hand slid up Mandy's thigh. The girl opened

her legs at the slight pressure from Anya's fingers and the older woman slid her hand onto the crotch of Mandy's knickers. Her fingers began a gentle circling motion on the material. As Anya was busy working on Mandy's erogenous zones, she began to caress Anya's body, her back, neck, breasts and belly. Anya sat up next to her again and they began to kiss once more. Long passionate, breathless kisses that made Tony's prick uncomfortable against the restriction of his tight jeans.

As they kissed, Anya guided Mandy's hand to her centre. She opened her legs wide, giving Tony and Dominic the perfect view of Mandy's delicate fingers stroking Anya's cunt. Under Mandy's tender ministrations, it opened like a flower in bloom. The pink inside was clearly visible as Mandy spread the cunt lips and ran her fingers teasingly over the gentle membrane. Tony could see that Anya was dripping wet by then. Mandy's fingers slid in and out of her soaking hole and their kisses became longer and even more loving, if that were possible.

They broke apart once more and Anya said, 'I think you've done this before, you naughty girl. Were you teasing me?'

Mandy smiled and nodded.

'I knew it,' said Anya. 'I knew it the first time I saw you.'

She pushed Mandy's knickers over her hips, down her legs, and Mandy kicked them off. Then Anya slid down the satin bedspread and put her mouth between the younger girl's legs. The girl screamed softly as Anya's tongue found her sex. She lay for a minute loving the ministrations, then she too slid round until her mouth could reach Anya's honeypot and she fastened her mouth to it.

Tony watched their wild, wanton *soixante-neuf* until he could hardly bear it.

The women rolled over and started kissing again, licking their own juices off the other's faces. Mandy lay back and Anya climbed on top of her and began rubbing her wet pubic hair against hers. She straightened her arms and lifted herself up off the girl and looked down to where their pussies were rubbing together, then looked straight at the mirror and winked and mouthed a kiss to whoever was watching the lesbian love session.

'Bitch,' said Dominic.

Anya ground her pubis into Mandy's and the girl began to moan. Her moans became louder, harder and more breathless as she came near to climax. Anya rode her like a man until, with one final scream, Mandy clutched at Anya's back with her fingers and came.

The older woman dropped down beside her, breathless. 'That was wonderful,' she panted and leant over and kissed the girl.

'What about that?' said Dominic. 'That girl of yours has hidden talents. Did you know she swung both ways?'

'Sure I did,' said Tony.

'Was it worth the price of admission?'

'I should say so,' said Tony. 'Watching that has made me horny. I'm going to find a woman for myself.'

'Good luck,' said Dominic. 'There's plenty to choose from. I think I'm going to join the ladies. You don't mind do you?'

'No,' said Tony. 'Good luck to you, too.' And with

one last look through the mirror at the two exhausted women lying together on the damp satin bedspread, he left the room.

30

Dominic stood up, rewound the film, fitted a fresh spool and threaded it through, pressed the button that started the camera recording and left the room, locking the door carefully behind him. He took another door key from his pocket and went along the corridor to the room where Anya and Mandy were together, quietly unlocked it and opened the door.

They were still lying side by side and Anya was gently rubbing the girl's upper thigh.

'What's all this?' said Dominic, feigning surprise.

Both the women looked up startled. Mandy pulled the edge of the bedspread over her nakedness.

Dominic closed the door behind him, and slipped the lock. 'I said, what's all this?' he demanded angrily.

'We were just having a lie down,' said Anya.

'A likely story,' said Dominic and walked over and tugged the bedspread off Mandy. He looked down at her nakedness and licked his lips.

'What have you been doing to this girl?' he demanded of Anya. 'What's she done to you?' to Mandy.

'N-nothing really,' stammered Mandy, confused at Dominic's intrusion when she'd been lying there half asleep, thrilling to the touch of Anya's hand on her thigh, as her long brown fingers teasingly moved up close to her cunt and then, equally teasingly, away again.

' "Nothing really" – what exactly?' said Dominic.

Mandy gave Anya a puzzled look. 'Nothing really, Dominic.'

Dominic looked sternly at her.

'Mr Edwards?'

Again the look.

'Sir?'

'That's better,' said Dominic. 'This has all the ingredients of a schoolgirl prank gone too far. And now the teacher has caught you.'

'We're so sorry, sir,' wheedled Anya. 'I don't know what came over us. It must have been the champagne.'

Dominic picked up the bottle. It was still chilly. He poured some into a glass and took a sip, seemingly deep in thought. His gaze passed over the two women. One, a naked teenager, her skin dewy with youth with its peaches-and-cream complexion, blonde hair and matching curly pubic thatch. The other in her thirties, wearing just a strappy black suspender belt and black nylons. Her skin was tanned all over, without a bikini mark, and her blue-black hair perfectly matched the thick, lustrous bush between her legs.

In their ages they could have been mother and daughter. But he'd just watched them making steamy, passionate lesbian love together. And now he knew they were in his power.

As he looked at them, he felt his cock thicken and push against the material of his trousers. Under his gaze, Mandy moved her hand to cover her maiden hair, but Anya just grinned and scissored her legs together to focus attention where they joined in the wet swamp of her cunt.

'You're my wife, Anya,' said Dominic. 'And you've been very naughty. And as for you, Mandy. You encouraged her.'

'No,' denied Mandy.

'*Yes*,' said Dominic firmly. 'And you're both going to have to take your punishments.'

'What punishment?' asked Mandy in a small voice, but Dominic noticed that she took her hand off her mound and reached over and took Anya's fingers in hers. Anya squeezed them reassuringly.

'I'm going to spank you both soundly,' said Dominic and took off his jacket. His cock was even harder now and strained against his fly. He saw Mandy's eyes move to it and stay there. 'You first Mandy,' he said.

He sat on the slippery material of the bedspread and pulled Mandy's naked body across his thighs, face down. She wriggled as his cock pressed into her belly. He looked down at the perfect orbs of her buttocks and raised his right hand and brought it down onto her flesh.

She screamed in pain and Dominic looked at the red mark his hand had made on her skin.

'That hurt,' she said.

'You deserve it, you naughty girl,' said Dominic. 'Don't you?'

'Yes, sir,' she whispered. He raised his hand again and gave her another stinging blow on her arse. Then he slapped her again and again. She was rubbing herself against him with pleasure as he hit her. When he paused, she cried, 'Don't stop, sir, I deserve it.'

Dominic smiled and looked over at his wife who was playing with her clitoris as she watched her husband dole out punishment to her new lover. Dominic slapped Mandy again. She became more excited as the punishment continued, until eventually it was too much for her and she orgasmed with a long pent-up cry, rubbing herself even harder onto the bulge in his trousers.

Dominic gently eased her off his lap, then stood up and began to undress. Mandy and Anya watched as he disrobed.

Naked, he was huge. But what Mandy had taken for fat was muscle. And his muscle of love was long and thick and reared out of a thicket of tight black pubic hair.

As he stood before the two women, Anya slid her hand around Mandy's shoulders. 'Kiss your master's prick,' she whispered.

Mandy looked at her, then smiled and scrambled off the bed and knelt in front of Dominic in a supplicatory position on the carpet. She took his cock in her right hand and kissed the end with her lips. She licked around the hole with her tongue, then opened her mouth and accepted the huge rod into it. It filled her throat perfectly and she wondered what it would feel like as he shagged her, because eventually she knew that that was to be her fate. She sucked at Dominic's prick until he cried out with pleasure then she stood up and, holding his knob end between her fingers, she led him to the bed where Anya lay smoking a cigarette and sipping at a glass of champagne.

Seeing her, Dominic said, 'I want a drink first.' He lay Mandy on her back, picked up the champagne bottle and began to pour the liquid over her pubic hair. He put the bottle back on the table, then got down between her legs and began to lap at the mixture of wine and female juices he found there. Then he lifted himself above her and guided his weapon between the lips of her cunt. She opened her legs wide to accept him. When he was astride her and comfortably inside her sticky cunt, he began to move on her as his wife had done half an hour previously.

Mandy crossed her legs across his back and together they found the sexual rhythm that suited them perfectly. As he humped her, she humped him, their faces less than an inch apart. Dominic battered at her slim body but she called for more, harder fucking. He rose to the occasion. As Anya watched, they beat at each other until Dominic froze and she watched as he spasmed into Mandy's pussy. As the last drop splashed her womb, she too came with a cry of excitement.

Dominic slumped over Mandy's slim form, then rolled over onto his back with a sigh of satisfaction.

Anya looked at her husband lying between her and Mandy and said, 'Me now, Dominic. Aren't you going to punish me, too?'

'In good time,' he replied. 'I need another drink first. Get me a glass of champagne.'

Anya did as she was told, and Dominic lay on the bed and sipped at the wine as his knob slowly grew between his legs again.

Anya slid down and started to lap at the wetness of it in her mouth and tasted Mandy's juices mixed with Dominic's come.

'Mmm,' she purred. 'This is delicious.'

Dominic lay back and relaxed and drew Mandy to

him and kissed her gently on the lips as his wife took his cock fully into her mouth and sucked it even harder.

'I'm sorry, my dear,' Dominic said to Mandy, 'but I must chastise my wife. The filthy bitch needs regular beatings to keep her in line.'

He disengaged himself from the younger girl's embrace and pushed Anya roughly off him, then got off the bed. He went over to the chest of drawers in the corner of the room and opened the top drawer. From inside he took out a leather belt, held the buckle in his hand and wrapped a foot or so of it around his knuckles and returned to the bedside.

Anya rolled over and lay face down, turning her head so that she could see what was going on and pushed her luscious arse in the air.

Dominic raised his arm and brought the end of the belt down over his wife's beautiful twin buttocks with a crack.

Anya gasped, smiled and said, 'Harder, you bastard. I could hardly feel that.'

Once again Dominic brought the leather strap down over her bottom. Then again and again until the smooth, honey-coloured skin was red with parallel welts.

'More,' cried Anya in delight. 'More.'

Dominic continued to beat her until he was sweating and out of breath, but still she cried for more.

Eventually, Dominic became so excited that he threw the belt across the room and forced his wife's legs wide and pushed his prick into her from behind, and pumped his body in and out of hers so hard that she screamed with a mixture of pain and pleasure. He literally pounded her body into the mattress until the bed was in danger of collapse, and still he pounded into her.

Mandy was transfixed with the sight and longed to be impaled on his mighty love organ again, and to feel the ecstasy that Anya was so obviously experiencing.

Dominic was panting with the exertion of his efforts and Anya was begging him to fuck her harder, to fuck her arse off, to fuck her to death, when with one last effort he came into her cunt with such force that it triggered off a come of her own and Dominic collapsed, totally spent, onto the exhausted body of his wife.

31

As Tony and Dominic climbed the stairs to the first
floor, Craig Sinclair came out of the dining room,
where he had been talking to the roadie from the
equipment hire company, and walked across the hall
into the drawing room. He saw that the place was really
humming and snaked across to the bar to get a drink.
Then he stood, glass in hand, and looked round the
room to see who was about.

The first person his eyes fell on was Jane. She was
vaguely familiar and he'd been watching her through
dinner and knew that she'd been watching him. She
was standing by the window talking to David Powell
from The Getaways. Craig thought she looked
extremely sexy in the short, hippy-print dress she was
wearing that showed off her long shapely legs to their
best advantage. And Craig had always liked blondes.
He vaguely wondered what the relationship was
between her and the bass player, as he knew from the
papers that David Powell was a heavy item with
Jade Dollar, the model. Craig kept looking at Jane
and eventually she looked over in his direction and, as
their eyes met, she smiled and waved and beckoned to
him.

He took his drink and walked through the crowd in her direction.

When he got to where she and David were standing, she said, 'Hi, I'm Jane Price. I work for Zenith.'

Craig snapped his fingers. 'I thought I recognised you,' he said. 'I think I've seen you round the office.'

'It's quite possible,' she said. 'I get around.' And she smiled invitingly.

I bet you do, thought Craig. And I'd like to get you around my cock.

'Do you know David Powell?' she asked.

'Only from the papers and TV,' replied Craig, and stuck out his hand in David's direction. 'Pleased to meet you. And congratulations on doing so well in America.'

David took the proffered hand. 'Pleased to meet you too,' he said, 'and thanks. That was a good set. I like your stuff. You've got a couple of great tunes there. I hope they do well.'

'Me too,' replied Craig. Then to Jane, 'Do you work on The Getaways?'

'Yes,' she replied. 'Who's handling your PR at Zenith?'

'A cat called Barry. Know him?'

'Sure,' said Jane. 'But he's leaving. Did you know?'

'Yeah. Going to the States. It's a bit of a worry, what with the single coming out and all.'

'Maybe I could squeeze you onto my list,' said Jane. 'How would that suit?'

'Great,' said Craig. Thinking that being squeezed by her in any way would be most exciting. 'If you've been working on The Getaways . . .' He didn't finish the sentence.

'I can't take the credit,' said Jane, smiling at David. 'I haven't been working on them for that long. Besides it's what's in the grooves that sells. But I'll speak to the promo director on Monday. If I tell him we've met, I'm sure he won't have any objections.'

'As long as The Getaways don't mind you working on my stuff.'

David shook his head. 'Not at all,' he said, 'we've got our own PR company now. I'm sure that Jane's getting bored with nothing to do. I know she's looking for a new challenge. Something to really get her teeth into.'

Jane nodded in agreement. Getting her teeth into Craig would suit her just fine.

'Terrific,' said Craig.

'We'll have to get together to plan a strategy,' said Jane.

'When?'

'Why not now? You don't mind do you David?'

David shrugged. 'No,' he said. 'Not a bit. I've got a few people to see myself. You two have a talk and I'll catch up with you in a bit.'

'Great,' said Jane.

'Thanks,' said Craig, 'I appreciate it.'

'No problem,' said David. 'See you later.' And with a smile he left them. He had a pretty good idea what was going on in Jane's mind but he didn't care. She was only a stop-gap after all.

'Nice guy,' said Craig.

'A sweetie,' replied Jane. 'It's a pity he's spoken for. His girlfriend's giving him a hard time right now. I only came down here to keep him company.'

Not strictly true, she thought, but it showed that she was available. And she'd always known that David wasn't going to be a permanent thing.

She looked admiringly at Craig's broad shoulders inside his silk shirt, then down to his faded jeans and the huge bulge in the crotch.

'I like the gear,' she said. 'Plain and simple, but effective.'

'This shirt cost a bomb,' said Craig proudly.

'I can tell,' said Jane.

'Yeah,' he went on. 'I got it in Kenny Market. A friend of mine's got a stall there. He sells really good stuff. You should come with me sometime. I could get you a good discount.'

'I'd like that,' said Jane. 'It's silk, isn't it? I just love silk, it's so sexy.' And she touched his arm and felt a thrill run through her body at the contact.

Craig felt it too. And realised that Jane had engineered them being alone together.

'Shall we go somewhere quiet to talk?' she asked.

'Sure.'

'The garden?'

'Can I get my guitar first? I hate to leave it lying around.'

'Course. Where is it?'

'In that gallery place,' replied Craig.

'Let's go then,' said Jane.

They walked together back to the dining room where the equipment roadie was just carrying out the last box of cables and leads.

'I put your guitar behind the curtain up there,' he said to Craig. 'Don't want any light-fingered bastard to rip it off. I'm going now. See you again, I hope.' And with an appreciative glance in Jane's direction, he left.

'Cheers, mate,' said the singer to the roadie's retreat-

ing back. 'Same here,' and he and Jane climbed the
circular staircase to the minstrel's gallery.

Craig pulled back the curtain and found his guitar
case, then hitched himself up on the balustrade and
said, 'So you think I could have a hit?'

'Sure,' replied Jane. 'Like David said, you've got a
couple of great songs there.'

'And you'll be my personal PR?'

'If you want me.'

Right then there was nothing that Craig wanted more
than that.

He nodded. 'I sure do,' he said.

'Then have me,' she said.

Craig reached over and pulled Jane close to him. So
close that he could feel her heart beating against his
through the thin material of their clothes.

He kissed her deeply and she felt the hardness of the
muscles in his arms and the difference in the smell of
him filled her nostrils, and she actually went weak at
the knees and had to lean against him for support.

'Careful,' he said, gripping the rail he was leaning
against. 'We don't want to fall over into the remains of
the dinner. We've got more important things to do.'

'Sorry,' she said. 'Men don't usually have that effect
on me. Even handsome men like you.'

'You think I'm handsome?' he asked.

She pulled back and looked up into his face.

'I do,' she said. 'You're beautiful. A photographer's
dream.'

Craig opened his mouth and laughed out loud,
exposing a mouthful of gleaming white teeth.

'Well, thank you, ma'am,' he said. 'I'm much
obliged.' And he leaned down and kissed her again.

To Jane the kiss seemed to last forever and she felt herself going weak again. She pulled back. 'Craig,' she said. 'I think you're going to be a dangerous man for me to know.'

'I hope so,' he said.

Craig led Jane across the gallery to where a leather sofa stood next to the window. Outside, twilight was coming and a gentle diffused light fell across the floor. Craig pushed the sofa round so that the back was facing the top of the stairs and anyone standing there would not be able to see over the back of it.

'Sit down with me,' said Craig. 'I think we need to get acquainted properly.'

Jane smiled. She couldn't have agreed more.

She joined Craig on the sofa and they cuddled up together and started kissing again. Craig ran his hands down the front of her body and she shivered in anticipation of what was going to happen next.

Their kisses got more passionate and Craig pushed up the short skirt of her dress to expose the peach-coloured panties she was wearing beneath it. He looked longingly at the mound of her pubis and slid his hand between her legs and felt at the crotch of her underpants.

'That feels lovely,' she said and wriggled round so that she could open her legs to allow him easier access.

She looked down and marvelled at the contrast between the black skin on the back of his hand and the whiteness of the skin on her thighs. The sight made her more excited and she could smell her own sex in the warm, still air that filled the deserted room they were in.

She put her own hand down to the bulge in his jeans and said, 'Is it true?'

'What?' he asked in reply.

'You know,' she said. Suddenly shy.

'What?' he asked again, but this time she saw him smile.

'About black men's cocks.'

'What about them?' he teased.

'*You know.*'

He laughed out loud then. 'Say it,' he insisted.

'No,' she said. 'I can't.'

'Yes, you can.'

She plucked up courage. 'That they're *huge*,' she said.

He put on an exaggerated southern American accent, 'And dat we got natural rhythm.' He laughed again after he said it and gathered her up in his arms.

'You'll have to tell me, Jane honey. I ain't had that much experience of other men's cocks myself. Why don't I show it to you and you can let me know.'

Jane was breathless with excitement as he peeled off his shirt to expose the beautiful physique of his chest, then unzipped his jeans and pushed them down his legs. He was naked underneath the denims and she could hardly believe the size of his prick as it sprang up before her eyes.

'Christ!' she said. 'It is true. Do you expect to get all of that inside me?'

'I haven't had any problems before. Or any complaints.'

'I bet you haven't,' she said as she looked down at his swollen penis. It stood straight up, proud and erect before her. It had to be fully a foot long and easily as thick as her own wrist. His pubic hair was dense and black, with an oily sheen to it that glistened in the light, and underneath his balls were fat and round and hard-looking. The skin on his prick was darker than that on the rest of his body and, at the end of the huge weapon, the knob of it seemed to be as large as a tennis ball; the narrow slit in the end was open and, inside, the flesh was the colour of raspberry ice-cream.

She touched it almost fearfully. It was as hard as a rock and she could feel the heat of it so intensely that she imagined that it almost burnt her fingers.

She looked up into his eyes and said, 'It's the most beautiful thing I've ever seen. I want it, Craig. I want you to fuck me.'

He grinned back. 'It'll be a pleasure, Jane, believe me.'

'But you won't hurt me, will you? Promise you won't hurt me.'

'I'll never hurt you. Take my word on it.'

'I do,' she said.

'But first I'm going to pleasure you in a different way.'

'Anything,' she breathed.

Craig pulled her dress over her head and dropped it onto the floor beside the sofa. Underneath, as he had guessed, she was wearing no bra. Her breasts moved slowly in time with her breathing and he reached out and touched the creamy skin on them, and her nipples reddened and hardened. He moved from the sofa onto the thick carpet that covered the floor, lifted Jane's legs, removed the brief material of her panties and dropped them carelessly on top of her dress.

She was running her hands over her breasts, her eyes

closed, when he knelt between her legs. Sharp sounds came from her throat and she arched as his mouth and tongue moved on her. It was only seconds until her muscles tightened against him and she cried out. Craig continued, and soon she began to move spasmodically again, more slowly this time, the urgency gone. Quieter, but more intense, noises emerged from deep within her.

She lay back and Craig joined her on the sofa again. Soundlessly she reached for his hard cock and held it in one hand. She tried to close her fingers round it but they wouldn't meet. 'God,' she whispered. 'Dominic said you were going to be massive, but not this massive.'

Craig smiled at her tenderly. 'Did you like what I just did?' he asked.

She nodded. 'It was beautiful. Will you fuck me now?'

'Yes, babe,' he said, and pushed her back onto the cool, slick leather of the sofa, spread her legs and mounted her in one smooth movement.

Jane felt his huge prick poking at the lips of her cunt and she put her hands down and found the knob of it. Once again she marvelled at the size.

'It'll never fit,' she said fearfully. 'It's too big for me.'

He pushed down urgently. 'I want you,' he said. 'Trust me.'

With a mixture of trepidation and longing, she guided the tremendous ball of blood-gorged flesh into the centre of her and suddenly she could feel her cunt being stretched by its hugeness.

'No, Craig,' she cried, frightened once again.

257

'Relax,' he said. 'Groove on it,' and he pushed himself into her gently.

She felt her flesh and muscle resist for a second, then open. There was a stab of intense pain and she tensed, then suddenly he was up inside her and she could only feel pleasure – pleasure like she'd never known before with any other man. It felt as if his cock was filling all her body. The heat of it spread from her womb, up through her breasts to every pleasure point in her brain and she almost swooned at the sensation.

'Christ!' she cried. 'Christ, Craig. That's wonderful.'

He began to move inside her. Slowly at first, then faster. With every movement of his prick, the pleasure increased, until her whole world consisted of the foot-long piece of flesh that filled her cunt and womb.

She called his name again and again and her fingernails ripped at the smooth black skin of his back until they drew blood.

Still he fucked her. Harder and harder until his body was just a blur in the fading light. Then he stopped, his cock buried deep inside her body, and as his spunk jetted into her like boiling oil, she pulled his head down and mashed her mouth to his and came over him with a savage intensity that she had never known in her life before.

Afterwards, they both lay as if dead, Craig's body covering hers, his cock still deep inside her and dribbling more hot spunk to join the river of it that coated the inside of her. She loved the feel of the weight of him on top of her. After a few minutes she began to stroke the back of his head.

He raised it and looked into her eyes. 'Good?' he asked.

'The best. The best ever,' she said.

'Did I hurt you?'

'Only for a second.'

'Then?'

She scrunched up her face and grinned. 'Then it was magnificent.'

'I think you took most of the skin off my back,' he said.

She bit her lip. 'I'm sorry, darling,' she said. 'Did I hurt *you*?'

'Only a little,' he replied.

He eased himself off her body and pulled his cock out of her. It had hardly softened at all and she was amazed at his staying power. The black skin was covered in a mixture of his come and her lubricant and it gleamed like the paintwork on a new car. She reached out and ran her fingers down it and collected some of the juice which she licked off her fingers. It tasted delicious. Sweet, salty and pungent all at once. And she told him so.

'What do you want to do?' he asked. 'Go back to the party?'

'I want to stay here all night with you and make love till dawn,' she said.

'What about David Powell?' he asked. 'Won't he be looking for you?'

'Who cares if he is? He can take care of himself.'

Craig smiled. 'I hoped you'd say that. Does that mean you're my woman now?'

'For as long as you want me,' she said, and he reached out and gathered her up in his strongly muscled arms and kissed her on the mouth again.

32

After he left Jane and Craig, David made his way out into the hall and wandered down a corridor towards the side of the house. He didn't know where he was going and couldn't have cared less. Jade's absence had got to him more than he cared to admit. Bitch, he thought as he went. And that bastard of a photographer. It would be a long time until he trusted a woman again. As for Jane, what the hell? It had been fun while it lasted, but nothing goes on forever. Especially not in the rock-and-roll business. David had seen the way she looked at the black guy. He was welcome to her.

David went through a set of swing doors and saw a flight of stairs leading downwards. He took them. When he reached the bottom another corridor dog-legged away and he followed it.

He sniffed the air as he went and could smell chlorine. Then he remembered Sly mentioning a swimming pool in the basement. David fancied a dip. It might relax him and take his mind off his worries. Not that he should have any. A number one single in Britain. An album that would soon join it at the top of the LP charts and what looked like one of the biggest hits by a UK band in the States for ages.

Everything he'd always wanted – and for what?

Sod Jade, he thought again, as he came to another set of swing doors which he opened, and found himself in the pool itself.

There were only two people inside. One was Donkey and the other, a dark-haired girl he didn't recognise.

Donkey was lying on the diving board, dressed only in his underpants. As far as David could tell through the green opaqueness of the water where the girl was swimming, she was naked.

'Hello, Dave,' greeted Donkey. 'How's it going?'

'Crap,' replied David.

'It's all right down here,' said Donkey. 'All the comforts of home.'

'Since when did you have this at home?' asked David.

Donkey laughed his unique honk. 'Never. But who knows? Now you blokes are international stars.'

'Save it,' said David. 'Who's she?'

'Derek's bird. But he's not about, so I've taken her over.'

'What's her name?'

'Fuck knows. I call her Boiler.'

David laughed and felt his mood lighten. 'You're such a wanker, Donkey,' he said.

'But good value for money.'

'You can say that again.'

As David spoke the girl surfaced, shook the water out of her hair and stood at the shallow end looking at David. 'Hi,' she said.

He looked at her. Her hair was short, and the water plastered it close to her scalp. She had a pretty, gamine face with a tiny, pert nose and full lips. And he'd been right. She was naked. As she stood bobbing up and down in the water, her tiny breasts bobbed with her. A most diverting sight, he thought. And he could now clearly see the dark triangle of hair between her legs.

'Hi yourself,' said David.

'You're David Powell, aren't you?'

'I was the last time I looked in the mirror.'

'I'm Sunshine.'

'Is that right? I thought your name was Boiler.'

'That's just Donkey's idea of a joke.'

'You came down with Derek?'

'Yeah. I pulled him last night. Then he brings me down here to a pop group's party. Great isn't it?'

David shrugged.

'I loved that dinner we had,' she went on. 'Kinky, or what?'

'Depends what turns you on.'

'Drugs and men mostly,' she replied.

'Fair enough,' said David. 'Why you hanging out with roadies, then?'

'They're cool,' replied Sunshine.

'What, him?' asked David, gesturing in the direction of Donkey, who exploded with laughter again.

'Leave him,' said Sunshine. 'He's OK.'

David laughed too. 'If you say so,' he said.

'Except he can't swim,' said Sunshine. 'Can you?'

'Sure. That's why I came down.'

'Come on in then, there's room for one more.'

David took off his clothes except for the brief underpants he was wearing and prepared to dive into the water.

'Are you chicken?' asked Sunshine.

He shook his head.

'This pool is for skinny-dippers only.'

David shrugged, peeled off his briefs. Threw them at Donkey, who caught them one-handed, and jumped into the water.

It was warm and refreshing and he ploughed across in the direction of Sunshine. He loved the feel of the water on his bare genitals and felt his prick harden as the current he caused with his passage gently caressed it.

She watched as he made for her, then dropped back into the water and swam along the side of the pool away from him.

He saw her going and changed direction. The pool was big, Olympic size, and she was a strong swimmer. But he was stronger. David caught her halfway up the length of it and grabbed her ankle. She turned and tried to kick away but he had her. His other hand ran up the length of her leg and he felt the silkiness of the hair between her legs, before she managed to escape. She swam away again, but he soon caught her and that time his hand unerringly found the curve of one breast. She trod water and pushed him away, but once again he was too strong and caught her up in his arms and kissed her, half underwater. She kissed him back and they both reared out of the water, laughing.

Donkey was running along the side of the pool waving David's briefs in the air. 'Leave her, Dave,' he shouted and his voice echoed round the vast room. 'She's mine.'

'Not in here, she isn't,' said David through a mouthful of water. 'She's my water baby. You should have taken swimming lessons.' And he kissed Sunshine again.

264

She kissed him back firmly and her hands ran down to his cock and balls. Then she turned in the water and dived down until her mouth found them. She was only underwater for a moment before she had to resurface, blowing water.

'Don't drown,' he said.

'I won't, but I might choke.'

Donkey was dancing on the edge of the pool above them. 'Not fair,' he cried.

'Bollocks,' said David. 'All's fair in love and war. Come on, Sunshine,' he whispered in her ear. 'Let's find somewhere private.'

'The changing rooms,' she whispered back. 'Down there,' and looked towards the opposite end of the pool from where David had entered. Then they swam together across the width of the pool and pulled themselves up onto the side, then ran in the direction she'd indicated. Donkey tried to head them off, but they were too quick for him, and ran into the first changing room they came to, where David slammed the door behind them and slipped the lock.

Donkey was only seconds behind them and started banging on the door. 'Open up, Dave,' he demanded.

'Go away, Donkey,' David shouted back. 'Go and fix some amps or something.'

'You bastard. I'll get even with you for this.'

'Go away,' repeated David. 'This is your master's voice speaking.'

The banging ceased and in the silence that followed David looked round the room. Towels hung on heated rails and there were lockers and a long padded bench to sit on.

'That seemed to work,' he said and Sunshine giggled.

'You're wicked,' she said.

'You'll soon find out *how* wicked,' he promised her and dragged her over to the bench.

They sat down together and kissed. Her skin was slick, wet and hot, and tasted slightly of chlorine.

Their mouths glued together, then they kissed each other's necks, and David's mouth went down to her small, round breasts and he felt the nipples grow hard on his tongue.

Sunshine's hand found his balls again and gently cupped them and stroked the wet pubic hair with her thumb. His ministrations at her breasts increased. He bit the soft skin until she gasped with pleasure and her fingers wanked his cock until he was afraid he would come. He pushed her hand away, slid off the bench, knelt between her legs and kissed her pussy. She opened her legs and he stuck his tongue deep inside her where the taste of female replaced that of the chlorine. She leaned back against the wall as he continued to suck and kiss her. After a few minutes when the only sound in the room was the slurping of his mouth on her cunt, and her excited breathing, he pulled her down onto the cool stone floor and turned so that she could put his cock into her mouth. She did as he wished without him asking and sucked on his prick until he was within a few seconds of shooting his load down her throat. He pulled away, slid her round, pushed her legs apart and drove his cock into her love slit. She cried out as he roughly entered her, then put her ankles onto his calves as he began to hump her. They kissed excitedly as he rode her. Then within a few strokes he climaxed.

'What about me?' she demanded as he pushed himself to his feet.

'I told you I was wicked, didn't I?' he said and opened the door and saw Donkey sitting dejectedly on the diving board again. 'She's primed and ready, Donk,' said David. 'As long as you don't mind taking sloppy seconds.'

'Who me?' said Donkey in reply. 'I love it.'

'I just knew you would. Get in there, son, and fill your boots.'

Donkey jumped up from where he was sitting, as David gathered up his clothes and left the pool room.

The roadie ran down to the changing room, where Sunshine was still lying, legs apart, with David's sperm dribbling out of her open pussy, down her legs and dripping to the floor.

Donkey stood at the door and looked at her.

'What are you waiting for?' she asked. 'A written invitation? Come and finish me off, I'm as horny as hell. That selfish bastard just left me like this.' And she opened her arms and legs even wider in willing anticipation.

Donkey didn't have to be asked twice. He pulled down his underpants and took David's place on top of Sunshine's body.

His cock was rigid and her cunt was open and he was inside her and pumping within a second.

His balls were banging against the cheeks of her arse as he screwed away at her slender body.

Sunshine loved the different feel, movement and texture of his body, and was soon moving with him eagerly. Her cunt was like a swamp of come and slippery lubricant, and when Donkey's prick rubbed against her clitoris she came with a yell. Goaded to greater heights by her eagerness, Donkey crashed his body against hers and she wrapped her legs around his waist and hung onto his neck as his pace increased.

'Let me get on top,' she gasped. 'You're breaking my back.'

Donkey ceased his endeavours and, still joined at the groin, they rolled over on the floor so that Sunshine could ride him. She sat astride his body, knees on the floor, back straight, head up, with both hands on his shoulders, so that his cock was sticking right up through the middle of her, and manipulated her cunt on top of it until he could bear the feeling no more and his come boiled up inside her like a fountain.

She looked down and grinned into his face. 'That's much better, Donkey,' she said. 'Who needs a rock star when there's a roadie around?'

33

When Tony left the room where he'd watched Mandy and Anya consummate their affair, he went straight downstairs to look for Sonja, pausing only to grab a fresh joint from Sly.

'What's going on?' asked the rhythm guitarist.

'What I told you.'

'What? Your bird and Anya?'

Tony nodded.

'Fuck me, Tone, you promised you'd come and fetch me.'

'Sorry, mate. It all happened too quick. But don't worry, it's all down on film. We'll have a look another time.'

'I'll say. World premier. Ice cream, Kiaora. The lot. What are they doing now?'

'Christ knows. Dom's gone to sort them out.'

'Lucky bleeder,' said Sly. 'I wish I was there.'

'Where's Sylvia?' asked Tony.

'Gone for a slash. She'll be back in a minute unless that dirty Ozzie bastard's got 'old of her again. I'd better go and see. Where are you off to?'

'Unfinished business with our new promoter's little sister.'

'Oh well, son, Good luck.'

'Cheers, mate. See you in a bit.'

Sly winked. 'I don't think so. Here comes old Sylvia now. I'm going to drag her off for a bit of the other. And the way I feel it could take all night. Eyes down for a full house.'

Tony grinned at his cockney friend. 'Have fun,' he said and, still holding the joint, he headed in the direction of the bar.

'Sir?' said the barman at his approach.

'Got a bottle I could have?' asked Tony. 'Something that'll fit in my pocket.'

The barman reached under the table and brought out a half bottle of white wine. 'Would this do, sir?' he asked. 'It is chilled.'

'You're a marvel,' said Tony and slid the bottle into the pocket of his jacket.

'Do you need an corkscrew?' asked the barman.

'It's sorted,' said Tony and moved through the crowd towards the window and into the garden.

He found Sonja where he'd left her, still on the bench by the trees talking to Derek and Vanessa.

'Hello, you lot,' he said. 'I'm glad I found you.'

'Hello, Tony,' said Derek. 'Everything OK?'

'Never better,' said Tony. 'Who wants some of this?' Holding up the joint.

'You're a life-saver,' said Derek and grabbed a quick toke before passing the joint to Vanessa, who was already looking a little glassy-eyed and unsteady on her feet from what she'd had previously. 'She's not used to all this,' said the roadie.

'I hope you don't take advantage,' said Tony.

'What, me?' asked Derek. 'No, mate. Not my style.'

270

'You can if you like,' said Vanessa, with a giggle in her voice. 'I don't mind.'

'What *can* you do?' said Derek and reached over and pulled Vanessa closer to him and kissed the tip of her nose.

'What did your manager want?' asked Sonja.

'Nothing much. Business, you know,' replied Tony.

Vanessa passed the joint to Sonja so that she could put her arms round Derek, and Sonja took a drag before passing it back to Tony.

'Shall we leave these two to it?' he asked.

Sonja looked at her friend. 'Will they be all right?'

'You heard her,' replied the guitarist. 'She wants to be taken advantage of.'

'She's very naive.'

'She won't be after Derek's taken care of her.'

'That's what I'm worried about,' said Sonja.

'Come on, leave them,' urged Tony. 'He won't hurt her. He's a good bloke. She might just learn a bit about life.'

'I don't know,' said Sonja. 'Vanessa. Are you OK?'

She and Derek were snogging busily at the other end of the bench and, when she heard her name, the brown-haired girl looked up. 'Lovely,' she said. 'I do like this man.'

Sonja shrugged. 'I'm going for a walk with Tony. OK?'

Vanessa nodded.

'Be careful,' warned Sonja, but Vanessa was already kissing Derek's neck again and appeared not to hear.

Sonja shrugged again. 'Well, I did warn her.' Then she took Tony's hand and they walked together across the lawn and into the woods.

271

Inside the bank of trees it was quite dark and Tony pulled Sonja closer. 'Be careful,' he said. 'Don't trip over.'

'I'm a country girl,' said Sonja. 'I know woods at night.'

'Do you? How interesting.'

Sonja slapped his arm. 'Don't you start,' she said. 'You know what I mean.'

'Do I?' he replied.

'I wish we had something to drink,' said the girl.

'No probs,' said Tony and took the cold bottle of wine out of his pocket.

'Hey, that's great.' Then her face fell. 'I bet you haven't got an opener.'

'Are you kidding? I haven't been on the road all these years without carrying one of these with me.' And from his trouser pocket he took a penknife with a corkscrew attachment.

'You're marvellous,' said Sonja.

'Hold that thought,' replied Tony as they entered a small grassy clearing, where the rising moon that could be seen above the tops of the trees threw a yellow light on a circle of darker grass in the centre.

'A fairy ring,' said Sonja. 'How fabulous. Can we stay here?'

'Wherever you want,' replied Tony.

'Have you got any glasses?' asked the girl, as she sat in the centre of the circle.

'No. Where I come from you drink from the bottle.'

'Suits me,' she replied.

Tony wrestled with the cork and the bottle opened with a slight pop. He took a swig and said, 'Most acceptable,' and passed it to Sonja before joining her on the grass that was still slightly warm from the heat of the day.

'This is great,' he said. 'Whaddya say?'

'Excellent,' she agreed.

They sat in companionable silence for a few minutes and Tony took out his cigarettes and lit two and gave one to Sonja.

'Tony,' she said.

'What?'

'What's the story?'

'How do you mean?'

'With me.'

He took the bottle back and sipped from the neck, then said, 'I don't know what you're talking about.'

'You don't have to impress me to get Joseph to put you on the tour.'

Tony laughed. 'Forget it. I wouldn't bother. It's you I'm interested in. There's loads of tours. Loads of promoters.' And he leant over and gently kissed her on the mouth. 'But there's only one of you.'

'How sweet of you to say that,' she said.

'Not really. I'm not generally noted for my sweetness. Just the opposite in fact. But it's true. Here and now. No strings. No commitments. It's you I'm interested in. Maybe tomorrow it'll be different. That's the way I am, the way this business has made me. If you can handle that, fine. If not, you'd better get up and go back and rescue your friend from Derek.'

'You're very cynical,' Sonja said sadly.

'No, I'm not. It's a fact.'

She sat and smoked her cigarette and looked at him in the moonlight. 'That suits me,' she said. 'Here and now is OK. We might all be blown up tomorrow.'

'My sentiments entirely.'

'So what do you want to do?'

'Fuck,' he replied.

Vanessa and Derek stayed on the bench kissing after Tony and Sonja went into the woods. Vanessa was extremely drunk and stoned and the earth seemed to be spinning around her as Derek's mouth glued itself to hers. Derek, on the other hand, was used to taking vast quantities of drugs and drink and was well in control of himself.

He pulled himself back from Vanessa and said, 'I fancy you.'

'I fancy you too,' she replied.

'Want to do something about it?'

She hesitated, then nodded.

'Where?'

She shrugged.

'I've got a room,' he said.

'What about Sonja?'

'Don't worry about her. She'll be cool with Tony.'

'Are you sure?'

'Sure I'm sure.'

'OK then.'

Derek stood up and pulled Vanessa to her feet. Then led her back across to the house and round the side to a door he'd discovered earlier. They went through and up some narrow stairs to the second floor where the roadies had been given a room each. He unlocked a door and led Vanessa inside.

The room was small but comfortably furnished with a double bed, wardrobe and chest of drawers. Derek went over and switched on a small lamp on the bureau next to the bed, then drew the curtains at the window tightly.

'Drink?' he asked.

'Have you got any water?'

'Just what's in the tap.' He gestured at the hand basin fixed to one wall. 'Are you sure you don't fancy a Scotch?'

Vanessa pulled a face. 'I don't think so,' she said. 'I'd probably pass out. Water will do fine.'

'Help yourself,' he said.

She went to the basin and rinsed out the glass that stood on the shelf above it and filled it with water.

Meanwhile Derek went to the chest, opened the top drawer and took out a half bottle of Scotch.

'I don't know how you can,' said Vanessa.

'Years of practice,' replied Derek, and sat on the bed. 'Come and join me.'

Vanessa did as he said.

'Are you feeling OK?' He asked.

Vanessa nodded. 'You're nice,' she said.

'Don't let too many people hear you say that. I've got my reputation to think of.'

She put the glass on the bureau next to the lamp and said, 'I'm a virgin.'

'Crikey,' said Derek. 'That's rare.'

She blushed. 'I'm sorry,' she said.

'Don't be,' he replied.

'But I don't want to be. Do you think you could fix it for me?'

The roadie laughed. 'With pleasure. And I mean that.'

'You won't hurt me too much, will you?'

'I'll try not to.'

'I'm sure you won't. Do you want me to undress?'

'It's a start, I suppose,' replied Derek.

Vanessa stood up and pulled the simple dress she was wearing over her head. Underneath she was dressed in a white bra and matching bikini briefs.

'Very virginal,' said Derek.

'Don't you like them?'

'Course I do. Don't be paranoid.'

'It's just that all my friends have done it,' said Vanessa. 'I've told them I have too. But I've never met anyone I liked enough.'

'And you like me?' said Derek. 'I've only known you five minutes.'

She shrugged. 'I always knew I'd know as soon as I saw the right man.'

'I'm flattered.'

'So you should be.'

'Come here,' he said.

She did as she was told and sat on the bed next to him. She smelled fresh and clean.

Derek kissed her on the side of her mouth and she kissed him back with great vigour. His hands ran down her back and found the fastening of her bra. He opened it one-handed, exposing her breasts. He slid the straps off her shoulders and the garment fell into her lap, and he tossed it onto the chest of drawers. Her breasts were round, soft and full. The nipples hot and pink. He took one between his finger and thumb and gently teased it to hardness. Vanessa moaned with pleasure as he did it. They kissed again, open-mouthed, long and hard, and he dug his fingers in to her breast as he sucked at her tongue. She began to undo the buttons on his shirt and pulled it out of the waistband of his trousers. His cock was getting hard and she saw the bulge and ran her fingers along the length of it and made it grow more.

'Those trousers are so sexy,' she said. 'I love the feel of leather.'

'Me too,' said Derek and leant down and caught one nipple in his mouth and sucked, licked and gently bit it until Vanessa cried a small cry. He smiled to himself and came up for more kisses on her lips, neck, ears, eyes and nose.

As he was kissing her, he caught her breasts up in one hand and flattened them together and against her rib cage. The flesh flowed between his fingers like rubber.

She pushed his shirt off and the air in the room felt sticky and warm on his naked skin. She raked his spine gently with her fingernails, down to the waistband of his trousers, then round the front to find the button that fastened it. She popped it open and gently slid the zip down. His cock was hard inside the tightness of the skin and it was a relief to allow it some freedom.

He reached down and pulled off his boots and socks and slid the trousers under his buttocks and down his legs and kicked them off his feet. His cock poked up through the material of his underpants and he saw Vanessa eyeing the lump.

'Like it?' he asked and his voice was husky.

She nodded. 'It scares me,' she said.

He smiled into her face. 'Don't be frightened,' he said. 'I told you I wouldn't hurt you.'

'I know. It's just that I've never seen one before. Close up. In the flesh.'

He smiled again at her choice of words. 'You haven't seen this one yet,' he said.

'I know.'

'Do you want to?'

'Of course.'

'I'll show you mine, if you'll show me yours.'

'I haven't got one . . .' Then she stopped and giggled.

'You know what I mean, silly,' he said. And kissed her again.

They both stood up and, looking at each other, they slowly peeled off their underpants.

Vanessa's pubic hair was light brown and very fine. Derek's was ginger-coloured, thick and wiry, and the fat flesh of his knob stuck up out of it fully erect.

Vanessa shyly moved her hand to cover her mound.

'Don't do that,' said Derek. 'It's beautiful.'

'No it's not,' she replied. 'It's all lopsided.'

'Who's isn't?'

'I don't know.'

'Take my word for it.'

'Are you sure?'

'Sure I am.'

'Are you telling the truth?'

He nodded.

Her face lit up. 'That's great,' she said. 'You don't like to look at other girl's ones, if you know what I mean.'

'It's the same with men,' he said. 'They're all different shapes and sizes. Don't worry about it.'

'Yours is beautiful,' said Vanessa.

'My what?'

'You know.'

278

He shook his head, then said. 'No. You tell me.'

'Your thing.' She gestured in the direction of his groin.

'My *what*?'

She reddened with embarrassment. 'Your cock,' she whispered.

'That's better. Call it what it is. It turns me on.'

'Does it?'

'Sure.'

'What do you call mine?'

'Your cunt.'

'I hate that word.'

'There's nothing wrong with it.'

'It's horrible.'

He shook his head. 'It's not. You say it.'

It was her turn to shake hers. 'I couldn't.'

'Sure you can. It's just a word.'

'It's dirty.'

'Only if you've got a dirty mind. It's a beautiful word. Go on. Say it. That'll turn me on too.'

'Will it?'

'Sure.'

'Cunt,' she whispered.

'Louder.'

'Cunt,' she said.

'Louder.'

'*Cunt*,' she almost shouted, and he pulled her into his arms and kissed her again and she felt the heat and hardness of the skin of his prick push into her belly.

'That's better,' he said. 'I like to hear you talk dirty.'

'Do you?'

'Sure I do.'

'I'll do whatever you like. Always.'

'Anything?' he asked.

'Anything you want.'

'Promise.'

She nodded.

'Suck my cock.'

She slid down his body to her knees and took the length of hot flesh in her hands and shyly touched her lips to the tip of it.

'Open your mouth,' he ordered.

She did as she was told and he felt the warm wetness of her saliva on the knob of his weapon.

'Take it right in.'

She opened her mouth wider and allowed his knob into it. Her tongue touched the hole and Derek's whole body stiffened at the sensation. She parted her lips still wider and as he looked down he saw first a quarter, then half of the length of it disappear into her mouth until she almost gagged as the beast filled it and it started to slide into the back of her throat. He pulled gently back, then pushed his cock slowly into her orifice again, and felt the hardness of her teeth gently scratch the skin.

'Don't bite,' he said.

She mumbled something he couldn't understand and he pulled the slick length of his prick all the way out of her mouth and said, 'What did you say?'

She looked up. 'I wouldn't hurt it, Derek. I like it too much.'

'Come here,' he said and pulled her to her feet, then moved her in the direction of the bed where he gently lowered her onto the bedspread and lay next to her.

'You're beautiful,' he whispered.

'Thank you,' she breathed.

They began to kiss again, covering each other's faces with hot, wet saliva. Derek stuck his tongue in Vanessa's ear and she called out his name in passion.

He drifted his fingers down her body until he found her pubic mound and ran his fingers through the hair until he discovered her opening. It was wet and sticky, just as he knew it would be. He enlarged the hole with his finger, running it around the hot inside of her until she squealed.

He knew she was ready and so was he. Her hand was running up and down the hardness of his prick, and he climbed on top of her and she opened her legs wider to allow him easy access.

'Put me inside you,' he said.

He felt her move his cock until the knob pressed into the wet flesh and with one slippery motion it was in. He forced himself to slide it slowly down the length of her cunt, but even so she screamed one short scream of pain before he pierced her hymen and he was properly penetrating her.

'Oh God,' she said. 'That hurt.'

'Are you all right now?' he asked.

She opened her eyes and looked up into his. 'Yes,' she said. 'Oh yes. It feels so good. It was worth it.'

He smiled down on her and began to move his prick in and out of her pussy and he could feel the squelch of liquid between their skin. 'It feels so good,' he said. 'You're soaking.'

As he lifted his body off hers, he peered down the length of them and looked at the skin of his cock as it pulled out of her. It was pink with blood.

'Have you got your period?' he asked.

She shook her head.

'Then you're definitely not a virgin any more.' And he laughed and after a moment she joined in.

They carried on fucking. Derek trying to be gentle but all the time feeling the need to pump Vanessa hard until, as he felt the first tickle of orgasm in his scrotum, he began to move faster and faster. She grabbed his biceps with her fingers and dug the nails deep into the muscle. 'Yes,' she cried. 'Yes, baby. Go faster. I love it.'

Derek did as she said. He pushed his feet against the wooden end of the bed to gain purchase and rammed his cock as hard and deep into her as he could and the sound of squelching got louder.

Vanessa's breath shortened and he could feel the heat of it on his neck as his strokes became more gentle again, until he was only moving his cock inside her a fraction of an inch at a time to prolong the pleasure he was feeling. Eventually he could bear it no more. 'I'm going to come,' he shouted joyously and shot long, delicious spurts into the centre of her, before he collapsed on top of her body.

They lay there together for long minutes until Derek pulled himself clear and slumped next to her. His cock was red with blood and come and he wiped himself on the bedspread. 'Was it good?' he asked.

'Very.'

'Did you come?' Although he was sure she hadn't.

'I don't know.'

'Then you didn't.' And he slid down until his face was over the heat and perfume of her quim and he licked at the pink liquid that oozed out from it until she stiffened as he found her clitoris.

'Christ!' she exclaimed, 'What are you doing?'

He didn't reply, being too busy concentrating on the small piece of erect flesh he was poking with his tongue.

She exhaled a long excited breath and her thighs opened and he licked at her until, from deep inside, he felt her begin to shake and shiver with delight as she began to feel her orgasm beginning. He tongued her harder, pulling out her clitoris with his lips and sucking it even harder.

Her hand grasped at his hair and her shivering increased until at last, almost painfully, she orgasmed into his mouth.

When Tony and Sonja had finished their cigarettes and most of the bottle of wine was gone, she reached over and pulled him closer. 'Give me a hug,' she said. 'I think it's beginning to cool down.'

He did as she said and took her into his arms and felt the warmth of her body melt into his.

Where they were under the trees, it was almost fully dark, with just a glimmer of the evening light permeating into the clearing. Just enough so that a little reflected off her skin and glinted in her eyes.

'You can if you want,' she said.

'What?'

'Fuck me.'

'Are you sure you want to? You seem a little sad.'

'I'm not sad. Just lonely.'

'What about all those boyfriends you were telling me about?'

He felt her shrug in his embrace. 'Just guys,' she said. 'Nothing special.'

'What about girlfriends? Vanessa, for instance?'

'She's cool,' replied Sonja. 'But I still get terribly lonely.'

'You don't have to be lonely tonight.'

'I know.'

He kissed her. A long sweet kiss that made him feel as sad as she had said she was. 'You're different,' he said.

'Is that right?'

'Yes.'

'Why?'

'I'm not sure. But I just know you are. You've got something. Something that I haven't seen in a long time.'

'Like what?'

'Like . . .' He ran his fingers along the skin on the back of her hand. 'Like magic,' he said.

'You're nice.'

'You too.'

'So shall we . . .?'

'If you want.'

'I do. I think you're magic, too.'

Tony pushed her back onto the grass and they started to kiss again. More long lingering kisses, as soft and sweet as the first, but with a backdraft of passion that neither of them could ignore.

He closed his eyes and felt the earth shift under him as the fairy ring seemed to spin slowly, taking them with it. 'God, it is magic,' he said.

'I told you,' she whispered, her breath rasping in his ear. 'The fairies are taking care of us.'

Tony ran his hand down the silkiness of her shirt towards the crotch of her jeans. 'Wait,' said Sonja and sat up and tugged off her boots and peeled off the white cotton socks she was wearing beneath them. 'That's better,' she said. 'You can carry on now.'

He rubbed her flesh through the tight denim and her breath caught in her throat. 'Undress me,' she said. 'I want to feel the grass on my body.'

Tony stripped off her shirt. Underneath it her breasts were naked and he could see in the gloom that they were small and pointed. He unfastened her jeans and rolled them over her hips and pulled them down her legs and off. Beneath her jeans she was wearing a pair of black, lacy pants, pulled up tight against her cunt.

Tony hurriedly undressed, filled with a mixture of lust and something else. Something he hadn't felt for a long time. A longing to be a part of Sonja's body. But also part of her mind. Part of the very essence of her. Her spirit.

He pulled her close, so that he could see her expression in the faint light. 'You are so beautiful,' he whispered, as if speaking loudly would break the spell.

'You too, baby,' she said.

He buried his head into the heat of her breasts and felt the skin of them slick against his face; he could hear her heart beating fast inside her rib cage.

Her hands stroked the back of his neck and all at once he knew that he had never felt as happy in his life. He smiled into the flesh and caught some between his teeth and bit on it gently and she wriggled in his embrace.

He moved his face down across the slight roundness of her belly and into the fragrance between her legs. The smooth lace of her underwear rubbed against the skin of his face and he breathed in the perfume of her. He lay with his head between her legs for long minutes and the material of her underwear dampened from her secretions.

Eventually he moved back up until they were head to head again and they kissed as their hands roved over each other's bodies, discovering the secret places and the parts that gave them pleasure.

At some point Tony peeled her panties off and, before throwing them into the darkness, put the wet gusset to his lips to taste her juices.

They kept moving round each other, finding new places to explore with their mouths and fingers until Tony was as hard as he could ever remember being and Sonja was wet and open for him.

They lay side by side and melted together as one, his prick sliding into her like a hot knife through warm butter.

They stayed as still as they could and both could feel the blood rushing through their veins. 'I am you,' he said.

'And I'm you,' she replied.

'I've never felt like this before.'

'Nor me.'

'I can feel every inch of your cunt.'

'And I can feel every inch of your cock.'

'I never want this to end,' he said.

'Me neither.'

'Will it ever be this good again?'

'We've got a lifetime to find out.'

'Do you mean it?'

'I knew from the moment I saw you,' she said.

'I didn't.'

'Just another conquest, was I?'

'Yes.'

'So, what's changed?'
'Being here with you.'
'I love you, Tony,' she said.
And with one huge push he came inside her, just as she covered his prick with her hot, sweet wetness.

34

When Sylvia got back from the loo, Sly grabbed her. 'You've been neglecting me,' he said.

She smiled a half-drunk, sticky, wet, lipsticky smile and said. 'No, babes. Not me.'

'You've been too busy with that faggoty DJ. Just because he's Australian, don't mean he can get it up, you know.'

'He's very interesting,' pouted Sylvia.

'Interested, more like. Interested in your tits. Too interested if you ask me.'

'I thought you said he was faggoty.'

'Some people swing both ways,' said Sly, and thought wistfully of Anya and Mandy together in some sultry room upstairs.

'I don't,' said Sylvia.

'You will if I tell you to,' replied Sly.

'Want to bet?'

He grinned. 'Maybe sometime. But not now. Fancy a fuck?'

'Why not?' she said. 'Best offer I've had all night.'

'Even from Jolly Roger over there.'

'I'll tell you when we're all alone,' said Sylvia and licked her lips.

'I knew it,' said Sly. 'Dirty bastard.'

'Can we go upstairs?' asked Sylvia.

'Sure.'

Hand in hand, they left the party and went up to the second floor of the west wing where their room was located. Sly unlocked the door to let them in and locked it tightly behind them.

Sylvia posed beside the bed. 'Do you want to know what that DJ wanted me to do to him?'

Sly nodded.

'He wanted me to be his daughter.'

'Do what?'

'It's these.' She gestured down to her white socks. 'He said they really turned him on. He said he wanted me to be his daughter and be really naughty with him. Then he wanted to spank my bottom, with me just wearing these socks.'

'The dirty sod. What did you say?'

'I said I'd have to ask you. I wouldn't do it unless you were there.'

Sly grinned. 'Come here first,' he ordered.

She did as she was told and he pushed up her skirt and fumbled with his fly. When he freed his cock it was hard and red. He pushed her pants aside and felt for her hole. It was damp and humid.

'You want to do it, don't you?' he asked.

She nodded.

'But I'm going to give you this first,' he said and, still holding the elastic of her knicker leg with his finger, he pushed his knob into the plumpness of her pussy.

Sylvia stood with her hands on his shoulders as he rammed his cock into her. Back and forth he went until with a grunt he shot his load inside her.

He pulled out and let the elastic snap back. 'Go and fetch him then.'

Sylvia pulled her skirt down, checked her make-up in the mirror and, once satisfied, got the key from Sly and left.

She was back within a few minutes with the Australian DJ in tow.

'Hi, Sly,' he said drunkenly, his Australian accent very pronounced.

'Hi, Roj.'

'My name's Mike.'

'Not in here it's not. It's Jolly Roger. Sylvia's daddy.'

The DJ smiled. 'She told you then?' he said.

'I told you I did,' said Sylvia.

'And you don't mind?' said Mike.

'Not at all,' replied Sly. 'I'm just going to sit over here in my chair and watch you two.'

'I brought this,' said the DJ and pulled a half bottle of vodka from his jacket pocket. 'And these.' He slid two joints from his top pocket. 'And this for my little girl.' Finally he took a white pill from his shirt pocket.

'What's that?' asked Sly accepting the first hit from the bottle.

'A Mandrax.'

'A Mandy makes you randy, huh Roj?' said Sly, still thinking of the *other* Mandy. 'Good enough. Should be fun.'

'I've never had one of those before,' said Sylvia, taking the pill and swallowing it without looking and washing it down with a hefty slug of booze.

'Well, you have now,' said Sly and, taking the bottle back and extracting one of the joints from Mike's hand, he did as he said he would and went and sat down.

Sylvia bent one leg like a little girl, put one finger in her mouth, and said in a breathless voice to Mike, 'What do you want me to do Daddy?'

He grinned salaciously. 'Get undressed down to your knickers and socks and get into bed. I hope you're wearing white ones.'

'I am, Daddy,' said Sylvia. 'I told you that before. Just like *you* like. But I've been naughty and wet them.' She looked over at Sly and winked, and he realised he had underestimated the girl he'd brought to the party with him.

'That is naughty,' said Mike. 'I might have to chastise you for that.'

'Goody,' said Sylvia and kicked off her shoes, tugged off her sweater and threw it into one corner, unhooked her bra and allowed her large breasts to swing free, tossed the garment at Sly and unzipped her miniskirt and let it drop to the floor.

She covered her breasts with one arm and ran over to the bed and jumped in, pulling the covers up to her throat.

The DJ walked over after her and perched on the edge of the mattress. 'Aren't you asleep yet, darling?' he asked.

'I can't, Daddy,' lisped Sylvia, getting into the part. 'I'm not tired yet.'

'You need to relax, darling.'

'Will you help me, Daddy?'

'Of course. I'll just rub your tummy.' And he put his hand under the covers and Sly watched them move as he caressed Sylvia's stomach.

'Ooh, that's good,' she said.

'And why did you wet your knickers today?'

'It was an accident.'

'Let me feel.'

Sly saw her open her legs under the eiderdown and the DJ's hand moved lower.

'You are a *naughty* girl,' he said.

'I know, Daddy. I'm sorry.'

'I'm going to have to teach you a lesson.'

'What are you going to do?'

'Spank your bottom. But not yet.'

'What are you going to do first.'

'You'll see. Come and sit on my lap.'

'Must I?'

'Don't you want to?'

She nodded eagerly.

The DJ jumped up and ripped his clothes off, then lay on top of the eiderdown. Both Sly and Sylvia saw that his big, veined cock was rigid. 'Come on then,' he said.

Sylvia threw back the covers and got out of bed. The DJ had already half pushed her knickers down over her thighs and she finished the job, and holding them in one hand she straddled him. Almost before she was sitting over his groin she moaned and his cock jumped as she mounted it and sank down with a scream of pure pleasure. She rode him until he cried out too and shot into her.

'Oh Daddy,' she said as she got straight off him. 'That *was* naughty. Are you going to smack me now? I've kept my socks on specially for you.'

'Yes,' he said and rolled off the bed after her.

'You'll have to catch me first,' she said, laughing, and ran towards the bathroom door. But Mike was too quick for her. He caught her before she made it and dragged her back to the bed where he sat on the edge of the mattress again and tugged her over his naked lap and began to hit her bottom with the flat of his hand. She screamed and laughed at the same time as he beat at her naked flesh, until eventually he bent down and began to kiss the skin where Sly could clearly see the red fingermarks from his smacks.

Sylvia rolled over and soon the pair of them were kissing for real.

Sly watched as their kisses got deeper and Mike pulled Sylvia onto the eiderdown and mounted her. They were soon rocking together in a long slow fuck until Mike climaxed for the second time into Sylvia's cunt.

He rolled off her and was soon snoring deeply.

Sylvia got up and pulled her clothes onto her sticky body. 'He'll catch his death if he's not careful,' she said.

'He'll survive,' said Sly.

'Coming downstairs,' she said. 'I fancy another drink.'

And hand in hand they left the sleeping DJ to his erotic dreams and walked out of the room together.

35

After the fiasco in the car and the embarrassment that followed, Jud and Judy abandoned the party after dinner and went upstairs to Jud's room to talk.

'This is crazy,' said Judy when the door was shut behind them.

'Isn't it?' agreed Jud.

'We've only made love in bed once.'

'Now's our second chance,' he said.

'Are you sure you want to?'

He nodded.

'And then you don't call again. Is that how it goes?'

He made a clean breast of what he felt. 'I didn't think you wanted me to,' he said.

'I don't say things I don't mean.'

'I didn't know that.'

'Just another rock-and-roller's scalp for my belt, you mean?'

Jud shrugged. 'Like I said, I didn't know.'

Her face softened. 'I'm not just another groupie, Jud. I don't need to be. I've got power in this business. In swingin' old England anyway.'

'I'm beginning to realise that.'

'Then will you shut up and make love to me, before I burst.'

Jud took her in his arms and kissed her. He felt her breasts pushing against his chest and his cock hardened and he felt her ride it with her belly.

She pulled him towards the bed and they lay down together, her skirt sliding up to expose her crotch. Her white panties were stained from their previous exertions and he thought he'd never seen anything so horny in his life before.

'Undress me,' she said.

He tugged her dress over her head and helped her release her breasts from the white bra that matched her briefs and all at once he remembered what a beautiful figure she had. Her breasts were lush and the nipples were red and enlarged. He put them in his mouth one by one, wetting the tips with his saliva and sucking them up into his mouth until the hard gristle touched the back of his throat.

As he was concentrating on her tits, she was tearing at his clothes and buttons flew from his shirt as she pulled it out of the waistband of his trousers.

'Steady,' he said when he looked up. 'We've got all night.'

'I haven't,' she said. 'Get naked and screw me.'

Jud stood up, took off all his clothes and rejoined her on the smooth material of the eiderdown of the bed. It felt deliciously cool beneath the heat that Judy was generating in his skin.

She reached for his cock and began to tickle where the foreskin was joined at the top. It was a most delicious feeling, and he felt himself shiver from head to toe. 'Cold?' she asked.

'No,' he replied. 'Hot. Hot for you.'

'That's what I like to hear. Take my knickers off.'

As she continued her ministrations on his cock, he moved so that he could roll the thin material of her panties over her bottom and off her, and he put his face between the cheeks of her arse and found her arsehole with his tongue.

She giggled as he stuck it as deeply as he could into the orifice. 'That tickles,' she said.

He pushed her flat on her tummy and, using his own saliva as lubricant, he inserted his forefinger into the hole and gently wiggled it around until it opened and he could push his finger down as far as the knuckle and further.

He heard her breath catch in her throat and he said, 'Does that tickle, too?'

'No,' she said. 'You are naughty. Who taught you that?'

'No one. I just thought about it after watching your bottom all night.'

He opened the hole further until he could insert two fingers, then three.

'It hurts,' she panted.

'Shall I stop?'

'Don't you dare.'

As he pushed his fingers deeper into her, her breathing became more ragged and when she turned her head he could see that she was biting down on her lip. The thought that he was giving her pleasure and pain at the exact same moment excited him even further and he pressed deeper into her until, to his amazement if not hers, she began to rub her pussy on the mattress, bucking and heaving like a wild animal under the pressure in her anus. Suddenly, with a piecing scream, she orgasmed.

He withdrew his fingers and leaned over her and said, 'Are you all right?'

Judy rolled over onto her back. 'Are you kidding? That was amazing. Christ knows what you found in there, but it did the trick. Now, fuck me.'

'You're a glutton for punishment.'

'You ain't seen nuthin' yet.' And she pulled him down next to her and stuck her tongue in his mouth. He responded with deep kisses of his own then moved his mouth around her forehead, face and neck, and felt her kissing him where her mouth landed too. He kissed her shoulders and back, then round to her breasts again, and her hand began to play with the knob of his cock again.

'Fuck me,' she pleaded. 'I feel all empty inside. Like there's a vacuum between my legs and only you can fill it.'

'No,' he said.

'What?'

'You heard.'

'Oh Jud, don't tease me.'

'I'm not.'

He saw that there was genuine fear on her face at what he said.

'Have you gone off me?' she asked.

'No. I was just teasing,' he said. 'Honest.'

Then he realised that she was crying.

'Don't, sweetheart,' he said. 'Don't cry.'

'I'm sorry,' she sobbed. 'It's just . . .'

He gathered her up into his arms and felt her tears on his shoulder, then gently laid her head back onto the pillow and mounted her in one movement.

She hugged him close and he felt his cock slide gently into the swamp between her legs.

'Oh yes,' she breathed in his ear. 'Oh yes, Jud.'

They began to move together as if they'd been making love for years. Faster and faster they went. Deeper and deeper. Until their bodies were slapping together and the sweat broke out all over them. And faster still they moved until, simultaneously, Judy stiffened and came and Jud burst into the soft heart of her with what felt like a gallon of boiling hot jism.

36

David was walking down the corridor away from the swimming pool when he met Gloria walking towards him. 'Good evening, sir,' he said politely.

'Evening,' replied David. 'What's cooking in your little corner of the world?'

Gloria pulled a wry face under his mask. 'What do you require, sir?'

'Something interesting. I'm bored.'

'Mister Malcolm's in the snooker room with some companions.'

'Where's that?' asked David.

Gloria turned and pointed back down the corridor in the direction he'd come from. 'That way, sir. Second, no, third door on the left.'

'I'll go and check it out. Thanks,' said David, and walked in the direction that Gloria had indicated.

He found the door he was looking for and pushed it open. The room was dark except for the light over a full-sized snooker table that stood in the centre of the floor. A record player was cranking out 'Aftermath', by The Stones. A girl he had never seen before was doing an enthusiastic bump and grind striptease to one of the slower tracks in front of Big Mal and the two naked women who'd been used as serving dishes for the caviar at dinner. They were still wearing the leather chokers with chains attached that they'd been wearing earlier and nothing else. Mal and the girls were sitting on a leather chesterfield holding bottles of spirits, which all of them seemed to have been sampling to excess. The girl stripping seemed to have no inhibitions at all. Her dress and shoes were lying on the floor and, as David entered, she unhooked her scarlet lace bra, pulled it off and threw it over the fixture that illuminated the green baize of the snooker table, exposing a pair of truly massive breasts tipped with purple nipples. As she continued to dance, her breasts bounced and wobbled in a most exciting way.

David watched them move in time to the music as he walked over to the sofa.

'Hello, David,' slurred Mal. 'How you doin'?'

'Can't complain. Who the fuck is that?'

'Wendy, I think her name is. A friend of a friend of a very good friend of mine who I just met and seems to have vanished. I told her I reckoned she'd make a good stripper and she started taking her clothes off.'

'Makes sense,' said David. 'As much sense as anything else I've seen today. What are you drinking?'

'Rum,' said Mal. 'There's a bar over there somewhere.' He pointed off into the darkness that filled the corners of the room. 'What do you fancy?'

'I don't care,' replied David. 'Scotch, Bourbon. Anything.'

'I'll get you a bottle,' the big man said, levered himself up from the sofa and wandered unsteadily off into the shadows.

As the first song finished and the next one started, Wendy kept dancing without missing a beat. The next tune was faster and she began to dance faster herself, in time with the tempo of the music. Her eyes were closed and she caressed her body from neck to thighs as she moved, paying special attention to her pubic area, which was covered in a thin pair of scarlet lace panties which barely concealed the hairy bump at the front, or the twin orbs of flesh at the back. Her fingers ran up and down the clearly visible crack between her legs and teased the material of her panties down, then pulled them up again. David felt his prick harden at the sight of her, and it also seemed to be having some effect on the pair of women sitting on the chesterfield who were moving their naked bottoms on the upholstery in time to the music.

Mal reappeared carrying a bottle of Jack Daniel's which he gave to David. 'Enjoy,' he said.

David cracked open the bottle and raised the neck to his lips and took a jolt, the fiery liquid burning right down to his stomach. 'She don't give a shit, does she?' he said.

'No,' replied Mal. 'But that's what it's all about, isn't it?'

'You're right, mate. Absolutely. And what about these two then?' He asked pointing the bottle at the two naked girls sitting on the sofa and bouncing up and down to the beat of the music.

'Just part of the show,' said Mal.

'Do they smell a bit fishy to you?' David asked.

'So would you if you'd been covered in caviar all night. Anyway, all women smell fishy. You get used to it.'

'Yeah,' said David contemplatively and took another mouthful of Bourbon.

The two men stood and looked as Wendy continued her erotic dance.

'She's got some fucking tits, tell you what,' said David. 'I don't know how you do it, Malcolm.'

'Just trust your old uncle,' said Mal. 'Come on, Wendy,' he shouted. 'Don't take all night getting your knickers off. We all want to see what you've got.'

Wendy began to dance closer to David and Mal, moving in a slow circle in front of them, thrusting her pelvis and backside in their direction as she moved round.

'She's dying for a fuck,' said Mal. 'Feel like obliging, Dave? I fancy going case with this pair here. It's been years since I've had a threesome.'

'You want to watch?' asked the musician.

'If you don't mind.'

'Couldn't care less, mate. The way I feel right now, I'll do anything for a laugh.'

'Go for it, then,' said Mal and clapped the younger man on the shoulder, then moved away in the direction of the sofa.

As the track that was playing finished, Wendy wobbled over to David and pushed her groin into his. She grabbed the bottle of bourbon he was holding and took a deep swallow, spilling half of it down her chin. David licked the residue off her face and she kissed him messily. He made a grab for her but she moved away towards the snooker table. She jumped up onto it and continued to dance as the next track on the album began.

David jumped up to join her. He tore off his shirt

and unzipped his trousers, hopping about as he pulled them off, to expose his naked penis.

Wendy's eyes widened at the sight of it and she stopped dancing. 'Nice,' she said drunkenly.

'Go on, Dave,' shouted Mal, who had stopped halfway between the table and the sofa to watch what was happening. 'Give her a treat.'

David grabbed Wendy and kissed her roughly, his prick digging into the flesh of her belly. She kissed him back enthusiastically and they stood on the table, locked in a long embrace. As they kissed Wendy could feel David's cock growing harder and her cunt became wetter as it secreted the lubricants to make its passage easier, until the crotch of her pants was hot and dripping.

David pulled her down onto the green baize and they continued to kiss, oblivious of Mal and the two naked girls whose hot eyes watched their every move.

As the kisses continued, Wendy wrestled off her panties and David slid his hand into her pubic hair, found the entrance to her sex and inserted his middle finger. She pushed against it and found his member with her right hand and smiled at the thought of it filling her box to bursting point.

She lay back and David hoisted himself above her, found her entrance with the knob of his cock and bore down on her. Inch by inch she accepted his organ. The lips of her cunt rolling back as the weapon went deeper and deeper.

The two girls on the sofa could contain themselves no longer and, with a clank of chains, threw themselves into each other's arms.

Mal didn't know where to look first. His eyes moved

from the couple on the snooker table to the couple on the chesterfield.

David and Wendy were fucking enthusiastically, and the two girls were sixty-nining each other with their tongues deep in each other's muffs.

Mal grinned and took another swig of rum from the bottle he was holding and contemplated what he was going to do to the two girls after they'd finished licking each other out.

What a life, he thought. Rock and roll, I love it.

37

The sky began to lighten around four in the morning and as the brief darkness of the night lifted from Lambert House, it revealed the partygoers in various stages of undress scattered around the house and grounds.

Tony and Sonja were in the clearing in the woods where they'd made love. Their clothes were hanging on branches and littered across the soft grass where they lay.

Dominic was in bed between Anya and Mandy. The room was silent except for their breathing and, in the locked room next door, the empty reel of film in the movie camera mounted in front of the two-way mirror clicked softly as it continued to run sightlessly behind the lens.

Jud and Judy lay together in the double bed in his room, zonked out from too much booze, dope and sex.

David lay asleep in Wendy's arms on top of the snooker table where they had screwed each other. Both were still naked. Big Mal and the two girls in chokers and chains were also asleep in a heap on the chesterfield after Mal had fucked them both, one after the other.

Derek and Vanessa cuddled together in the bed in Derek's room where he had taken her virginity, as close as two spoons under the bedclothes.

Craig and Jane slept together on the sofa where they had made love. His hand covered the blondeness of her cunt and her hand rested on his groin.

Gloria had locked himself into a small cupboard he had found close to the attic. He sat on the bare wooden floor with his back against one of the walls thinking about all the things he had seen and done during the party, and fell asleep with a satisfied smile on his face.

Mike, the Australian DJ, slept on in Sly's room, sprawled on the satin bedspread, that was stained and sticky with come, dreaming of yet more perverse pleasures he hoped to enjoy in the future.

Donkey and Sunshine had gone back to his room, where they had made love again before they, too, fell asleep in each other's arms.

The only one of the band still conscious was Sly, who was standing outside the french windows of the drawing room sucking on a bottle of beer and looking at the bodies scattered around the lawn, as if war had broken out and the revellers had been mown down by gunfire.

Sylvia came out behind him. Her face was puffy from lack of sleep and too much sex. She touched him on the shoulder. He lowered the bottle from his mouth and turned round to face her. He was missing Nancy for some reason.

'Everyone's crashed out,' she said petulantly. 'Let's find somewhere where you can fuck me again.'

'You want more?' he asked in amazement.

'Always,' she said, and with a shrug he followed her back into the house and upstairs to look for an empty bed.

More Erotic Fiction from Headline:

Lustful Liaisons

Erotic adventures in the capital city of love!

Anonymous

PARIS 1912 – a city alive with the pursuit of pleasure, from the promenade of the Folies Bergère to the high-class brothels of the Left Bank. Everywhere business is booming in the oldest trade of all – the trade of love!

But now there is a new and flourishing activity to absorb the efforts of go-ahead men-about-town: the business of manufacturing motor cars. Men like Robert and Bertrand Laforge are pioneers in this field but their new automobile has a design defect that can only be rectified by some cunning industrial espionage. Which is where the new trade marries with the old, for the most reliable way of discovering information is to enlist the help of a lovely and compliant woman. A woman, for example, like the voluptuous Nellie Lebérigot whose soft creamy flesh and generous nature are guaranteed to uncover a man's most closely guarded secrets...

More titillating reading from Headline:
AMOROUS LIAISONS
LOVE ITALIAN STYLE
ECSTASY ITALIAN STYLE
EROTICON DREAMS
EROTICON DESIRES

FICTION/EROTICA   0 7472 3710 7

A selection of Erotica from Headline

FONDLE ON TOP	Nadia Adamant	£4.99 □
EROS AT PLAY	Anonymous	£4.99 □
THE GIRLS' BOARDING SCHOOL	Anonymous	£4.99 □
HOTEL D'AMOUR	Anonymous	£4.99 □
A MAN WITH THREE MAIDS	Anonymous	£4.99 □
RELUCTANT LUST	Lesley Asquith	£4.50 □
SEX AND MRS SAXON	Lesley Asquith	£4.50 □
THE BLUE LANTERN	Nick Bancroft	£4.99 □
AMATEUR NIGHTS	Becky Bell	£4.99 □
BIANCA	Maria Caprio	£4.50 □
THE GIRLS OF LAZY DAISY'S	Faye Rossignol	£4.50 □

All Headline books are available at your local bookshop or newsagent, or can be ordered direct from the publisher. Just tick the titles you want and fill in the form below. Prices and availability subject to change without notice.

Headline Book Publishing PLC, Cash Sales Department, Bookpoint, 39 Milton Park, Abingdon, OXON, OX14 4TD, UK. If you have a credit card you may order by telephone — 0235 831700.

Please enclose a cheque or postal order made payable to Bookpoint Ltd to the value of the cover price and allow the following for postage and packing:
UK & BFPO: £1.00 for the first book, 50p for the second book and 30p for each additional book ordered up to a maximum charge of £3.00.
OVERSEAS & EIRE: £2.00 for the first book, £1.00 for the second book and 50p for each additional book.

Name ....

Address ....

....

....

If you would prefer to pay by credit card, please complete:
Please debit my Visa/Access/Diner's Card/American Express (delete as applicable) card no:

Signature ....Expiry Date ....